TWISTED JUSTICE

INSPECTOR WEST

PETER MULRANEY

Copyright © 2019 by Peter Mulraney

ISBN-13: 978-0-6482661-1-2

Cover image: Filip Mroz on Unsplash

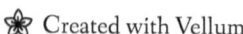 Created with Vellum

For those people standing quietly in the wings supporting me.

MAJOR CRIMES TEAM

DCI Rankin (Chief)
DI West (Carl)
DS Fuller (Harry)
DC Beard (Nigel)
DC Paterson (Wayne)
DC Templar (Lisa)

Supporting Officers

Dr Jonas (Mike) Pathologist
Dr Worthington (Emma) Pathologist
Sgt Lang (Dean) Forensics
SC Head (Charlie) Uniform
PC Chan (Lily) Uniform
PC Monks (Adam) Uniform
PC Highland Community Liaison

CHAPTER ONE

Several new admissions and a death had kept Kelly Palmer busy since she'd signed on as the intensive care duty sister at midnight, which was the way Kelly preferred her shifts to go.

With the end of her shift in sight, she was looking forward to a good sleep before coming back to do it all again. And, being Friday, she knew she'd need all the sleep she could get before returning to face the rush of patients Fridays always seemed to deliver.

Kelly looked across the city skyline to the hills through the third-floor windows of City Hospital. The morning sky was heavy with grey rain clouds. She hoped it wouldn't start raining until she'd reached her car, parked a two-minute walk away from the hospital in the West End of the city. She glanced at her watch. It was almost time for the morning shift to arrive.

Kelly walked back to the nurse station from the bedside of the patient she had gone to check to start preparing for the shift change.

As she gathered her notes, the elevator doors opened and the sound of bright voices drifted across to her. The nurses of the morning shift stepped onto the floor and walked towards the nurse station across from the elevators. Kelly greeted her replacement and went through the handover routine required to bring her up to speed on the status of the patients in their care.

When she'd completed the handover, Kelly went into the staffroom. She slipped on her coat, took her handbag out of her locker, and checked her face in the mirror of her compact. Satisfied with her appearance, she headed for the elevator.

Kelly stepped into the elevator and pushed the button for the ground floor. While she waited for the doors to close, she pulled her mobile phone out of her handbag and switched it on. There were two missed calls. Both from Ian. She dropped the phone back into her handbag.

She had no intention of returning Ian's calls. She'd told him it was over and she'd told herself that, this time, she wasn't giving into his puppy dog pleas.

It had taken another fight with her sister, but she'd finally come to terms with the fact that Ian was never going to change, no matter how many promises he'd make. Besides, her sister had gone to great lengths to remind her that she'd heard them all before and that every time she'd forgiven him and let him back into her life, they'd ended up in the same place.

In the end, she'd agreed with her sister that five years of living with Ian's idea of how relationships worked was more than enough and decided there was no way she could put up with any more of his abuse. Now, having mustered up the courage to kick him out, she knew living on her own was better than living with him, even if he hadn't yet come to terms with their new arrangement. She hoped he'd get the message soon and leave her alone, otherwise, she'd have no choice but to take her sister's advice and get a restraining order.

When she reached the foyer, she looked around to make

sure Ian wasn't waiting for her. There was no sign of him. She crossed the open expanse between the elevators and the main doors of the hospital and headed towards the parking station where she'd left her car.

She wrapped her arms around herself and looked up into the sky. The clouds were black. A couple of raindrops splashed onto her face. She hurried across the intersection in front of the hospital, rebuking herself for leaving her umbrella in the car, and made her way to the laneway that led to the car park.

At eight o'clock on a Friday morning, the city was coming to life but the West End, away from the commercial heart of the city, was still all but deserted. Businesses in the West End didn't open until nine, and the little shops that serviced visitors to the hospital remained closed until just before ten, when visiting hours started.

Kelly hurried down Grant Lane, hoping she'd get to the car park before it started raining in earnest. A man dressed in black swept past her on a bicycle. Kelly jumped; startled. She hadn't heard him coming. She thought it had to be Ian.

She took a couple of deep breaths and told herself to calm down.

Once she'd recovered from her initial fright, she realized there was no way Ian would be riding around the city on his bike at eight o'clock in the morning. He started work at seven-thirty and, besides, he hated riding in the rain. She shook her head. It was just a man on his way to work.

Kelly turned into the entrance of the car park and climbed the stairs to level one, where her car was waiting for her in bay 1-B, the spot outside the stairwell door she'd managed to secure when she'd first started working at City Hospital.

CHAPTER TWO

Trent had agonised about what he was planning to do for a long time but it hadn't helped. It had only made thinking about what had happened to Helen all the more painful.

It wasn't his fault that it had happened to her, but it had happened, and nobody had been held accountable. In his mind, that wasn't right. The powers that be hadn't listened to him when he had raised his concerns. They had dismissed his accusations as unfounded, and advised him to seek help with managing his grief. He'd stuffed it all down into the dungeons of his mind and tried to get on with his life.

But she wouldn't leave him alone.

Helen wanted justice and, after another night of haunted dreams, he understood she had chosen him to administer it and that she would not leave him in peace until he did. Seven years of nightly torment had worn down his resistance. He wanted peace more than anything else, and she'd told him how he could get it.

He sat at the kitchen table and wrote each of the five names he'd memorised onto a small square of paper, using the biro he used for making his weekly shopping list. He folded each square after he'd written a name on it and dropped the folded piece of paper into Helen's coffee mug.

Trent couldn't remember why he'd kept Helen's mug. He'd discarded everything else that had belonged to her years ago. Now, as he dropped the name bearing pieces of paper into the mug, he understood why he'd kept it. She wanted to determine the order of his executions.

He picked up the mug in his left hand and held it above his head.

'You choose, sweetheart,' he said to the empty room, before blindly pushing the fingers of his right hand into the mug and pulling out a piece of paper.

He lowered the mug onto the table and opened the folded square. He read the name: Kelly Palmer.

Trent put Helen's coffee mug with the remaining names in it back into the cupboard above the refrigerator, opened his laptop, and started researching Kelly Palmer.

The number of entries for Kelly Palmer surprised him but what he knew about her helped him narrow down the field of possibilities.

He signed-in to LinkedIn and read the profile of the Kelly Palmer working at City Hospital. She was still working in intensive care.

He signed-in to Facebook. There was a profile for a Kelly Palmer living in Morton Sands. The profile picture matched his memory of her face.

He opened White Pages and searched for K Palmer in Morton Sands. The search result listed two entries. He wrote down the addresses.

Trent made himself a thermos of hot coffee and two ham, cheese, and tomato sandwiches. Then he drove his van to Morton Sands.

The first address was a house in Whale Street. There were two cars in the driveway. He parked across the street from the house and waited.

He'd almost finished the coffee in his thermos when the front door of the house opened and a woman with grey hair stepped out onto the veranda with a dog on a leash. As he watched them walk towards the beach at the end of the street, he decided Kelly had to be living at the other address.

He drove around to Dune Avenue and parked outside the apartment block at number fifteen. He got out of the van, walked across the street and looked at the cars parked in the numbered parking bays. There was no car in the bay for apartment three. He returned to the van and waited.

Trent went home after watching the sun slide into the ocean and take its light from the sky in a spectacular display of oranges and pinks that slowly faded to black.

He came back to number fifteen Dune Avenue at two o'clock the next morning. There was a car parked in the bay for apartment three. He wrote down the details and figured she must be working the four to midnight shift.

He returned at three o'clock in the afternoon and watched Kelly Palmer get into her car. He followed her into the city. At three forty-six, he watched her turn into Grant Lane, opposite the main entrance to City Hospital, and enter the car park halfway down the lane.

He followed her to and from work for a week. At the end of that week, she started leaving for work at eleven pm and going home at eight the next morning. He decided on the car park, as there were always too many people around at her apartment building and there were no security cameras in the car park.

Trent spent several mornings observing the comings and goings in the car park around the time Kelly retrieved her car before driving home. She arrived at five minutes after eight most mornings and was the only person on level one for the next ten to fifteen minutes, which was more than enough time for what he had in mind.

On the Friday morning of the week Kelly had started on the midnight shift, Trent rode his bicycle into the city and waited opposite the hospital until he saw her leave the building. When she crossed the street and started down the lane, he followed her on his bicycle and rode past her before she'd reached the entrance into the car park.

He rode up the ramp to level one, dismounted, and leant his bicycle on the wall next to parking bay 1-B, and waited for Kelly to come through the door from the stairwell.

CHAPTER THREE

Detective Inspector Carl West stood on the platform at Morton Sands with the crowd waiting to catch the seven-ten train into the city. He and Nina had moved to Morton Sands a few months after the birth of their daughter, Sophie, trading their near-city apartment for a family home with a yard in the popular seaside suburb.

It had taken Carl several weeks to get used to the forty-minute train ride to work every morning, which was quite a change from the ten-minute drive he'd been accustomed to for years. But, now that it had become part of his morning routine, he took advantage of his commute to prepare for the day ahead, except for those mornings when he struggled to keep his eyes open after a night of disturbed sleep.

He watched the city bound train pull into the station and come to a halt. Then, like everyone else on the platform, he entered the nearest carriage, swiped his travel card on the ticket machine, and found himself a seat. When the train started moving, he took his iPad out of his briefcase and scrolled through his emails to get an idea of what the day had in store for him. Nothing stood out. His inbox was full of the routine administrative tasks that came with managing a team of detectives. The excitement for the day looked like being Harry Fuller's return to work from his honeymoon.

Carl wondered how Harry and Jessika had enjoyed their ten days in Hawaii, and smiled as he thought about his own honeymoon there with Nina. They had certainly enjoyed themselves after Nina's close encounter with death. In fact, they'd had such a good time he'd been tempted to turn in his badge and stay, but tourists could only stay so long, so they had come home. Besides, Nina had reminded him he wouldn't know what to do with himself if he left the force.

It all seemed like a long time ago now that they were the parents of an energetic one-year-old, and Nina had decided to resign from the force to be a full-time mother.

Things had been relatively quiet while Harry was on leave. The team was still working on the same stolen cars case they'd started in the days before Harry's wedding, and didn't seem to be getting anywhere. Expensive cars were vanishing into thin air, much to the disappointment of their owners, their insurers, and the team. Carl hoped a fresh insight from Harry might help them crack the case.

He put the iPad back into his briefcase and spent the rest of the ride into the city reading the morning's paper.

At seven-fifty, Carl disembarked at City Station and set off on the ten-minute walk that took him through the city to Police Headquarters.

———

Carl dropped into the coffee shop next door to Police Headquarters and bought himself a coffee, before making his way up to his office on the third floor.

The team was standing around Harry's desk drinking coffee and catching up on his holiday news.

'Morning, all,' said Carl.

The banter of jovial voices stopped.

'Morning, Inspector.'

'How was Hawaii?'

'As good as you said it would be, Boss,' said Harry.

'Well, I'm glad you had a good time, then.' Carl smiled. 'Team meeting in ten, folks.' He left them to talk and went into his office to log on and start his work day.

At eight twenty, Carl called the team together around the whiteboard on the wall outside his office.

'Okay, Wayne, let's bring DS Fuller up to date on where we're at with these cars.'

'Still going?' said Harry. 'Thought you'd have that one wrapped up by now.'

Carl shook his head. 'No such luck, I'm afraid, Harry. Wayne?'

DC Paterson took out his notebook. 'We've got fifteen cars that fit the pattern. Expensive, near new, all with remote keyless entry, and taken from driveways while their owners were asleep inside. And, the owners still have their remote key fobs, so the thieves have managed to disengage the onboard security and somehow start the cars.'

'How are they doing that?' said Harry. 'Thought those cars were supposed to be theft-proof.'

'We're not sure, Sarge. Those remotes send some sort of shortwave radio signal to the computer in the car that controls the locks and the ignition,' said DC Paterson, 'and, you have to be close to the car, like five to ten metres, to unlock the doors and start the engine.'

'So, how are they doing it?' said Harry.

'Even if you had a duplicate key to open the door, you'd

have to hot-wire the ignition if you could get past the security lock on the steering. Those cars don't have anywhere to insert a key to start them,' said DC Beard, 'and, nobody makes duplicate remotes. You have to get them from the manufacturers.'

'Any word on the street?' said Carl.

'Not even a rumour as to who might be involved or where the cars are going,' said Wayne.

'Any luck with those parts dealers you spoke to yesterday, Nigel?' said Carl.

'They reckon the parts for those fancy cars have serial numbers on them these days,' said DC Beard. 'The bloke I spoke to yesterday told me legitimate dealers wouldn't touch second hand parts for expensive foreign cars like these without verifying the serial numbers.'

'Maybe the resale market is interstate,' said Harry.

'Or offshore,' said DC Templar, 'in places where they can't import parts or vehicles thanks to sanctions.'

Carl's mobile phone rang. He looked at the display. The call was from Operations. He held up his hand for silence.

'DI West.'

'We have a body in the car park off Grant Lane, Inspector. Patrol says it looks like a homicide. We're looking for a man on a bicycle seen leaving the area about fifteen minutes ago.'

'Okay, I'm on my way.'

Carl slipped his mobile back into his pocket.

'Looks like we have a homicide. Harry, you come with me. I want everybody else on standby until we know the full details.'

'Where?' said DC Paterson.

'Grant Lane, down by City Hospital,' said Carl.

———

The entrance to Grant Lane was blocked by a patrol car with flashing blue lights. Carl produced his ID and the constable controlling access let them into the lane. When Harry had parked the car, they slipped into their crime scene suits and walked to the pedestrian entrance to the car park, where a second constable stood controlling access to the crime scene.

Carl signed the control sheet.

'You'll need to go up the ramp to level one, Inspector. The stairs open into the crime scene.'

'Who found the body?' said Carl.

'A nurse from the hospital,' said the constable. 'She's pretty upset.' He pointed to the patrol car parked a short distance from where they stood. 'She's given us a statement.'

'Okay, we'll speak to her after we've had a look at the crime scene,' said Carl.

When they reached level one, they found the area immediately outside the stairwell door roped off with crime scene tape. Sgt Dean Lang and his crime scene investigators were still unpacking equipment from their vehicle, which was parked in the opposite corner away from the white Toyota Corolla inside the crime scene.

As they approached the line of tape, Carl spotted Dr Mike Jonas, the police pathologist, kneeling beside a body on the floor between the car and the wall holding the stairwell door.

'Morning, Mike.'

Dr Jonas stood. 'Definitely not accidental, Carl. Poor girl's been garrotted.'

'Do we know who she is?'

'We'll have to wait for Dean's people to take their photographs before we go through her things, but she's obviously a nurse from City Hospital.'

Carl thought he should have asked the nurse downstairs before coming up to take a look.

They stood next to the crime scene tape while the body and its surroundings were photographed.

'How was Hawaii, Harry?' said Mike.

'A lot warmer than this.'

'Was it as good as Carl reckons?'

'It was great. You should go,' said Harry. 'Scenery is fantastic. You'd come back with a thousand photos.'

'You might not come back at all,' said Carl. 'I was tempted to stay.'

'Be nice to be somewhere warm,' said Mike.

'It's even warm when it rains over there,' said Harry. 'Not like here.'

'How's that girl of yours, Carl? She walking yet?' said Mike.

'Won't be long now,' said Carl. 'She's pulling herself up on the armchairs.'

Mike laughed and slapped Carl on the back. 'Fun's about to begin, mate.'

'All yours, Doc,' said the photographer.

They pulled on their latex gloves and stepped inside the cordoned off area with Mike.

'The body is still warm,' said Mike.

'How warm?' said Carl.

'This girl was alive less than an hour ago,' said Mike.

Carl picked up her handbag and looked inside. It held a mobile phone, a ring of keys, a wallet containing several plastic cards and fifty-five dollars in notes, and a driver's licence in the name of Kelly Ann Palmer of Unit 3, 15 Dune Avenue, Morton Sands.

He handed the licence to Harry, who photographed it with his phone, and pressed the unlock button on the car key. The lights of the Corolla flashed.

'Looks like robbery wasn't the motive, then' said Harry, handing back the licence.

Carl put the handbag back on the floor next to the body for one of the CSI officers to bag.

Mike pointed out the purple line embedded in the victim's neck. 'Some sort of ligature, probably a rope.'

'Bastard has a nerve,' said Carl, 'killing her here at this time of day.'

'Must have been waiting for her,' said Harry. 'I wonder if the woman that found the body is the person who saw the man on the bike.'

'I'll see you at the post mortem, Mike,' said Carl.

'I'll let you know if I find anything else here,' said Mike.

They stepped over the crime scene tape back into the public domain.

'Anything, Dean?'

'Nothing obvious, Inspector. This door is covered in prints, but you'll need to catch him first if they're to be of any use.'

Carl and Harry walked back down the ramp to the front of the car park.

'Does this place have CCTV, Constable?' said Carl.

'I don't think so, Inspector. I haven't seen any cameras.'

'Is there an attendant?'

'No. This place is monthly parkers only. You need a four-digit code to open the barrier to get in or out.'

'Check for CCTV with the operators, Harry. You never know your luck,' said Carl, as they walked over to the patrol car.

'Right, Boss.'

———

Carl introduced himself to the constable standing next to the patrol car parked outside the car park.

'How is she?'

'A bit shaken up, Inspector.'

'Did she see anyone?'

'A man on a bicycle. I put out an alert as soon as she told me.'

'Good work, Constable. Let's hope we find him,' said Carl. 'Did she get a look at him?'

'Not really, Inspector. She said a man rode past her going towards the hospital as she was walking down the lane to the car park, but she didn't take that much notice.'

That made sense to Carl. He probably wouldn't have taken much notice of a man on a bike either as he was walking towards the railway station thinking about home.

'What's her name?'

'Mary Howe. She's a nurse at the hospital, Inspector. She knows the victim.'

Carl opened the back door of the patrol car and slid in beside Mary Howe.

'I'm Inspector West,' said Carl. 'We won't keep you much longer, Ms Howe. Do you want me to arrange for someone to take you home?'

Mary Howe turned to face Carl. 'I think I'll be alright to drive by the time they're finished in there.'

'How well did you know Kelly?' said Carl.

'We'd worked together a few times.'

'Where's your car?' said Carl.

'It's on the same floor as Kelly's. I found her when I opened the door from the stairs.'

She's a nurse, thought Carl. She would have tried to help someone lying on the floor.

'Did you touch the body?'

'I checked for a pulse. I thought she must have fainted or something. Then I saw her neck. No way we can bring people back from that.' Mary blew her nose in the tissues she held in her hand.

Carl waited. He felt her discomfort but needed to ask his questions while things were still fresh in her mind.

'What time was it when you found her?' said Carl.

'I left the hospital at ten past eight, so I guess around a quarter past.'

'Any idea what time Kelly left the hospital?'

'Couldn't have been much before I did. The shift ends at eight.'

Carl realized the killer had taken a calculated risk and decided he'd probably watched Kelly to work out the timing of her morning routine.

'Do you always leave at ten past eight?' said Carl.

'Most mornings. It usually takes me that long to get out of the building. I work in the West Wing.'

'What do you remember about the man on the bicycle?' said Carl.

Mary Howe looked at her hands. 'I'm sorry, but I really didn't take any notice of him.'

'Any colors come to mind?'

'Black. He was wearing black. It was all fairly quick.'

'Did you see where he came from?' said Carl.

'No. I didn't see him until he was going past, and I only saw him out of the corner of my eye. To be honest, I hardly saw him at all. I was looking at my phone.'

'One last question, Ms Howe. Did you seen anyone hanging about the car park on any other morning this week?'

'No, but this morning's the first time I've ever seen anybody on a bike in this lane, Inspector, and I've been parking here for years.'

Carl wished Mary Howe had been a few years older and less attached to the screen of her mobile phone, but realized they were lucky she'd noticed the man on the bike at all.

'Thank you, Ms Howe. The constable will let you know when you can retrieve your car.'

Carl got out of the car and closed the door. He looked up and down Grant Lane. The entrance to the car park was the only opening in the narrow canyon of bricks formed by the blank walls of the warehouses that lined either side of the lane. He pointed at the windowless walls. 'Easy to see why he chose this spot.'

Harry rubbed his chin and looked down the lane towards the hospital. 'I'm pretty sure there's a traffic camera at that intersection down there in front of the hospital.'

'Let's hope it was working this morning,' said Carl. 'It might be our only window into what went on here.'

CHAPTER FOUR

Leaving their car parked in the lane, Carl and Harry crossed the street and walked into City Hospital. The reception lobby was deserted, apart from the store holders preparing for the daily influx of visitors that would begin at ten.

Carl showed his ID to the woman sitting at the reception desk. 'Inspector West, City Police. I need to talk to someone senior from HR.'

'Can I say what it's about?' said the receptionist.

'Tell them it's an urgent police matter,' said Carl.

Carl tapped his fingers together while she made the call. He'd never liked being in a hospital, and City Hospital, with its connection to Nina's brush with death, especially unnerved him. He took a deep breath and waited.

'Mr Nelson will be down in a moment, Inspector. He's the head of HR.'

'Thank you,' said Carl.

A couple of minutes later, a tall middle-aged man, wearing a grey suit supported by a sky-blue tie on a white shirt, stepped out of one of the elevators and approached the reception desk.

'Inspector West?'

'Yes,' said Carl, extending his hand. 'This is my colleague, Detective Sergeant Fuller.'

'David Nelson, head of HR. How can I help you, gentlemen?'

Carl guided the HR Manager away from the reception desk. He didn't want the receptionist listening in on their conversation.

'We're after the next of kin details for one of your nurses, Mr Nelson. I'm afraid her body's been found in the car park across the street,' said Carl.

'I guess that explains the police car with flashing lights,' said Mr Nelson. 'Who is she?'

'Kelly Ann Palmer,' said Carl.

Carl saw a look of recognition flash in the HR manager's eyes.

'You'd better come up to my office, Inspector.'

Mr Nelson turned and led them over to the elevators. They rode up to the administration centre on the ninth floor.

'How long has Ms Palmer worked here at City Hospital?' said Carl.

Mr Nelson keyed her name into his computer and brought up her file. 'Ten years, Inspector. She's one of our intensive care specialists. We are going to miss her.' He looked up from his monitor. 'That's a skill set that's hard to replace in a hurry.'

'Do you have a next of kin contact for her, Mr Nelson?'

The HR manager looked at his screen. 'She's given us her sister's details. I'll print them for you.'

They waited while Mr Nelson retrieved the printout from a printer located a short walk from his desk.

'I'd appreciate you keeping this confidential until we've notified her next of kin,' said Carl.

'How will I know when you've done that?'

'Give me your number,' said Carl. 'I'll call you.'

Mr Nelson handed Carl a business card.

'I'd appreciate a list of the people she worked with on her last shift. We'll need to speak to them,' said Carl, handing him his card. 'Can you email it to me?'

Mr Nelson looked at the email address on Carl's business card. 'That shouldn't be a problem, Inspector.'

———

Carl called the number David Nelson had given him for Tyler Virgo.

'Lawrence and Peters. This is Tyler. How can I help you?'

'Is this Tyler Virgo, Kelly Palmer's sister?' said Carl.

'Yes. Who's this?'

'Inspector West from City Police. I need to speak to you about your sister. Where are you at the moment?'

'We're in Long Street. Number three hundred and twenty-one. What's this about my sister?'

'It's not something I can discuss on the phone, Ms Virgo. We'll be there shortly.'

Carl ended the call. 'Three twenty-one Long Street, Harry.'

A little under five minutes later, Harry parked outside the offices of Lawrence and Peters, Chartered Accountants, at three twenty-one Long Street.

The woman sitting at reception looked up when they walked into the building. Carl thought she and Kelly had to be twins.

'Tyler Virgo?' said Carl, showing her his ID.

Tyler nodded. 'Is Kelly in trouble?'

'Is there somewhere we can talk in private?' said Carl.

'I can't leave the phones,' said Tyler.

'Is there someone who can take over for you?' said Carl. 'I'm afraid we have bad news.'

'Has that bastard hurt her?'

Carl wondered who she meant. 'I'm afraid it's worse than that. Kelly's dead.'

'Noooooo!' Tyler dropped her head into her hands on the desk.

A dark-haired woman in a navy-blue suit came out of an office into reception. She looked at Tyler, who was crying, and at Carl and Harry.

'What's going on?'

'Police,' said Carl, showing her his ID. 'Who are you?'

'I'm Tyler's manager,' said the woman.

'You'll need to get someone to take over here,' said Carl.

'Why?'

'I'm afraid we're bearers of bad news,' said Carl.

'Oh. I see.' The woman took a deep breath and let it out slowly.

'Is there somewhere we can talk to Tyler in private?' said Carl.

The woman turned and opened a door. 'You can use this meeting room, if you like.'

Harry put his arm around Tyler and guided her into the meeting room. Carl closed the door behind them.

There was a knock on the door and the woman handed Carl a box of tissues. 'You might need these.'

'Thank you,' said Carl, placing the box of tissues on the table in front of Tyler.

They waited while Tyler blew her nose and dabbed at her eyes.

'It's okay,' said Carl. 'Take your time.'

'What happened?' said Tyler, twisting a tissue around her fingers.

'It looks like she was attacked on her way home from work this morning. Her body was found in the car park over the road from the hospital,' said Carl.

'I told her to stop using that place,' said Tyler. 'It's got no security.'

'Who did you think had hurt her?' said Carl.

'Ian.'

'Who's he?' said Carl.

'The bloke she'd been living with for the last five years. He's a complete arsehole.'

Carl looked at Harry, who had taken out his notebook, and wondered whether Kelly had become another statistic in the sad tale of women being killed by people they knew.

'Had they split up?' said Carl.

'Yeah. She tossed him out last month. He's been pestering her ever since but she told me she'd decided to end it for good, this time.'

'Had they broken up before?' said Carl.

'Several times, but she'd always given in and taken him back. He'd treat her nice for a while and then he'd get stuck into her again.'

'Did he hit her?' said Carl.

'No. Ian's into verbal abuse. He's one of those bastards that gets his kicks out of making women feel like shit.'

'What's his full name?' said Carl.

'Ian Holden.'

'Do you know where we can find him?'

'I don't know where he went after Kelly kicked him out, but he's a mechanic at Bayside Auto,' said Tyler.

'How can we contact your parents?' said Carl.

'They're on their second honeymoon in New Zealand,' said Tyler. 'They left on Wednesday.'

'Do you know where they're staying? We'll get someone in New Zealand to break the news to them.'

'I've got all that stuff at home,' said Tyler.

'How do you get to work?' said Carl.

'On the bus.'

'I'll arrange for someone to drive you home and you can give them your parents' contact details. I'm sorry to be the bearer of such bad news,' said Carl.

'Just make sure you catch the bastard!'

'We will,' said Carl.

Carl stepped out into reception and explained the situation to Tyler's manager. Then, while Harry arranged for Community Liaison to take Tyler home, Carl called Wayne and asked him to pick up Ian Holden from Bayside Auto and bring him in for questioning.

They waited with Tyler Virgo until PC Highland from Community Liaison arrived to drive her home.

———

As they were driving back to Police Headquarters, Carl's mobile phone rang. Carl looked at the display before answering.

'What's up, Wayne.'

'Holden's on leave, Inspector. Hasn't been at work all week,' said DC Paterson.

Interesting, thought Carl. 'Did you get an address?'

'A unit at Portside. We're on our way there now.'

'Okay. Let me know if you find him at home.'

Carl slipped his phone back into the inside pocket of his coat.

'Holden's apparently on leave,' said Carl.

'He's going to need a good alibi after what her sister told us,' said Harry.

'Let's not jump to conclusions, Harry.'

'You know what the chances are that he did it, don't you?' said Harry.

'I've read the statistics, Harry, but we can't convict him with statistics. We need something concrete,' said Carl. 'That's why I want to talk to him.'

Carl was back in his office coordinating the retrieval of the recordings from the traffic cameras in the area around City Hospital when DC Paterson called again.

'He's not home, Inspector. One of the neighbours said he'd seen him going for a bike ride around seven this morning. Apparently, he's a keen cyclist.'

Carl looked at his watch. It was ten thirty-seven. 'Bloody long time for a bike ride, Wayne, especially in the rain.'

'Maybe the silly bugger's fallen off his bike,' said Wayne.

'Or he's done a runner,' said Carl.

'What do you want us to do, Inspector?'

'Come back to the office. There's probably no point waiting there.'

Carl walked over to DC Templar's desk. 'Lisa, see if you can get an image of Ian Holden from Registrations. He was living at Unit 3, 15 Dune Avenue, Morton Sands. Wayne can give you an address at Portside if that doesn't work.'

'Is he a suspect, sir?'

'Let's say he's a person of interest until we can speak to him and verify his whereabouts.'

On the way back to his office, Carl stopped at Harry's desk. 'Give the Ambulance Service a call, Harry. See if they've picked up any male cyclists this morning in the Portside area.'

'Who are we looking for in particular?' said Harry.

24

'Holden went for a ride on his bike this morning around seven o'clock and hasn't come back', said Carl.

'That's not going to do much for his alibi,' said Harry. 'He could easily have ridden into the city by eight from there.'

'Traffic are sending over this morning's recordings from the cameras on North Terrace that cover the intersections adjacent to City Hospital. If he came into town, they should have a picture of him approaching and leaving the laneway.'

Carl's mobile phone rang.

'DI West.'

'Charlie Head, Inspector. Think I might have something for you.'

'What would that be Charlie?'

'A stolen vehicle. An S Class Mercedes to be precise,' said SC Head.

Carl hoped this was the breakthrough they'd been waiting for in their stolen cars investigation.

'And where did you find that?'

'On the back of a truck involved in a fatal collision on Port Road this morning.'

'Tell me we have the driver in custody, Charlie,' said Carl.

'We do, Inspector. A bloke named Ian Holden. He's not very happy about it either.'

Carl smiled. He didn't think anyone driving a truck with a stolen car as cargo would be happy about being involved in an accident and being arrested.

'What time was this accident?' said Carl.

'Just after seven thirty.'

That would give Holden an alibi if he was the Ian Holden he was looking for, thought Carl.

'What's this Holden fellow saying about the car?' said Carl.

'Says he won't answer any questions without his lawyer.'

'Where is he now?'

'Downstairs. I thought you might want to ask him a few questions when his lawyer gets here.'

'Ask him if he knows a woman named Kelly Palmer. She's a nurse at City Hospital,' said Carl.

'Just a minute.'

Carl waited.

'Says she's his ex,' said Charlie.

'I'll be right down.'

Carl turned back to Harry. 'We've got Holden downstairs. He's got an airtight alibi so he might be able to help us.'

———

The Custody Sergeant opened the door to let Carl and Harry into the holding cell where Ian Holden sat on the bunk. Carl put his fingers to his nose. He'd never enjoyed interviewing prisoners in these holding cells. The overpowering smell of urine and body odour reminded him of an open sewer.

'Who are you?' said Ian, as the door closed behind his visitors.

'Detective Inspector West. I'd like to ask you a few questions,' said Carl

'I'm not answering any questions without my lawyer?' said Ian.

'We'll talk about why you're here when your lawyer arrives, Mr Holden. Right now, I want to talk about Kelly Palmer.'

Ian looked up. 'Has she made a complaint about me?'

'No. She's dead,' said Carl.

Ian opened his mouth and then shut it. He looked at Carl and then at Harry. 'And you think I had something to do with it?'

'Not unless you're some kind of magician.'

'What do you mean?'

26

'Where were you between eight and eight fifteen this morning?' said Carl.

'Sitting in a police car on Port Road, but I guess you already know that.'

Carl nodded. 'Kelly was still alive at eight o'clock this morning but she was dead by eight fifteen, so I know you didn't kill her, Mr Holden. I'm not here to accuse you. I'm asking for your help.'

Ian let out a long, slow breath. 'What do you want to know?'

'When was the last time you saw her?'

'She kicked me out about a month ago. I haven't seen her since. She wouldn't even answer my calls.'

'Any ideas on who might have killed her?' said Carl.

'No,' said Ian. 'I didn't think she had any enemies.'

'Did she ever mention she'd been threatened by anyone or followed home from work?' said Carl.

Ian shook his head. 'I think the only person she thought was giving her grief was me. She told me often enough.'

'Notice anyone hanging about the place when you were living with her?'

'Not really. There's a fair bit of foot traffic in Dune Avenue with people going to and from the beach, even at this time of the year.'

'Anyone you think we should talk to that she might have confided in?'

'Her sister. She was always talking to her.'

'Would that be Tyler?'

'Yeah. Mind you, she won't have a good word to say about me.'

Carl smiled as he remembered what Tyler had said to them earlier in the day.

'What about friends at work?'

'She didn't talk much about work. Too many people die where she works.' Ian leant back against the wall of his cell. 'You'll have to ask someone at the hospital who her friends were there.'

'What was she like?' said Carl.

'She was a good person, Inspector. Too good for someone like me. I tried to love her but I wasn't very good at it I'm afraid.' Ian looked at the floor.

'I'm sorry you had to find out this way. We'll do our best to find her killer.'

'Thanks for telling me, Inspector. It's better than hearing it on the radio.' Ian looked Carl in the eye. 'Bloody Tyler wouldn't have told me.'

The door of the cell opened and the Custody Sergeant announced the arrival of William Maynard, Ian's lawyer.

'You're supposed to wait for me,' said William Maynard.

'Mr Holden is assisting us with a separate matter, Mr Maynard,' said Carl. 'We'll give you fifteen minutes with your client before we start the formal interview on the matter for which he's been arrested.'

CHAPTER FIVE

'Harry, while I'm talking to Holden, I want you to search his apartment. Take Nigel with you, and send Wayne down here. He knows more about this case than anyone else.'

'Okay, Boss. What are we going to do about the murder now Holden's out of the picture?'

'Get Lisa to start on the recordings from Traffic,' said Carl. 'We'll regroup when you get back from your search.'

While Carl waited in the interview room down the corridor from the holding cells, he read Charlie Head's notes on the accident on Port Road. It appeared the elderly driver of the other vehicle had pulled out in front of the truck Holden had been driving.

A few minutes later, DC Paterson joined him. 'This is a bit of a surprise, Inspector.'

'Let's hope we get something useful out of him,' said Carl. 'I doubt he's the mastermind.'

'If we tap into his network, you never know what we might find. Perhaps we should start with Bayside Auto,' said Wayne.

'Yes, and follow up on the ownership of the truck,' said

Carl. 'I'll need you and Nigel to run with this case for the time being. I'll have to focus on this morning's murder.'

There was a knock at the door. The Custody Sergeant poked his head in. 'Are you ready, Inspector?'

'Show them in, Sergeant,' said Carl.

Wayne turned on the video recorder when Ian Holden and his lawyer entered the interview room and took their seats at the table opposite Carl.

Carl stepped them through the formalities and waited for Ian to state his full name and acknowledge that he understood his answers had to be verbal.

'I understand you work at Bayside Auto,' said Carl. 'Is that right?'

'Yeah.'

'Any connection between Bayside Auto and the truck you were driving this morning?'

'I dunno,' said Ian.

Carl wondered whether Holden was going to play dumb or cooperate.

'Who owns the truck you were driving this morning?' said Carl.

'Can't say,' said Ian.

Carl leant back and crossed his arms on his chest. 'And, why's that, Mr Holden?'

'Coz I don't know.'

'So, it's definitely not your truck, then?'

'No.'

'So, how did you end up driving it on Port Road this morning?'

Ian shrugged his shoulders.

'Can you answer the question for the recording, Mr Holden?' said Wayne.

'A mate asked me to drive it down to the port for him,' said Ian.

'Who's this mate?'

'I don't know his name,' said Ian. 'A bloke I met at the pub.'

Carl smiled. He knew he could trace the owner from the registration number of the truck.

'You do realize the seriousness of the predicament you're in, don't you?' said Carl.

'It's not my bloody fault some stupid shit drove in front of me and got himself killed,' said Ian.

Carl smiled and glanced at William Maynard.

'Perhaps you'd better explain to your client, Mr Maynard, that he's not here because of the accident. From what I've been told, it looks like the other driver was at fault. I'm not interested in that. Tell your client he's here because of what was on the back of the truck he was driving.'

'A bloody car?' said Ian. 'What's that got to do with anything?'

'Did your mate tell you what you were delivering?'

'Yeah. Said the owner wanted it shipped interstate.'

'Where were you taking it?' said Carl.

'The address is in the truck. Some warehouse near H dock.'

Something to follow up to see if he's telling the truth, thought Carl.

'This is the problem we have, Mr Holden. That car, which you were transporting to the port this morning for your mate, happens to be a stolen vehicle.'

'I didn't know that,' said Ian, looking from Carl to his lawyer and back.

Carl thought Holden's eyes were going to pop out of his head and wondered if he was telling him the truth or spinning him a yarn with added dramatic effects thrown in.

'So, who's this mate, then?' said Carl.

'Look, I only know him as Jim,' said Ian. 'I was doing him a favour.'

'Just so you know,' said Carl, 'I have a team searching your apartment. Anything you want to tell me about what they might find there?'

'There's nothing there to find,' said Ian.

'We'll see,' said Carl. 'Is this the only time you've done this mate a favour and driven his truck down to the port?'

'Yeah.'

'I hope you're telling me the truth, Mr Holden, because I've got more cars like this one to locate.'

'What happens now?' said Ian.

'You'll be charged with being in possession of stolen goods and for being an accessory to theft of a motor vehicle. If I find out you're involved with any of the other cars, additional charges will be added. If I find out your story is true and you were duped, I'll ask for the charges to be withdrawn.'

'I don't get the benefit of the doubt?' said Ian.

'Look at it from my perspective, Mr Holden. You were caught with the goods. For all I know, what you're telling me is the truth. On the other hand, it could be nothing but lies. Until I find out which one it is, you get to stay here.'

'Don't I get bail or something?' Ian looked at his lawyer.

'We'll apply for bail,' said William Maynard. 'You have a good chance but it's still up to the magistrate.'

'How long do I have to stay here?'

'We can't get you before a magistrate until Monday morning,' said Carl.

'There goes my weekend,' said Ian.

'Look on the bright side,' said Carl. 'You could have ended up in the hospital or the morgue.'

'You think this place is any better?' said Ian.

After interviewing Holden, Carl and Wayne made their way back to their offices on level three.

'Get hold of that address from the truck and find out what's going on in that warehouse down at the port,' said Carl.

'They're probably aware we've got one of their cars by now,' said Wayne.

'Don't do anything silly. Just have a look around. Then go pick up the owner of the truck and bring him in for questioning.'

———

'Okay, folks, we're back to square one with the Palmer murder,' said Carl. 'Holden is definitely out of the picture. He was with SC Head on Port Road at the time of her death, so he couldn't possibly have killed her. He is, though, a person of interest in the cars case, seeing as he was transporting one of our missing vehicles at the time of his accident.'

'Is he still here?' said DC Beard.

'He'll be in custody until at least Monday morning,' said Carl. 'What happens after that will be up to the magistrate. His lawyer is applying for bail.'

'Will we be opposing that?' said DC Beard.

'Depends on what we uncover between now and then,' said Carl. 'Any luck with your search, Harry?'

'Nothing obvious, Boss,' said Harry. 'We'll have to follow up with his associates.'

'Wayne and Nigel can do that, 'said Carl.

'Where is Wayne?' said Harry.

'He's having a look around down at the port and chasing up the owner of the truck Holden was driving this morning,' said Carl. He looked at DC Templar. 'Any luck with those recordings from Traffic, Lisa?'

'We've got pictures of a man following the victim into the lane at eight and exiting again at eight sixteen, but he's wearing dark glasses and a baseball cap. There's no clear shot of his face, sir,' said Lisa.

'Which way was he heading?'

'Towards the port.'

'He must have turned off somewhere,' said DS Fuller, 'otherwise Uniform would have picked him up on Port Road.'

'Maybe he had a vehicle parked close by,' said Lisa. 'That would explain how he managed to disappear so quickly. It's not like he had a lot of time to get away before Uniform started looking for him.'

'Perhaps he lives in the West End or just off Port Road,' said Carl.

'We might have to look at recordings further out from the city on Port Road,' said Harry.

'I'm not sure that would do any good, Harry. If he'd stayed on Port Road one of the patrols would have spotted him. Can we identify the brand of the bike he's riding, Lisa?' said Carl.

'It's one of those expensive looking racing bikes, so I should be able to,' said Lisa.

'Anything else you can tell us about him?'

'I'd say he was about as tall as DS Fuller and lean, like Nigel,' said Lisa.

'Okay, select some shots we can release to the media. We might get lucky,' said Carl. 'Then, follow up with the victim's mobile service provider and get a listing of her call log.'

'Right, sir,' said Lisa.

'Harry, I've arranged to speak to the nurses she worked with at the end of their shift in the morning. Eight o'clock at the hospital. I'll meet you there.'

Carl's mobile phone rang. He glanced at the display. 'What's up, Wayne?'

'The truck Holden was driving belongs to a bloke called Jim Nolan. His missus reckons she hasn't seen him since six this morning, when he left for work in his truck. And, get this, Inspector. She's Holden's sister. Apparently, Holden drives the truck on weekends.'

'So, Holden wasn't exactly being honest with us,' said Carl, thinking he'd have to interview Holden again before Monday morning. 'Where does this Nolan work?'

'He's self-employed. Does local and interstate deliveries,' said Wayne. 'His missus says he's interstate. She's expecting him back some time tomorrow afternoon.'

'Something doesn't add up there, Wayne. Why was Holden driving Nolan's truck on Port Road this morning if he's supposed to be driving it interstate?'

'What do you want me to do?' said Wayne.

'Get his details and issue an APB,' said Carl.

'I'm on it,' said Wayne.

'Before you go, Wayne, what did you see down at the port?'

'An empty warehouse, Inspector, but the security guard on H Dock told me he'd seen a few trucks going in and out of it over the last month, and a semi-trailer leaving the place just after nine this morning,' said Wayne.

'Text me the address,' said Carl. 'Think we'd better take a look inside. We'll meet you there as soon as I've arranged the warrant.'

'There's no-one there, Inspector.'

'That may be so, Wayne, but we still need to play by the rules if we want things to stack up in court.'

Carl slipped his phone back into his pocket.

'Harry, get on to Forensics. We need a team to search a warehouse down at the port and I want you and Nigel to come with me.'

'What about me?' said DC Templar.

Carl smiled. 'You get to go home, Lisa. We'll see you in the morning.'

———

It was dark by the time they arrived at Warehouse 66 on H Dock.

'Where did Wayne say he'd meet us?' said Carl.

'At the back door of the warehouse,' said Nigel.

Harry drove slowly along the side of the warehouse and pulled up behind a white van with police plates.

Carl showed the search warrant to the sergeant from Forensics.

'Okay, Reg, open her up,' said the sergeant.

Five minutes later, they were standing in an empty warehouse flooded in light.

'What are we looking for, Inspector?'

'Anything that will tell us what's been stored in here recently,' said Carl.

The Forensics team spread out across the open space of the interior of the warehouse. Carl and his detectives made their way to the office along the wall from the door they'd entered through.

'Gloves on, boys' said Carl.

The office was empty, apart from three chairs and a table with a clean top. The floor was covered in dusty footprints. Harry walked around the edge of the room to the door that opened into the restrooms and flicked on the light.

'There's nothing in here,' said Harry. 'Not even any rubbish.'

'This place doesn't look like it's been used much,' said Nigel. 'There's dust all over the work benches out there.'

Carl went out into the warehouse to speak to the sergeant from Forensics.

'Motor vehicles,' said the sergeant. 'The floor is covered in tyre marks.' He pointed to a thick set of tracks on the floor that came to an abrupt end. 'Looks like cars were loaded onto a truck here, Inspector.'

'Anything we can use?' said Carl

'Some of those fancy cars you're looking for come with specific tyres, Inspector. I'll get the boys to photograph any treads that stand out.'

'And see if you can get any prints from the office or the restrooms. It looks like they've taken everything that wasn't bolted down but you never know your luck, Sergeant. They may have missed something if they left in a hurry.'

'I'll let you know if we find anything, Inspector.'

Carl joined his detectives and walked them outside.

'They're photographing the tread marks on the floor and I've asked them to sweep for prints,' said Carl.

'That could take them all night,' said Harry.

'Did you get any details on the truck seen leaving this morning, Wayne?' said Carl.

'Plain trailer without signage, I'm afraid, but the prime mover is a dark green Mack with local plates.'

'Well, that gives you a place to start, and find out who owns this warehouse. That might help us work out our next step,' said Carl.

CHAPTER SIX

Carl was back on the platform at Morton Sands in time to catch the seven-ten on Saturday morning. As he waited for the train to arrive, he leafed through the pages of the paper he'd purchased on his way into the station. The photograph they'd released of the man on a bike coming out of Grant Lane was on page three, along with their request for anyone who'd seen him to contact the Crime Stoppers Hotline.

On the trip into the city, he checked through his email and learnt that Forensics had lifted several sets of prints from the restrooms inside Warehouse 66. He wondered if they'd get any hits from the database that would give Wayne and Nigel someone to focus on.

When the train reached the city, Carl caught a cab to City Hospital, where he found Harry waiting for him outside the main entrance.

They made their way up to the third floor where the intensive care nurses who had worked with Kelly Palmer were waiting to be interviewed.

'Thanks for staying back to speak to us,' said Carl. 'I appreciate you'd be wanting to head home, so I won't keep you long.'

'What do you want to know about Kelly?' said one of the nurses.

'Had she mentioned anything about being followed or threatened by anyone?' said Carl.

The nurses exchanged glances. 'I guess it's okay to say she'd been having trouble with her partner,' said one of the nurses. 'She told me she'd kicked him out.'

'Ian Holden?' said Carl.

'That's him,' said the nurse.

'He was sitting in a police car on Port Road at the time Kelly was killed,' said Carl. 'He'd been involved in a traffic accident, so we know it wasn't him. Did she mention anybody else?'

'We don't get threats, Inspector,' said another of the nurses. 'Mostly, we get thanks from people we've looked after or from their families.'

'Have any of you been followed or threatened?' said Carl.

The nurses looked at each other and shook their heads.

'What about when a patient dies?' said Harry. 'Do you get blamed?'

'Not us, personally,' said one of the nurses. 'Those cases end up with the coroner, and people usually sue the hospital or the doctor. Everyone knows we don't get paid enough to be worth suing.'

'Do any of you park in the car park in Grant Lane?' said Carl.

'Most of us use public transport,' said one of the nurses. 'Parking in the city costs a small fortune, unless you're lucky enough to be allocated a spot in the hospital's car park.'

'Anyone know why Kelly chose to park there?' said Carl.

'She didn't like taking the train home at night,' said one of the nurses.

Carl handed each of them one of his cards. 'If you notice

anything out of the ordinary, or if you think of anything, please contact me.'

'Are we in any danger?' said one of the nurses.

'I don't know, to be honest,' said Carl, 'but I suggest you keep your wits about you until we find out who killed Kelly.'

Carl and Harry took the elevator down to the lobby and walked out into the sunshine.

'Did you bring a car?' said Carl, glancing up into the clear blue sky.

'Jessika dropped me off,' said Harry. 'She's spending the day with her mother.'

'Hard to believe it was raining yesterday,' said Carl. 'Let's walk.'

They crossed the intersection and walked down Grant Lane towards the car park.

'How's Nina?' said Harry.

'She's got her hands full,' said Carl. 'Sophie's into everything.'

'Wait until she's walking,' said Harry. 'My mother reckons that's when a parent's life gets interesting.'

'She's almost there,' said Carl. 'She walks if I hold her hand.'

They stopped outside the entrance to the car park.

'Pity there's no CCTV here,' said Harry.

'He obviously picked this place on purpose,' said Carl, 'so he must have scouted the place. I wonder if Uniform has had any luck talking to people around here.'

'Hopefully, we'll have some statements from them today,' said Harry. 'The lot we just spoke to didn't help much but it seems everyone knew about her problems with Holden.'

'Makes me think she would have talked about anybody else causing her grief,' said Carl. 'Don't like our chances with this, going on what we know.'

'Guess we'd better talk to her sister again,' said Harry.

They walked to the end of the lane, turned left, and headed towards the centre of the city.

———

There were two reports on Carl's desk when he arrived at Police Headquarters.

'Get the team together, Harry,' said Carl, picking up the report from Crime Stoppers.

He scanned the contents. Crime Stoppers had received several calls from people saying they'd seen a cyclist dressed like the man in the picture on Port Road early Friday morning, but no-one had called to suggest they knew who he was.

The second report was an update from Uniform, telling him they had failed to find anybody in the vicinity of Grant Lane that had seen anyone in the lane or hanging around the car park, apart from a patient in the hospital, who'd told them she'd seen a man dressed in black waiting with his bike at the bus stop opposite the hospital on Friday morning while she'd been having breakfast. She'd told the interviewing officer she'd watched him get on his bike and enter the lane after a woman had crossed the street and disappeared into the lane. The officer had noted that the window in the patient's room did not allow a view down the lane from the patient's bed and that the patient had not seen the man exiting the lane.

Carl went out to where the team was waiting for him.

'We don't seem to be getting very far with this one,' said Carl.

'We've identified the bike,' said DC Templar. 'It's an Allez Sprint DSW. They retail for around two thousand dollars, so he's probably a serious cyclist.'

'Well, until something else comes up, get a list of their local distributors and work on finding out who owns one,' said Carl.

'And, I've got the call log for her mobile phone,' said DC Templar. 'The only incoming calls over the last few days are from Holden, her sister, and her mother.'

'We might have to start looking deeper into her past. Maybe a previous boyfriend,' said Harry.

'Talk to her sister,' said Carl. 'What have you got, Wayne?'

'I spoke to the property manager for the warehouse. He's let the place out on a casual basis to a small transport company that's using it as a storehouse for its shipments.' Wayne looked at Carl and smiled. 'Nolan Transport.'

'When's he due back from his interstate trip?' said Carl.

'Sometime this afternoon,' said Wayne.

'Pay him a visit,' said Carl, 'and bring him in for a chat.'

'That's if he turns up,' said Wayne. 'If his wife's told him we've been around asking questions, he probably won't want to show his face, especially if he's part of the gang taking the cars.'

'Check anyway, Wayne. If he doesn't show, we'll know he's not someone who was simply contracted to shift the cars.'

'What's happening with Holden?' said Wayne.

'Waiting for his lawyer,' said Carl. 'When he shows, we'll see what he has to say for himself.'

'I reckon he's in it up to his neck,' said Wayne. 'There's no way they'd let just anyone transport those cars around, after all the trouble they've gone to getting them.'

———

Carl took Lisa into the interview with him to operate the recording equipment and fulfil the requirement for having a second officer present.

Carl looked at Holden. His demeanour suggested he hadn't enjoyed his first night in the holding cells.

'This had better be important,' said William Maynard.

'Police work is always important, Mr Maynard. Besides, we wouldn't be here if your client hadn't lied to me yesterday,' said Carl.

'I didn't lie to you,' said Ian.

'You weren't exactly honest with me, Mr Holden,' said Carl. 'Take your mate Jim, the bloke that owns the truck you were driving. Why didn't you tell me his full name and that he's married to your sister?'

William Maynard rolled his eyes.

'I knew you'd work it out from the rego on the truck,' said Ian. 'I didn't want to do your bloody job for you.'

'Or that you drove his truck most weekends?' said Carl.

'Only when he needs a hand,' said Ian.

'Any idea where we might find him?' said Carl.

Ian crossed his arms on his chest.

'Looks like he's dropped you in it,' said Carl. 'He's done a runner; happy for you to take the blame, I'd say.'

'It's like I said,' said Ian. 'I didn't know the car was stolen. Jim said he'd picked it up from the owner.'

'Why were you driving his truck?' said Carl.

'He was driving the other truck, the one he uses to take cars interstate,' said Ian.

'What sort of truck is that?' said Carl, hoping Holden would confirm it was a green Mack.

Ian shrugged his shoulders. 'Never seen it. He was going to meet me down at the port.'

'Does he own it?' said Carl.

'I don't think so.'

'So, what was the plan for yesterday?'

'I was supposed to take the car down to the warehouse and

help him load the truck,' said Ian, 'then, we were going interstate.'

'Where?' said Carl.

'He didn't say. All he said was we'd be away overnight.'

Carl wondered if Holden was being deliberately evasive or really didn't know where Nolan had planned to go.

'Did you contact him after the accident?' said Carl.

'Yeah.'

'How?' said Carl.

'On me bloody phone.'

'What did he say?' said Carl.

'I don't think I can repeat that with a lady present,' said Ian, flashing a smile at Lisa.

'My client wouldn't have told you where he was taking that car if he was involved,' said William Maynard.

Carl thought that was possible but he wasn't convinced. He'd listened to too many criminals selling out their mates to make themselves look innocent, and his gut instinct was telling him not to trust Holden.

'Have you been to the warehouse at the port before, Mr Holden?' said Carl.

'Nah, this is the first time I'd taken a car down there. That's why I had the address written down in the truck with me. Jim wouldn't have asked me to do it if I hadn't been on holidays and, besides, he only asked me because his offsider's crook.'

'Does this offsider have a name?' said Carl.

'Some bloke called Greg. I've only met him a couple of times. My sister will tell you who he is.'

'I hope for your sake you're telling me the truth,' said Carl.

'I'm not a thief,' said Ian. 'I've never pinched a thing in my life.'

Carl knew he should be giving Holden the benefit of the doubt on that as he didn't have a record, but a little voice in his head was asking whether that was true or if the truth was he'd simply never been caught until now.

'What's Nolan's mobile number?' said Carl.

'It's in my phone,' said Ian.

'What's your access code?' said Carl.

Ian turned to his lawyer. 'Can I give him that?'

'It would help your case,' said William Maynard.

———

After interviewing Holden, Carl called Wayne and asked him to find out from Nolan's wife who his offsider was. Twenty minutes later, as he was finishing his notes on the interview for the case file, Wayne called him back.

'There's no-one home at Nolan's, Inspector. The neighbours reckon she drove off shortly after we were here yesterday.'

'Sounds like we might be onto something, Wayne. Add her to your APB for Nolan.'

'Did Holden change his story?'

'Still claims he had no idea the car was stolen,' said Carl. 'See you when you get back.'

Carl slipped his phone back into the inside pocket of his jacket and wondered if Holden had told him the truth or spun him a yarn. He was inclined to believe the voice in his head telling him he'd been lied to, but he knew they'd need something a little more concrete than a gut feeling to convince a judge Holden was involved.

He walked out to the squad room where DC Templar was sitting at her desk.

'Lisa, get Nolan's mobile number out of Holden's phone and put a trace on it. We might find out where he's been if nothing else.'

CHAPTER SEVEN

On the morning after he'd administered justice to Kelly Palmer, Trent made himself a coffee and sat down with the paper.

He felt refreshed. He'd enjoyed a good night's sleep; a night free of the nightmare that usually interrupted his slumber.

He was feeling good about himself. He'd finally acted and executed the first name on his list, instead of sitting around agonising over whether it was the right thing to do or not. In Trent's mind, retribution was the purest form of justice he could administer, and he had administered it. But, he was under no illusion that what he was doing was within the law. He was doing it because the system and its laws had not served him. The system had let him down. The powers that be had refused to punish those who had denied Helen her dreams and taken her from him.

It felt good knowing he was setting things right. He no longer cared about what would happen to him. He only cared about doing what Helen wanted.

Curious to see what they had made of his first execution, he pulled the paper towards him and removed its plastic wrapping.

There was nothing about Kelly's death on the front page of the paper. He opened to page three and confronted the picture of him leaving Grant Lane on his bike.

'Fuck!'

He'd forgotten to check if there was a traffic camera at the intersection in front of the hospital. Too late now. He put down his coffee and examined the photograph with care.

After several nervous moments, he decided there was no way anybody would recognize him as the man on the bike, thanks to the hat and sunglasses he'd chosen to wear.

Trent leant back in his chair and resumed sipping his coffee while he read the story that accompanied the photograph. It seemed to him the police had no idea who'd killed her or why.

He told himself things were going to plan and God was keeping his side of the bargain by looking out for him while he delivered Helen's divine justice.

When he'd finished his coffee, he took Helen's coffee mug out of the cupboard above the refrigerator and placed it on top of the newspaper on the table. He didn't see any point in waiting. After all, the police weren't looking for him. They didn't even know he existed.

'Time to choose the next one, sweetheart.'

Trent closed his eyes, dipped the fingers of his right hand into the mug, and pulled out one of the folded pieces of paper. He placed the small wad of paper onto the table and unfolded it to see who she'd chosen: Christine Viking.

He remembered her. She was the older woman, the one that had talked to him and tried to console him. She was the one that had told him she was planning to retire on the South Coast, at Carrick. He smiled to himself. That was nearly seven years ago. She'd be retired by now and Carrick wasn't a very big place.

Trent started his research with White Pages.

That was bloody easy, he thought, when the listing for C Viking appeared. He flipped over the piece of paper with her name on it and wrote her address on the back. He opened Google Maps and keyed in 5 Squall Avenue, Carrick. When the red marker appeared on the map, he switched to the satellite view and studied the surrounding area.

Squall Avenue was three streets back from the ocean, on the northern edge of the town and close to the caravan park. He thought the houses looked like they were holiday homes. He smiled as he realized most of them would be unoccupied at this time of year.

Straight away, he knew taking out this one was going to be easier than Kelly Palmer. Christine Viking was a sitting duck waiting for him. All he had to do was go to Carrick and knock on her front door.

He looked up the website for the caravan park and booked himself a cabin for the following week. He'd stayed there several times before. He liked spending time in quiet places like Carrick and decided he may as well turn his visit into a break away from the city.

Trent put Helen's coffee mug back into the cupboard above the refrigerator and went into his bedroom to pack a bag for his seaside holiday.

CHAPTER EIGHT

First thing Monday morning, Carl met with DCI Rankin to discuss his cases.

'We've got little to go on, Chief, apart from that image of a man on a bike coming out of Grant Lane around the time of the murder,' said Carl, 'and a statement from a patient in the hospital saying she'd seen a man dressed in black standing around with a bike opposite the hospital and following a woman down the lane around the time our victim left the hospital.'

'Sounds like he's your man, then,' said DCI Rankin.

'I can't argue with that, Chief, but we still have to find him,' said Carl. 'I'd like to know how he disappeared so quickly. We had patrols in the area looking for him within ten minutes.'

'Makes you think he must have had a vehicle parked nearby,' said DCI Rankin. 'Did I hear correctly that Lisa has identified the bike as one of those expensive models?'

Carl nodded. 'She's working her way through the shops that sell them to construct a database of owners, but we could still miss him, especially if he bought the bike privately.'

'It's a place to start, Carl, and you never know your luck. I doubt many people pay cash for that sort of bike,' said DCI Rankin.

'I hope you're right, Chief. But, it's still like looking for a needle in a haystack,' said Carl.

'At least you have the haystack,' said DCI Rankin. 'Are you following any other lines of enquiry?'

'With her immediate ex out of the picture, we're exploring previous boyfriends with the victim's sister,' said Carl.

'Nothing from your chat with her colleagues?' said DCI Rankin.

Carl shook his head. 'They all knew about her troubles with her boyfriend, so I guess she wasn't the sort that would have kept a stalker or someone threatening her secret.'

'There will be something in her background, Carl. There has to be a reason why someone wanted her dead. Keep looking.'

'I guess we're going to have to talk to more people that knew her,' said Carl. 'It could be related to her life outside of her relationship and work.'

'Keep at it, Carl. You'll crack it,' said DCI Rankin. 'Any luck with that Nolan character you're trying to find?'

'The boys are searching the registrations database for green Mack trucks. Nolan doesn't own one, so he must have hired one to pull his trailer interstate or wherever he took it,' said Carl. 'Another needle in a haystack but at least we know the needle's in this haystack.'

DCI Rankin laughed. 'Keep me posted, Carl.'

Carl left the chief inspector's office and headed to the Magistrates Court for Holden's committal hearing.

———

The committal hearing ended with the magistrate releasing Holden on bail, to appear again on Tuesday, the seventh of November, to answer the charge of being in possession of a stolen motor vehicle. Carl returned to Police Headquarters to attend Kelly Palmer's post mortem.

Mike Jonas looked at the photographs taken at the crime scene. 'Doesn't look like she put up much of a struggle, Carl. Her clothing is not torn or in disarray.' He examined the victim's finger nails and the bruising on her neck.

'I'd say he surprised her from behind,' said Mike. 'There's nothing under her finger nails and he certainly applied a lot of pressure to her throat. The larynx is crushed. She would have died quickly, with little time to struggle.'

Carl didn't think that was much consolation. She was still dead.

He waited while Mike worked his way through her body to satisfy the coroner's requirements.

'This was the body of a fit and healthy woman in her mid-thirties,' said Mike, 'until she met her killer.'

'Anything that might help me find him?' said Carl.

'I'd say he was taller than the victim. See how the bruises go up on the sides of her neck? And, he's probably fit. He's applied enough pressure to kill her almost instantly,' said Mike.

And he was quick, thought Carl. He'd left the scene before the body was found a little after eight fifteen, and the victim hadn't left the hospital until eight. 'What about the rope he used?'

'Standard garden variety, I'm afraid,' said Mike. 'Dark green nylon, we've got a couple of fibres, but what you need is a length of rope with traces of your victim's skin on it.'

After the post mortem, Carl returned to his office on the third floor.

'Get anything from her sister, Harry?'

'The name of every guy Kelly ever went out with but she doesn't think any of them would have the sort of grudge that would explain Kelly's murder,' said Harry. 'She also gave me the contact details of their tennis club. Apparently, that was Kelly's main social outlet apart from work.'

'Sounds like you have a few people to follow up, then,' said Carl.

'More than a few,' said Harry. 'Appears she was popular with the boys until Holden came onto the scene. Learn anything at the post mortem?' said Harry.

'Nothing we didn't already know. Mike reckons it was quick. I wonder if that means he's got a rope with handles on it,' said Carl.

'Could be knotted at the ends, I suppose,' said Harry. 'I've seen that done before. What did Mike say about the rope?'

'It's dark green nylon and the sort anybody can buy at a hardware store.'

'Think we might have better luck finding the bike,' said Harry.

'If we can trace him through the bike, we might get lucky if he hasn't tossed the rope,' said Carl, thinking about what Mike said he needed to find.

'If it was me, I would have tossed the rope,' said Harry, 'unless I planned to use it again.'

'Don't go there, Harry. That's all we need. How's that database of yours coming along, Lisa?' said Carl.

'I've got fifty-six names so far, Inspector, and five stores still to go,' said Lisa.

'Keep at it. By the way, where are Wayne and Nigel?' said Carl.

'They've gone to speak to Mrs Nolan,' said Lisa. 'She called Wayne.'

CHAPTER NINE

Jim Nolan lay on the bed in the dark, waiting. His hosts hadn't said much to him since bringing him to the house, relieving him of his phone, and showing him into the back bedroom.

He thought about Cynthia and how stressed she'd be not knowing where he was and what was happening to him. He didn't understand why they'd taken his phone. It wasn't like he'd be calling the police.

He cursed his rotten luck. This load was the last lot of cars he'd agreed to deliver, and the money he'd been promised would have seen them right for months. He sat upright. They hadn't paid him, even though he had delivered four of the five cars. He wondered if he'd get paid at all, seeing as he was being treated more like a prisoner than a service provider. Things certainly weren't going according to what he'd been told would happen when he delivered this load of cars. He lay down on the bed again and closed his eyes.

He thought he'd done the right thing leaving as soon as Ian had told him about the accident and the truck being out of action, but now he wasn't quite so sure.

Cynthia had called and told him Ian had been arrested before they'd taken his phone from him. He'd told her the police had made a mistake and denied dealing in stolen cars. Poor Ian. He'd been dropped right in it, hadn't he? If only he hadn't been involved in that bloody accident. He wondered how Ian was doing and if he'd be released, and worried about what he'd tell the police to save his own skin.

Jim gazed into the darkness and hoped Ian had stuck to the story they'd agreed to tell if asked about the cars. If not, he was in deep shit. It hadn't taken the police long to work out who owned the truck, which was why they'd been around to see Cynthia. Too late to cry over spilt milk now, he thought. The people they were working for had heard about Ian's arrest on the radio before he'd arrived, and they hadn't been impressed that his load was one car short. And, they'd made it clear they weren't happy with the police knowing about his connection to their operation.

He wondered if they'd expect him to take the fall for the entire operation, and shuddered as he thought they might decide silencing him forever was a better option. He sat up and held his head in his hands, wishing he'd never listened to Ian's solution for solving their financial problems.

Jim looked at the sliver of light around the edges of the locked door and wondered what they were waiting for, before realizing the two men in the room down the corridor weren't in charge. They were waiting for someone else to decide his fate.

He listened to the sound of muffled voices coming through the door and wondered if they were talking about him or watching the TV. As he listened, he heard the sound of footsteps approaching the door to his room. There was a rattle as the key was turned in the lock and the door opened. The room filled with bright light.

'Get your stuff, Nolan. Time to go.'

Jim blinked as his eyes adjusted to the light and picked up his overnight bag from where he'd dropped it on the floor next to the bed. He followed them outside.

'Get in.'

'Are you taking me back to the truck?' said Jim.

'We'll take you there later. The boss wants to talk to you first.'

Jim opened the rear door of the sedan, threw in his overnight bag, and slid onto the back seat. He heard the door locks click into place when the driver turned the key in the ignition. He looked out into the night. He had no idea where they were or where they were taking him, and hoped it wasn't to an early grave in the middle of nowhere.

———

After spending the weekend in the police holding cells, the first thing Ian Holden wanted to do after being released on bail was go home and have a shower.

He hailed a taxi in front of the Magistrates Court and slipped into the back seat for the ride to Portside. As the taxi rejoined the traffic stream, Ian switched on his mobile phone and waited for the display to light up, hoping there'd be enough juice in the battery to make a few calls. When the phone came to life, he called his sister to let her know he'd been released on bail and to ask if she'd heard from Jim.

'Nothing since I spoke to him Friday afternoon,' said Cynthia.

'Call the police and report him missing,' said Ian.

'Why should I do that?' said Cynthia. 'Won't that just make them ask more questions?'

'You need to play the worried wife,' said Ian, 'otherwise,

they'll think you're involved. And, remember, you know nothing.'

'That bit won't be hard,' said Cynthia. 'Where do you think Jim is?'

'Don't know,' said Ian, 'but I wouldn't expect him back anytime soon.'

'What are you going to do?' said Cynthia.

'I'm going home to have a shower, I'll call you later.'

Ian ended the call and hoped he'd given her the right advice. He needed the police to think Jim was the connection to the stolen cars and that Cynthia had no idea what was going on. He hoped she'd be able to play her part so the police would waste their time looking for Jim and leave him alone.

He paid the fare and exited the cab. He thought his phone had enough juice to make another call but he didn't want to make that call inside the taxi with the driver listening.

He stood on the footpath in front of his apartment building and soaked in the rays of the winter sun.

'Kurt, it's me,' said Ian.

'Where are you? Heard you'd been arrested.'

'Maynard got me out on bail,' said Ian.

'Has anyone told you about Kelly?' said Kurt.

'Yeah, the coppers told me Friday morning,' said Ian. 'At least they can't blame me for that.'

'You okay?'

'Not much I can do about it. It's not like she was talking to me.'

'You'd better come and see me,' said Kurt. 'We need to talk.'

'I need to freshen up. Give me a couple of hours,' said Ian.

Ian ended the call and opened the door to his apartment, pondering the possibility of the police making the charges stick. Be a nuisance if they did, he thought. He didn't particularly want to spend any more time in jail, especially if the stories he'd heard about what it was like doing time were true. It sounded a hell of a lot worse than spending a weekend in a holding cell at the Watch House.

He closed the door and wondered if he'd ever get to see Jim again. They'd been friends since high school, when they'd started stealing cars for a lark, taking them for a spin around the city until they'd run out of petrol. He knew his sister would be devastated when she finally understood Jim had done a runner to stay ahead of the police. He smiled. At least Jim had gotten a head start, even if it meant he'd been left holding the baby. As he plugged his phone into the charger, he hoped the magistrate would believe his story when he got his day in court.

When he walked into his bedroom, the photograph of Kelly he'd placed on his bedside cabinet caught his attention. He sat on the bed and picked it up. Tears welled up from somewhere deep within him and ran down his face as sobs of anguish and regret found voice in his throat.

She'd meant the world to him, and he'd done everything in his power to keep her and failed. Now she was gone forever. He wasn't sure he wanted to keep on living in a world without the possibility of winning her back.

He put the photograph back on the bedside cabinet and wiped his eyes with the back of his hand. He wondered how he'd find out about her funeral. He knew Tyler wouldn't tell him. She wouldn't even want him to attend. He hoped they'd publish a funeral notice in the paper as he wanted to be there for her one last time.

He looked at her photograph again. His fists clenched tightly. He stood and punched the air. He wanted to kill the sick bastard that had taken her from him. If he had to go to prison, he hoped the police caught the bastard. Tracking him down inside and killing him would make it worthwhile.

He spent the next hour going through his Tae Kwon Do

routines, before hitting the shower and heading off to meet Kurt.

————

Ian sat across the desk from Kurt Viking in the office at Bayside Auto.

'What do they know?' said Kurt.

'I was driving Jim's truck,' said Ian, 'but I played like I was the innocent party doing him a favour.'

'Did they buy it?'

'Who knows, but they have to prove otherwise,' said Ian, 'and Jim isn't around to tell them, is he?'

'No,' said Kurt.

'Have you heard from him?'

Kurt shook his head. 'Best if we don't know where he is.'

'So, he won't be coming back any time soon?' said Ian.

'Not if he doesn't want to go inside,' said Kurt, 'and we certainly don't want him spilling his guts to the cops, do we?'

Ian thought about his sister and wondered how she'd react when she realized Jim would not be coming home.

'My sister's going to be pissed,' said Ian, 'especially if she ever finds out I'm the one that talked him into this.'

'Well, you'd better not tell her.'

'She's not going to hear it from me,' said Ian. 'But what if Jim tells her?'

Kurt leant back in his chair. 'I don't think you need to worry about that. Jim knows the score.'

Ian glanced through the window at the stream of late afternoon traffic making its way past the workshop and watched a Mack truck slow to a stop as the lights at the intersection further down the road changed to red. 'What are we going to do about the truck? Jim was supposed to return it this morning.'

'When do you have to report in?' said Kurt.

'On Mondays, at ten.'

'Perhaps we can go up the river and bring it back tomorrow,' said Kurt.

'I don't want to miss Kelly's funeral.'

'Do you know when it is?'

'Not yet.'

'It won't be until the cops release her body' said Kurt, 'and then her family will need to arrange her funeral, so tomorrow shouldn't be a problem.'

Ian thought about how long it had taken to arrange his father's funeral, and he'd died in a hospital. 'I suppose you're right.'

'I'll give Eddie a call and get him to arrange an extension on the lease for the truck. We don't want them reporting it stolen,' said Kurt, 'and giving the cops any ideas.'

'They know Jim was driving another truck,' said Ian. 'I had to tell them something to explain why I was driving his truck.'

'What did you tell them about the truck?'

'Said I didn't know what sort of truck it was,' said Ian.

'Does your sister know about the Mack?'

'Not sure, but she knows not to say anything about it,' said Ian.

'Best if we get it back before the cops know what they're looking for,' said Kurt.

That sounded reasonable to Ian. 'What time do you want to leave in the morning?'

'First thing,' said Kurt. 'That way we can have it back before they close tomorrow.'

CHAPTER TEN

Cynthia Nolan sat in her mother's kitchen drinking coffee. 'Mum, the police have arrested Ian.' She looked at her hands. 'And they're looking for Jim.'

'What's Ian done?' said Mrs Holden.

'He was driving Jim's truck for him Friday morning. Greg's got the flu. Anyway, there was an accident. Some old fella pulled out in front of him and got himself killed.'

'Was Ian hurt?' said Mrs Holden.

'No, but the police are saying the car on the back of the truck was stolen. They came to see me. Wanted to know where Jim was.'

'What did you tell them?' said Mrs Holden.

'That he's interstate.'

'Is that true?' said Mrs Holden.

'Of course it's true, Mum! That's where he told me he was going.'

'Did you let him know the police were looking for him?'

'He said the police must have made a mistake and he'd sort it out when he got back, but he hasn't come home,' said

Cynthia. 'I was expecting him yesterday, and he's not answering his phone.'

'Do you think he could be involved in stealing cars?' said Mrs Holden.

Cynthia looked through the kitchen window into her mother's back garden. Her mother had never liked her husband but she'd never accused him of being a thief. A lazy bag of bones, maybe, but never a thief. She wasn't sure how to respond without sounding defensive. She didn't want another fight with her mother over her choice of husband.

'There's a lot of competition driving prices down, Mum,' said Cynthia. 'Some months, it's a struggle to make the payments on the truck. That's why Jim's taken a couple of interstate jobs for cash, no questions asked. This is the third time he's gone interstate in someone else's truck. It's good money but I'm scared something's happened to him. He always calls when he's going to be late.'

Mrs Holden put down her cup. 'Are you going to go to the police?'

'I don't know. What if he is taking stolen cars interstate?'

'Do you know who pays him all that cash?'

Cynthia shook her head. 'He said it was better I didn't know.'

'Have you spoken to Greg?' said Mrs Holden.

Cynthia nodded. 'He says he doesn't know anything. And, I'm worried about him too. He sounded like death warmed up when I spoke to him on Friday.'

'Do you believe him?' said Mrs Holden.

'He went with Jim on the other trips,' said Cynthia, 'he must know something.'

'You'd think he'd at least know where they went,' said Mrs Holden.

'Jim's probably sworn him to secrecy,' said Cynthia. 'They're as thick as thieves those two. Always have been.'

'I think you should talk to the police, Cynthia. What if Jim is in trouble?'

Cynthia drained her cup. She suspected her husband knew he was transporting stolen cars, even though he'd denied it when she'd spoken to him about Ian. There were too many signs pointing to that conclusion for her to discount it, but she still couldn't understand why he hadn't called her or returned her calls. She didn't want to believe something had happened to him. She wanted to believe he was being cautious.

'I'll give him another twenty-four hours,' said Cynthia. 'If I don't hear from him, I'll call the policeman that came to see me. He gave me his number.'

———

Wayne pushed the doorbell button and waited on the porch with Nigel. The door was opened by a woman with jet-black hair and white skin. Wayne thought he was looking at one of the living dead.

'Mrs Holden?'

'Yes.'

Wayne held out his ID. 'Detective Constable Paterson. This is Detective Constable Beard.'

'Please, come in. My daughter is expecting you,' said Mrs Holden.

She led them into the kitchen at the rear of the house where Cynthia Nolan sat at the table with a cup of coffee in front of her.

'Like to tell us what's going on, Mrs Nolan?' said Wayne.

'My husband hasn't come home,' said Cynthia. 'I'm afraid something's happened to him.'

There was something in her voice that made Wayne think she was genuine but he'd been had before by women spinning him tales of woe, so he remained a little skeptical.

'What makes you think that?' said Wayne, looking her directly in the eyes.

'Like I told you the other day, he went interstate. He was supposed to be back Saturday afternoon, and he's not answering his phone. He always calls when he's going to be late.'

Wayne wondered why she'd waited until Monday afternoon to call them but knew people didn't always act rationally, especially when they thought their spouse could be involved in something illegal, like stealing expensive cars.

'Does he do these interstate trips often?' said Wayne.

'You don't understand. This is only the third time he's gone interstate in that truck. Most times he drives our truck,' said Cynthia.

'What's so special about these trips?' said Wayne.

'I don't know, but we don't do invoices for them. He gets paid cash. That's not how the business usually works,' said Cynthia. 'I do the books. We send invoices and get paid electronically straight into our account. It's much easier that way.'

Wayne suspected they were onto something. Nolan might not be stealing the cars but it sounded like he was transporting them out of the city for whoever was.

'Where does this cash your husband gets come from?' said Wayne.

'I don't know,' said Cynthia. 'He wouldn't tell me.'

'Who else knows about these trips apart from your brother?' said Wayne.

'Greg. He works for us. He went with Jim on the first two trips,' said Cynthia.

This could be useful, thought Wayne. He glanced at Nigel, who had his notebook out.

'Greg who?' said Wayne.

'Sutton,' said Cynthia.

'Where can we find him?' said Wayne.

'He lives in Northfield. I've got his address in my phone,' said Cynthia.

Nigel wrote down Greg Sutton's address as Cynthia read it out.

'Do you know anything about this truck your husband drives interstate?' said Wayne.

Cynthia shook her head. 'All I know is he gets good money for driving it.'

'Do you know anything about the car that was on the truck your brother was driving?'

'No.'

'What about Warehouse 66?'

'That's where Jim told Ian to meet him Friday morning,' said Cynthia. 'I don't even know where it is.'

'The lease is in the name of Nolan Transport,' said Wayne.

'Is it?' said Cynthia. 'It's not being paid for by us. I do the accounts. I've never paid for that.'

———

Wayne and Nigel stood outside the house at the address Cynthia Nolan had given them for Greg Sutton. The front yard was overgrown. Lawn runners snaked across the driveway. Dead leaves lay in piles along the front wall of the house. The gutter had come off the front of the building and fallen onto the cement pathway that led from the driveway to the front door. An ancient Ford sedan was parked under the sagging roof of the carport attached to the side of the house.

'Can't be much money in whatever this guy does for Nolan,' said Nigel.

'Either that or he doesn't give a shit,' said Wayne. 'Come on, let's see if he's home.'

They made their way to the front door. Wayne banged on it with his fist. There was no response.

They walked through the carport to the rear of the house and peered through the windows.

'He could use a cleaner,' said Nigel. 'I don't know how anyone can live in a mess like that.'

They walked back to the front of the house and crossed over the street to the house opposite, where a woman was sweeping her yard. Wayne introduced himself and showed her his ID.

'Have you seen Mr Sutton in the last couple of days?' said Wayne.

'Who?'

'The man that lives in that house over there,' said Wayne, pointing across the street.

'Ambulance came for him Saturday night,' said the woman. 'Haven't seen him since.'

'Does anyone live with him?' said Wayne.

The woman shook her head. 'He's a bit of a strange one. Keeps to himself and, as you can see, isn't what you'd call house-proud. I've reported him to the council, but it hasn't made any bloody difference.'

Wayne called the Ambulance Service while Nigel piloted their car through the traffic heading into the city.

'They took him to City,' said Wayne.

Twenty minutes later, they walked through the main entrance of City Hospital and approached the reception desk. Wayne showed the receptionist his ID.

'We're looking for Greg Sutton. He came in by ambulance

on Saturday night,' said Wayne.

They waited while the receptionist queried the admissions records.

'What suburb?' said the receptionist.

'Northfield,' said Wayne.

'Yes. Here he is.' She clicked on the record to read the details. 'Oh!'

'Something wrong?' said Wayne.

'He died Sunday morning.'

———

Carl looked up from his screen when DC Paterson tapped on his office door and waved him in.

'How did it go with Mrs Nolan?'

'Nolan hasn't come back from his interstate trip,' said DC Paterson. 'She thinks something's happened to him.'

'Why's that?'

'Hasn't called, and she says he's not answering his phone when she calls,' said DC Paterson.

Carl wondered if Nolan had gone to ground and, in the process, incriminated himself and, perhaps, Holden as well.

'Pick up anything else, Wayne?'

'This is the third trip he's made using that particular truck,' said DC Paterson, 'and he's being paid cash, which I gather is not the usual way they do business.'

Carl thought Mrs Nolan probably wouldn't be talking to them if she knew her husband was involved in moving stolen vehicles.

'Did she know anything about the warehouse?'

DC Paterson shook his head. 'No, and she does the books, apparently.'

'What do you think? Is she telling us the truth?'

'Some of it,' said Wayne, 'but I'm not so sure she's totally in the dark about what Nolan's doing.'

'Any luck finding out who his offsider is?' said Carl.

'His name's Greg Sutton. Went on the first two trips with Nolan, according to Mrs Nolan, but he was admitted to City Saturday night with pneumonia.' DC Paterson smiled. 'Died Sunday morning, so we won't be getting anything from him.'

'Starting to think him being sick is the only thing Holden's told us that's turned out to be true,' said Carl.

'What happened with Holden this morning?' said DC Paterson.

'With no previous convictions, the magistrate let him out on bail,' said Carl. 'We need to know more about him. I'm not sure I buy his story. See what you can find out while you're looking for Nolan.'

CHAPTER ELEVEN

Gordon Sharp walked into his office in the Investigative Unit of the Forensic Medicine Department at City University, settled in behind his desk, and logged on to his computer.

Gordon, who had joined the unit after completing a doctorate in Forensic Medicine, enjoyed the research-based work they performed. It involved long hours sifting through data and clinical records looking for patterns and anomalies, which he found exciting, especially when his team exposed systemic errors others had failed to detect.

He checked his inbox. There was an email marked urgent from Professor Lincoln assigning him a new project to manage.

Gordon opened the attachment and read the description of the project. It was a request from the Health Department for a review of the reporting of deaths in City and University Hospitals to the Coroner's Office over the previous ten years. Gordon wondered what was behind the request. He hadn't heard any rumours of the under-reporting of hospital deaths to the coroner.

He clicked on the hyperlink to the legislation in the email

and read the criteria that were meant to trigger the mandatory reporting of deaths: unexpected, unnatural, violent, resulting from accident or injury, and during or resulting from an anaesthetic.

Gordon leant back in his chair. This was going to take his team the better part of a year and would involve liaison between his team, the hospitals, and the Coroner's Office.

A shadow fell across his desk. Gordon looked up. Professor Lincoln was standing in the doorway of his office.

'Morning, Professor.'

'Gordon.'

'What can I do for you?' said Gordon.

'We need to talk about your new assignment. They want the results before the end of the year.'

Gordon scratched his head. 'That could be a bit of a stretch. We don't have that many people we can devote to this job, and it's going to entail the reading of the clinical records of every hospital death over the last ten years.'

'The project comes with its own funding. Talk to my PhD students. They'll be able to help with the review of the clinical records. It'll look good on their CVs, and I'm sure they could use the money.'

'Okay. I'll do that, and then get started on my project plan. By the way, any idea why they want this done?'

'Someone's got into the minister's ear and convinced him doctors at both hospitals are covering up suspicious deaths and not reporting them to the coroner.'

'He thinks doctors are protecting themselves by avoiding scrutiny by the coroner?' said Gordon.

'Something along those lines,' said Professor Lincoln.

'Are they making a public announcement?'

'The minister is making a statement to the House next week.'

'Guess we can expect a bit of push back, then. The hospitals don't like us coming in asking questions even at the best of times.'

'We've been promised maximum cooperation by the Secretary for Health. She doesn't think there's a problem with the reporting but the minister won't take her word for it. He's demanding an independent review.'

'We can guarantee him that,' said Gordon.

CHAPTER TWELVE

On Saturday morning, Carl sat at his desk reading DC Templar's and DS Fuller's reports.

In the week since Kelly Palmer's murder, Lisa had interviewed thirty-two owners of Allez Sprint DSW cycles and confirmed their alibis with spouses, work mates, and friends. Harry had spoken to seven former boyfriends of Kelly Palmer, with the same outcome, and interviewed the members of the tennis club she had belonged to without uncovering any other angles they could pursue.

It seemed Kelly Palmer had been a fun-loving member of the community who'd gotten on well with the people she'd mixed with.

Carl had interviewed Kelly's parents on their return from New Zealand. They were as mystified as all the others as to why anyone would want to kill her. He squeezed his right earlobe between his thumb and index finger and stared into space. They were getting nowhere. He closed Harry's report and wondered if they'd ever get a lead they could follow to her killer. His thoughts were interrupted by the ringing of his mobile phone.

'DI West.'

'Got a minute?' said Mike Jonas.

'What's on your mind,' said Carl.

'I'm at a crime scene in Carrick,' said Mike. 'I'm looking at the body of a woman who's been strangled with a rope. Similar neck wound to that nurse we had last week.'

'Is the victim of a similar age?' said Carl.

'No. This woman would be in her sixties,' said Mike.

'Do we know who the victim is?' said Carl.

'Her name's Christine Viking. She's a retired nurse. Her daughter found the body this morning.'

Another nurse killed the same way, thought Carl. Too much of a coincidence to not be connected.

'Who's got the case?' said Carl.

'It's still with the locals.'

'I'll talk to the chief and call you back.'

————

Two hours after receiving the call from Mike Jonas, Carl and Harry arrived outside 5 Squall Avenue, Carrick. The CSI team from Forensics were packing up their equipment and the coroner's men were waiting to take away the body.

Sgt Dean Lang from Forensics looked up from his packing when Carl approached him.

'Pretty small crime scene, Inspector. I don't think your killer ventured beyond the area immediately inside the front door.'

'What makes you think that, Dean?' said Carl.

'Muddy footprints on the carpet,' said Dean, 'and it looks

like she let him in. There's no sign of a forced entry. Looks like he strangled her right there inside the door, and left.'

'Get anything on him?' said Carl.

'Only his footprints,' said Dean. 'We should be able to give you a shoe size and maybe a brand name.'

They went into the house with Mike Jonas to look at the crime scene. The body of a grey-haired woman, dressed in a pink tracksuit and white sneakers, lay on the floor of the hallway a few steps inside the front door. Mike pointed at the dark line across the victim's neck.

'This guy is either incredibly strong or driven by rage. I'd say he's crushed her windpipe.'

'How long has she been dead?' said Carl.

'A couple of days, at least,' said Mike. 'I'll have a better idea after the autopsy.'

While the coroner's men slipped the body into a body bag and carried it out to their van, Mike introduced Carl and Harry to Sgt Colin Whitelaw from the Carrick Police Station.

'What's the story?' said Carl.

'The victim's daughter, a Mrs Wendy Graham, found the body this morning, Inspector. She came down from the city to check on her mother when she couldn't get her to answer the phone. She'd been trying to call her since last night,' said Sgt Whitelaw.

What would we do without dutiful daughters, thought Carl. 'Did any of the neighbours see anything?'

'Most of the houses in this part of town are holiday homes, Inspector, but Mrs Dawson in number two across the street there,' Sgt Whitelaw pointed to a white house on the other side of Squall Avenue, 'says she saw a man delivering a package around ten o'clock Thursday morning. Unfortunately, it was raining, so she didn't get a good look at him or the rego of the van, but she's identified it as a Ford Transit. White, and probably a 2012 model.'

'Any markings?'

'Plain white, I'm afraid,' said Sgt Whitelaw.

'Many of them in town?' said Carl.

'There are white vans all over the place, Inspector, and we have a Ford dealership down here, so plenty of them are Fords. We also get a few couriers delivering stuff from the city, so you have a big haystack if he's the killer.'

'Sounds like we'll be building another database,' said Harry.

Sgt Whitelaw cocked an eyebrow.

'We're looking for a bike in the Palmer case,' said Carl. 'She was killed the same way.'

'Serial killer?' said Sgt Whitelaw.

'Too early to say,' said Carl. 'Do you know anything about the victim?'

'I understand from Mrs Dawson she bought the place last year. I can confirm that with Heads, if you like. They handle most of the real estate sales in town,' said Sgt Whitelaw. 'I gather from her daughter she's a recently retired nurse.'

'What have you done since the body was found this morning, Sergeant?' said Carl.

'I've asked Gunnings, that's the Ford place, for a list of customers with transit vans,' said Sgt Whitelaw. 'I've got one of my constables working on the list.'

'That's a good start,' said Carl, 'but you could also ask around if anyone's had a guest in the last week or so that was driving a white van.'

'Not that many visitors down here this time of year,' said Sgt Whitelaw, 'so that shouldn't take too long.'

Carl decided he'd leave the legwork to the locals and work with the results.

'Where's the daughter now?' said Carl.

'Over the road with Mrs Dawson,' said Sgt Whitelaw.

———

Carl and Harry crossed over to number two. The front door was opened by a white-haired woman with a sun-wrinkled face as they stepped onto the front veranda.

'Mrs Dawson?' said Carl.

'That's me.'

'Inspector West from City Police,' said Carl, showing her his ID. 'This is Detective Sergeant Fuller.'

'Come in' said Mrs Dawson. 'Go through to the kitchen.' She pointed across her sitting room to the doorway into her kitchen. 'Wendy's in there.'

They walked through the doorway into the kitchen, where a middle-aged woman in a dark blue coat sat at the table staring out into Mrs Dawson's rear garden.

'Mrs Graham?' said Carl. 'I'm Inspector West from City Police.'

The woman turned from the window and looked at Carl. 'Please, call me Wendy.'

'I'm sorry about your mother,' said Carl, sitting at the table opposite Wendy. 'Are you up to answering a few questions?'

'I hope so,' said Wendy.

'Where did your mother work as a nurse?' said Carl.

'She was at University Hospital when she retired but she worked at City before that,' said Wendy.

'Are you a nurse as well?' said Carl.

'No. I'm a teacher. I'm not good with sick people.'

You're not the only one, thought Carl. 'When was the last time you spoke to your mother?'

'Last Friday,' said Wendy. 'We spoke every Friday night,

unless one of us had an engagement. Then we'd talk Saturday morning.'

'Had she been worried about anyone hanging about or following her' said Carl.

'My mother was pretty independent, Inspector. She wasn't someone who scared easily.'

'Did she ever mention if she'd been threatened by anyone?' said Carl.

'Not to me.'

Carl looked through the window at Mrs Dawson's lush green garden and wondered if his would ever look anything like it. 'Why did she retire down here?'

'She was in love with the place. I can't tell you how many times we came here for the summer holidays when I was growing up,' said Wendy.

'Is your father still alive?' said Carl.

'As far as I know,' said Wendy. 'He left us when I was still in high school. I haven't seen him since my youngest son was born, and he's nearly sixteen.'

'Did your mother have any contact with him?' said Carl.

'I don't think so, but she did tell me a few years ago that he'd remarried,' said Wendy. 'I remember Mum being angry about the divorce for years, but I was surprised she was so upset when she found out he'd married someone younger than me.' Wendy smiled. 'To be honest, I don't think she ever forgave him.'

'What's his name?' said Carl.

'Kurt Viking. You don't think he had anything to do with this, do you?'

'I really don't know but anyone who knew your mother is a potential suspect,' said Carl. 'We'll need to talk to him and find out where he was around the time your mother was murdered.'

'My father may be a jerk, Inspector, but I don't think he'd kill anyone,' said Wendy, 'especially not my mother.'

Carl hoped she was right. 'Any idea who would want to kill your mother?'

Wendy shook her head. 'I have no idea who would do that to her. She was such a wonderful person.'

Carl waited while Wendy regained her composure and wiped away her tears.

'Anything taken from her house?' said Carl.

'Not that I could tell,' said Wendy. 'Her handbag with her credit cards and her mobile phone were on the table in the hall next to where I found her.'

Whatever's driving this killer must have something to do with them being nurses, thought Carl. He obviously wasn't interested in theft.

'Would you be able to give me a list of her closest friends,' said Carl. 'People she might have confided in.'

'Well, apart from me and her sister, I think the best people to talk to would be the people she worked with at the hospital,' said Wendy.

'What's your aunt's name?' said Carl.

'Kathleen French,' said Wendy. 'She's a nurse, too. She lives quite close to University Hospital.'

'Have you spoken to her?' said Carl.

Wendy nodded. 'They were very close. Mum's only two years older than Auntie Kathleen.'

————

Sgt Whitelaw was waiting for them when they emerged from Mrs Dawson's house.

'There was a bloke driving a white Ford Transit staying at the caravan park last week, Inspector. Arrived Sunday. Left

Friday morning. The manager says he was in and out of the park most days and that he's stayed here before. Comes every year, apparently.'

'Did you get a name?' said Carl.

'Trent Mitchell. Gave his address as 45 Harvey Street, Portside,' said Sgt Whitelaw. 'The rego is SRBC465. It's a 2012 model.'

'Get an APB on it,' said Carl. 'He's definitely a person of interest.'

They waited while Sgt Whitelaw spoke to Operations.

'Anybody else at home in any of the other houses in this street?' said Carl.

'Nobody that was here during the week, I'm afraid,' said Sgt Whitelaw.

'If it's the same bloke,' said Harry, 'he knows how to pick his spots.'

CHAPTER THIRTEEN

Carl waited for Harry to get off the phone.

'Uniform have Mitchell downstairs,' said Harry, slipping his mobile into his pocket.

'What do we know about him?' said Carl.

'He's clean, as far as the database goes.'

'Is he on your bikes database, Lisa?' said Carl.

'There's no-one named Mitchell on my list, sir,' said Lisa.

'Well, let's see what he has to say for himself,' said Carl.

Carl and Harry caught the elevator down to the ground floor and walked to the interview suite, where Trent Mitchell was waiting with two uniformed constables. Carl thought Mitchell had to be in his late thirties and looked like someone who spent time working out at the gym.

'Thanks for coming in, Mr Mitchell,' said Carl.

'Didn't think I had much choice,' said Trent. 'What's this about?'

'We're trying to identify the owner of a vehicle seen in Carrick last Thursday morning, Mr Mitchell. A white Ford

Transit like the one you drive,' said Carl. 'I understand you were in Carrick last week.'

'Yeah, I spent a week in a cabin at the caravan park,' said Trent. 'That's not a crime, is it?'

Carl thought Mitchell looked fairly relaxed for someone being interviewed by the police.

'No, that's not a crime, Mr Mitchell. Can you tell me where you were on Thursday, around ten in the morning?' said Carl.

'In the pub,' said Trent, 'and, no, I wasn't having an early morning tipple. The pub's the only place you can place a bet on the horses down there.'

'Any way you can verify that?' said Carl. 'Or is there someone who can confirm that's where you were?'

Trent pulled out his wallet and extracted several betting slips. He shuffled through them and handed one to Carl. 'These things have the date and time you place your bet stamped on them.'

Carl looked at the date stamp on the slip. The bet had been placed at ten minutes past ten on the Thursday morning they suspected Christine Viking had been murdered. He handed the slip to Harry, who photographed it with the camera in his phone and handed it back to Trent Mitchell.

'What were you doing in Carrick?' said Carl.

'Taking a break from life.' Trent smiled. 'I need to get away from the city every now and then. It's quiet down there.'

'What do you do for a living?' said Carl, thinking Mitchell must do something stressful if he'd needed to get away for a quiet break.

'I work in security,' said Trent. 'I do night patrols for Metropolitan Security, checking warehouses and workshops.'

'Whereabouts?'

'Around the airport. Down the port. Sometimes that industrial park in Northfield,' said Trent. 'Depends on the shift.'

Carl thought Mitchell's work sounded lonely, not stressful, and wondered why he'd choose to take a holiday in a place like Carrick in the offseason.

'Are you familiar with Squall Avenue in Carrick at all? It's not far from the caravan park where you stayed,' said Carl.

'Doesn't ring a bell, Inspector, not that I took much notice of street names,' said Trent. 'I followed the road along the beach when I went into town from the caravan park.'

Carl opened his folder and placed a photograph of Christine Viking on the table in front of Trent.

'Do you recognize this woman?' said Carl.

Trent glanced at the photograph. 'Can't say I know who she is, Inspector. Is it important?'

'Her name's Christine Viking. Her body was found in a house in Squall Avenue this morning,' said Carl.

'Why are you asking me about her?' said Trent.

'One of her neighbours reported seeing a van like yours outside her house on Thursday morning,' said Carl. 'We're speaking to the owners of all white Ford Transits that were in the area that day.'

'Oh, I see,' said Trent. 'Well, it wasn't me I'm afraid, Inspector. As I said, I spent most of Thursday morning at the betting counter in the pub. I'm pretty sure the guy behind the counter will remember me. There weren't that many of us there Thursday morning.'

'Just out of interest, Mr Mitchell, where were you around eight o'clock on the morning of Friday the twenty-sixth of May?' said Carl, closing his folder.

'Why are you interested in where I was that day?' said Trent.

'To see if you can help me with another of my unsolved cases,' said Carl. 'You'd be surprised how often people see things without realizing they're a witness to a crime.'

Trent leant back in his chair and crossed his arms. 'That was the Friday before I went to Carrick. I worked until six. At least, that's when I signed out at the depot, and I went straight home, so I would have been having breakfast,' said Trent, 'but, I live on my own.' He shrugged his shoulders. 'Maybe one of the neighbours will remember hearing me come home.'

'Well, that doesn't put you anywhere near the place I'm interested in, Mr Mitchell,' said Carl. 'Thank you for your time.'

Carl waited while Trent Mitchell was escorted out to reception.

'What do you think, Harry?'

'I'd like to check out this betting slip and talk to the staff in the Carrick pub,' said Harry. 'Bit of a coincidence him having that slip on him. Most people ditch their losing tickets as soon as the race is called, and there's nothing on this slip showing it was issued in the pub in Carrick.'

'Tight timing if it was,' said Carl. 'Be at least a five-minute drive to the pub from the victim's house.'

'Only if Mrs Dawson's given us the correct time, Boss. She could have it wrong.'

'I suppose her recollection is a best guess,' said Carl. 'It's not like the appearance of the van had any significance until this morning.'

'Do you want me to follow up with Metropolitan Security?' said Harry.

'Yes, and have a chat with his neighbours,' said Carl. 'I think we need to find out a bit more about Mr Mitchell before we cross him off the list. A little too cool, calm, and collected for me.'

'That could be because he's not our killer,' said Harry. 'I mean, if it was me, I wouldn't be staying in a caravan park around the corner from the victim under my own name.'

'That may be so, Harry, but I'd still like you to check him out.'

———

On the Monday morning following the discovery of Christine Viking's body, Carl took DC Templar with him to interview her sister, Kathleen French.

The garden of the house at the address they had been given contained a large silver birch, which had shed its autumn leaves over the well-maintained front lawn that separated the dwelling from the street. When DC Templar rang the doorbell, the door was opened by a grey-haired man wearing silver rimmed glasses and holding a newspaper in his hand.

'Inspector West, City Police,' said Carl, showing the man his ID. 'This is Detective Constable Templar. Is your wife home?'

'Come in, Inspector. Kath's in the family room.'

Mr French led them through the house to the family room, which opened onto the rear garden, and introduced them to his wife.

'My condolences on the death of your sister,' said Carl.

'Hard to believe someone's killed her,' said Kathleen.

'Yes,' said Carl. 'It's always a bit of a shock when someone you know is murdered.'

'Can I offer you something to drink?' said Kathleen.

'Coffee would be fine,' said Carl.

Kathleen turned to Lisa.

'Coffee's fine for me, too, thank you, Mrs French,' said Lisa.

Kathleen moved into the kitchen to make the coffee.

'Are you still working?' said Carl.

'No. I retired a couple of years ago,' said Mr French. 'I'd had enough of the bureaucracy by then.'

'Oh, what did you do?' said Carl.

'Worked in hospital administration,' said Mr French. 'I did the accounts for University Hospital.'

Kathleen came back into the room carrying a tray with their coffees. 'Be my turn soon. Another couple of years.'

'How long have you worked as a nurse?' said Carl.

'Be getting close to forty years,' said Kathleen. 'It was all different when we started. Not like these days when you need a university degree.'

'Did you work with your sister?' said Carl.

'We worked in the same hospitals, if that's what you mean, but we didn't work on the same wards very often, especially after Chris specialized in intensive care,' said Kathleen. 'She didn't come to University until five years ago. She spent most of her career at City.'

'What bought her to University?' said Carl.

'She was asked to mentor the newly trained intensive care nurses,' said Kathleen. 'She was good at her job.'

'What made her decide to retire to Carrick?' said Carl.

'Chris was very happy down at Carrick. She liked being on her own and she'd always wanted to retire down there. She just loved the beach.'

'What can you tell me about her ex-husband, Kurt?' said Carl.

Kathleen put down her cup. 'They never got on. I could never understand why she married him, and I was surprised they stayed together for as long as they did.'

'What's he like?' said Carl. 'Do you think he could have killed her?'

'Kurt?' said Kathleen. 'Couldn't fight his way out of a wet paper bag, Inspector. If anyone was abusive in that relationship, it was my sister. She had him wrapped around her little finger. Poor Kurt's one of those "Yes, Dear." husbands.' She formed air quotes with her fingers. 'Not like Roger here. I can't get him to say yes to anything.'

Roger French smiled. 'I wouldn't worry too much about Kurt, Inspector. He has to get his wife's permission to breathe. I can't see her letting him wander off to Carrick.'

'When was the last time you saw him?' said Carl.

'We see them at church,' said Kathleen. 'They've got two lovely little boys.'

'Do you have an address for Kurt?' said Carl.

Kathleen looked at Roger.

'They live next to the school in Crompton Street. Number fifty-one, I think. You can't miss it. It's one of those McMansions. About a five-minute drive from here,' said Roger, 'but you might find it easier to speak to him at Bayside Auto. Business belongs to his wife's father but Kurt manages the place.'

Small world, thought Carl. Bayside Auto was where Ian Holden worked. He waited while Lisa wrote down the details. 'When was the last time you saw your sister, Mrs French?'

'We spent the weekend before last with her. Roger looks after her garden,' said Kathleen.

Carl took a sip of his coffee. 'Did she mention anything about being threatened or anyone hanging about?'

Kathleen shook her head.

'Anyone ever threaten her when she was working?' said Carl.

'She would have told me if they had,' said Kathleen. 'We were close.'

'A man's secrets were never safe,' said Roger, picking up his coffee cup. 'They told each other everything.'

'That's what sisters do,' said Kathleen. 'Who am I going to turn to now?'

'Do you have any children?' said Carl.

'We have a son, but he's like his father I'm afraid. Keeps his secrets to himself.'

'Would she have confided in anyone at the hospital?' said Carl.

'I wouldn't think so, Inspector. She was too professional for that.'

———

After interviewing Kathleen French, Carl and Lisa went to University Hospital to speak to Judy McDonald, the manager of the hospital's human resources department.

'How can I help you, Inspector?' said Judy, as Carl and Lisa settled into the chairs in front of her desk.

'We're investigating the death of Christine Viking,' said Carl. 'I understand she worked here until she retired.'

'Terrible state of affairs when a woman is murdered in her own home,' said Judy, shaking her head. 'What is it you want to know about Christine?'

'Anything in her file that might shed light on why someone would want to kill her,' said Carl. 'Things like serious complaints or instances of patients or members of the public making threats that she reported.'

'I don't recall any of those but let me have a look.' Judy turned to her computer and searched through Christine Viking's file. 'As I thought, there's nothing of that nature here, I'm afraid. She has an exemplary record of service.'

'Does that file cover her years at City Hospital?' said Carl.

'Covers the last twenty years, since records were digitized. You'll have to get the department to pull the paper records from their archives if you want to go back further than that, Inspector.'

As they drove back to the city, Carl wondered if he was

dealing with a serial killer or two random attacks. There didn't seem to be anything connecting the victims apart from the fact they had both been nurses. He couldn't see a motive for their murders but, the fact they had both been strangled and their killer hadn't taken anything from them, apart from their lives, made him think they had to be connected.

'What do you think, Lisa?'

'There has to be something about the victims we don't know, Inspector,' said Lisa. 'I can't see why someone would kill them for no reason.'

'We need to find that reason, Lisa, and soon, before he kills someone else.'

———

At two o'clock on Monday afternoon, Carl stood alongside the steel table holding the naked body of Christine Viking waiting for Mike Jonas to begin his post mortem examination.

'There are no external injuries apart from the bruising to the neck, which is consistent with the victim having been strangled with a thin rope.' Mike measured the thickness of the dark line across the victim's throat. 'Probably five millimetres in diameter.' He picked up the magnifying glass and tweezers from the tray his assistant held and examined the wound through the magnifying glass. 'Dark green fibres are present in the wound.'

He lifted the fibres with tweezers and looked at them through the magnifying glass. 'They look similar to the fibres we found on Kelly Palmer's body, Carl. I'll get the lab to test them. This neck wound is similar as well. I'd say your killer is using a garrotte with handles. He's applied a lot of pressure very quickly.' He looked at the victim's finger nails. 'There's no sign she put up any resistance.'

Mike examined the area around the victim's vagina. 'There is no sign of sexual assault.'

Carl let his thoughts drift as Dr Jonas progressed through the internal examination of the body and wondered what was motivating the killer. He hadn't sexually assaulted either victim, assuming it was the same killer, and he hadn't taken anything from his victims, apart from their lives. There has to be some connection, thought Carl, but the only thing that connected the victims was they had both been intensive care nurses.

'Not much to go by, I'm afraid,' said Mike, as he stepped back from the table and peeled off his gloves.

'Enough to make me think it's the same killer,' said Carl.

As he made his way back upstairs to his office, Carl wondered if the victims had ever worked together at City Hospital. When he reached his office, he called David Nelson at City Hospital.

'How can I help you, Inspector?' said David.

'I was wondering whether Christine Viking and Kelly Palmer had ever worked together,' said Carl.

'I wouldn't be surprised if they had, Inspector. Christine was our senior intensive care sister before she transferred to the training program at University. Let me get someone to look through the rosters and get back to you.'

Carl knew it was a long shot, since Christine Viking had spent the last years of her career at University Hospital. If there was a connection to an event at City Hospital, it had to be something that happened more than five years ago. And, that would be another needle in another haystack, thought Carl, especially if they'd worked together on a regular basis.

CHAPTER FOURTEEN

At ten thirty-five on Tuesday morning, Carl and Harry walked into the office of Bayside Auto to interview Kurt Viking.

'Kurt Viking?' said Carl, feeling somewhat surprised that the solidly built man standing in the office was the man Kathleen French had described as someone who couldn't fight his way out of a wet paper bag.

'Are you the police?' said Kurt. 'You look like coppers.'

'Inspector West,' said Carl, holding out his ID. 'This is Detective Sergeant Fuller.'

Kurt crossed his arms on his chest. 'So, who killed the bitch?'

Carl had to stop himself from stepping back. 'We don't know yet.'

'Well, don't go getting any ideas it was me,' said Kurt. 'I didn't do it.'

Kurt's loud denial made little difference to Carl. Far too many women were killed by people they knew, and he'd interviewed more than enough killers to take a man's denial at face value.

'Any ideas who might have?' said Carl.

Kurt shrugged his shoulders. 'I haven't seen her for years. Not since my grandson was born, when I got the message I was no longer welcome.' Kurt smiled. 'I suppose people are telling you what a great person she was, but she was a vindictive bitch as far as I'm concerned. Everything had to be done her way.' Kurt shook his head. 'I'm surprised one of those nurses she trained didn't cut her up years ago. Perhaps you should question some of them.'

Carl wondered what sort of relationship Kurt had had with Christine to have such a different picture of her.

'For the record, Mr Viking, where were you last Thursday morning?' said Carl.

'Here.'

'Anyone who can verify that?' said Carl.

Kurt stepped over to the door that opened into the work-shop. 'Joe! Come in here!'

A young man dressed in blue overalls emblazoned with the Bayside Auto logo came into the office from the service bay.

'These guys are the police, Joe. They want to ask you a question,' said Kurt.

'Were you here last Thursday morning?' said Carl.

'Yeah.'

'What about Mr Viking? Was he here all morning that day as well?' said Carl.

'We were both here all day,' said Joe. 'We start at seven-thirty in the morning and don't knock off until four-thirty.'

'Thanks,' said Carl.

Carl pulled out one of his business cards and handed it to Kurt. 'If you think of anything, give me a call.'

'I doubt I'll think of anything,' said Kurt. 'My life's been better off without thinking about her for years.'

On Wednesday morning, Carl gathered the team around the whiteboard outside his office.

'How did you go following up on Mitchell, Harry?'

DS Fuller flipped open his notebook. He'd given up trying to take notes on his iPad when interviewing people. 'Metropolitan Security confirmed his employment and that he was on leave last week. Apparently, they do three weeks on and one week off, and Mitchell's a trusted employee, as far as they're concerned.'

'Speak to any of his neighbours?' said Carl.

'Spoke to the woman that lives in number forty-three. Sonya Harding. She remembers him coming home from work around six-thirty on the Friday morning Kelly Palmer was killed,' said Harry.

'Did she see him?' said Carl.

'Said she heard his van. He parks it in the street in front of his house, and the van was there when she went to work at eight,' said Harry, 'but she did tell me he rides a bike, although she couldn't tell me what sort.'

'Would he have to use the driveway to exit the property?' said DC Paterson.

'I suppose,' said Harry.

'Some of the older parts of Portside have laneways at the back of the houses,' said DC Paterson. 'Service lanes from the days of night soil collection last century.'

'Give me a minute,' said DC Beard, sitting down in front of his computer. 'What was that address again, Sarge?'

'45 Harvey Street,' said Harry.

DC Beard switched to satellite view on Google Maps. 'There's a laneway behind the houses in Harvey Street.'

'So, he could have slipped out through the lane on his bike without his neighbour seeing him,' said DC Paterson.

'Let's not get ahead of ourselves,' said Carl. 'What about the pub in Carrick where he placed those bets?'

'They remembered him,' said Harry. 'He'd been in every morning last week at ten or just after. They open the betting counter at ten.'

'Did they confirm they'd issued the slip he showed us?' said Carl.

'They issued the slip,' said Harry, 'but there's no way of telling who they issued it to. You have to present the slip to collect.'

'So, he could have picked up a discarded ticket when he got to the pub,' said Carl. 'Do they have CCTV covering their betting counter?'

'Afraid not,' said Harry.

'So, his alibi is not watertight,' said DC Paterson.

'That would take a bit of planning,' said DC Templar. 'Maybe that's why he was there every day.'

'We still have a timing issue,' said Carl, 'if the killer was seen outside the crime scene at ten, and then there's the question of motive.'

'Still think he's a person of interest,' said DC Paterson.

'We'd have to say he had opportunity,' said Harry, 'and, there's no certainty with that ten o'clock sighting outside the crime scene.'

'And, we know he's quick,' said DC Templar.

'Maybe,' said Carl, 'but we need to know more about him and find whatever connection he has to the victims before we can say he's our man.'

'Any luck with the hospital?' said Harry.

'They sent me a list as long as your arm,' said Carl. 'The

victims worked together hundreds of times while they were both at City.'

'Another bloody haystack!' said Harry.

———

Harry started his investigation into Trent Mitchell's background by requesting a review of his file by the Registrar of Births, Deaths, and Marriages. Then, he requested a review of admissions to both University and City Hospitals to see if Mitchell had ever been admitted as a patient.

The Registrar of Births, Deaths, and Marriages advised that Trent Mitchell had never been married or recorded as the father of a child. The hospitals reported that he had never been admitted to either hospital as a patient.

Harry reviewed the notes from the interviews they had conducted with the family and friends of both victims. There was no sign Trent Mitchell had been in either victim's life.

He interviewed Mitchell's neighbours. They told him Mitchell lived on his own and kept to himself. None of them had seen any sign of a partner or a girlfriend since he'd moved into the house in Harvey Street, where he'd lived for the last five years.

Harry reviewed the list of addresses linked to Mitchell in the Motor Vehicle Registrations database but none of the people living in the apartment block where he had lived prior to Harvey Street remembered him. Most of them had moved in since Mitchell had moved out.

Harry called the property manager of the apartment block, only to learn that the apartment had been let to Trent Mitchell for ten years before he'd moved out. There was no record of a partner or anybody else sharing the apartment with him, and the person who had been the property manager at the time was no longer with the company and the current property manager didn't know how to contact her.

As far as Harry could tell, the only thing linking Mitchell to Christine Viking was the fact he owned a white Ford Transit van and had been in Carrick at the time of her murder. There appeared to be nothing linking him to Kelly Palmer.

Harry walked into Carl's office.

'Mitchell looks like a dead end, Boss. I can't find anything linking him to either victim except for the fact he was in Carrick at the time of Viking's death and he drives a white Ford Transit, and I doubt that would hold up in court.'

Carl leant back in his chair. 'Keep him on the board, Harry. There's something about him I can't quite put my finger on. Having that betting stub in his wallet still doesn't gel with me, especially since it was a losing bet. I'm not ready to let him off the hook, just yet.'

'What do you want me to do?'

'Keep an open mind. There has to be something we've missed or not thought of yet.'

CHAPTER FIFTEEN

Carl read the report from Sgt Whitelaw and dropped it onto his desk.

The officers at Carrick had traced the movements of every white Ford Transit van registered to anyone living in the seaside town and placed them at locations away from 5 Squall Avenue on the morning Christine Viking had been murdered.

Carl scratched the back of his head and considered the implications of the report. If none of the locals could be placed at the scene of the murder, the killer had to be someone not from Carrick, and if the victim had opened the door to him, as Dean Lang had suggested, either she knew the killer or he was someone most people would open the door for, like a delivery driver with a package in his hands.

Carl walked out to Harry's desk with Sgt Whitelaw's report. 'The boys at Carrick have drawn a blank with their Ford transit van enquiries. If it wasn't Mitchell, it could have been someone making a delivery she was expecting.'

'Why do you think that, Boss?' said Harry.

'According to Dean, she opened the door to him, which

suggests she either knew him or he looked like someone most people would trust,' said Carl.

'Like a delivery driver with a package,' said Harry.

'Check out the local couriers,' said Carl. 'There can't be too many companies delivering stuff to Carrick.'

Carl felt his mobile phone vibrate inside the pocket of his trousers. He pulled it out and looked at the display: Operations.

'DI West.'

'Inspector, Portside have just called in. Ian Holden, hasn't reported in and they can't locate him.'

'Get an APB out on him and any vehicle registered in his name.'

Carl slipped his phone back into his pocket. 'Looks like Holden's playing games. Hasn't reported in and can't be located.'

'I'll let Wayne know,' said Harry.

———

Harry called the Post Office in Carrick.

'Who delivers packages to the residents of Carrick for you?' said Harry.

'We have a contractor who does that, Sergeant.'

'What does he drive?' said Harry.

'He drives a white van with our signage on it so people know who he is.'

'Do you have a record of any deliveries he made for you to 5 Squall Avenue?' said Harry.

'Just a minute, let me look that up.'

Harry waited.

'We haven't had a package for that address since January last year, Sergeant.'

'Do you know which other companies make deliveries in Carrick, by any chance?' said Harry.

'FedEx do most of them, Sergeant, as far as I know.'

'Thanks,' said Harry.

Harry looked up the number for FedEx and pressed the keys on his phone. It took him several minutes to work his way through the menu and find someone human to talk to.

'We haven't had a delivery for that address in the last twelve months, Sergeant.'

'Do you know if any other companies deliver to Carrick?' said Harry.

'We handle that region, Sergeant. Anything that doesn't go through the Post Office ends up here for delivery.'

Another dead end, thought Harry, as he typed 'deliveries to carrick' into his search bar and hit enter. The search returned the details of Coastal Express Deliveries beneath the entry for FedEx.

Harry called the number displayed on his screen.

'Yes, we deliver to Carrick, Sergeant. What do you want to send?'

'I'd like to know if you've delivered any packages to 5 Squall Avenue in the last month,' said Harry.

'That address doesn't ring a bell. Give me a minute, I'll look it up.'

Harry waited.

'Doesn't look like it, Sergeant.'

'What sort of vehicles do your delivery drivers use?' said Harry.

'Mercedes vans. We've just updated our fleet from Ford Transits.'

'When did you do that?' said Harry.

'In March.'

'And do your vans have signage on them?' said Harry.

'They sure do, we're proud of our business down here.'

'What happens to the signage on your old vehicles when you replace them?' said Harry.

'The company that sells them for us removes it before offering them for sale. We don't want other people driving around making out they're us. That would be bad for business.'

'Who handles the sale of your old vehicles?' said Harry.

'The last lot was done through Gunnings in Carrick. They're the biggest Ford dealer down here.'

'Thanks,' said Harry. 'You've been most helpful.'

Harry called Sgt Whitelaw at Carrick.

'Colin, we need to account for all the second-hand Ford Transits Gunnings had in their yard on the morning Christine Viking was killed.'

Sgt Whitelaw called back within the hour.

'Gunnings had five white Transits at the time, Harry. They have a system of recording whenever a vehicle is taken out of the yard and, according to their records, all five were in the yard that morning.'

Harry went into Inspector West's office and updated him on his delivery driver enquiries.

'Search Mitchell's house and van,' said Carl. 'He's either our man or we definitely need to eliminate him from our list.'

———

Harry knocked on the door of 45 Harvey Street and wondered if Mitchell was home. There was no sign of his van in the street.

The door was opened by a young woman dressed in a grey uniform.

'Police. I'm looking for Trent Mitchell,' said Harry, showing her his ID.

'You're too late, mate. I've just finished cleaning the place for the new tenants,' said the woman.

'Do you have the number for the property manager?' said Harry.

The woman pulled her wallet from her back pocket, extracted a card, and handed it to Harry.

'Did he leave any rubbish?' said Harry.

'It's all in the bins out the back,' said the woman.

'We'll take a look,' said Harry, showing her his search warrant.

'Try not to make a mess.' The woman smiled.

Harry signalled to Dean Lang and waited for him and his team to cross the street.

'She's already cleaned the house,' said Harry, 'but his rubbish is still in the bins in the back yard.'

'I'll take a look inside,' said Dean. 'Boys, go around the back and check out those bins.'

Harry stood on the front porch with the cleaner.

'When do the new tenants move in?' said Harry.

'Tomorrow,' said the woman.

Harry called the property manager and introduced himself.

'When did Trent Mitchell move out?' said Harry.

'Over the weekend, Sergeant.'

'Did he leave a forwarding address?' said Harry.

'Gave me a post office box in Portside, number 356.'

'Okay, thanks.'

Harry looked at his notes and called the number for Metropolitan Security.

'He finished up last Friday, Sergeant. Said he was going overseas for six months.'

Harry called Carl.

'Looks like Mitchell's done a runner, Boss. His employer said he told them he was going overseas, so you might want to get Lisa to run a check with the airlines. Dean and his boys are going through the rubbish he left behind, but the house has been cleaned by a cleaning service.'

'I'll get an APB out on him and his vehicle,' said Carl. 'Let me know if Dean's people find anything.'

Sgt Lang came out onto the porch and smiled at the cleaner. 'You've done a thorough job cleaning this place.'

'That's what I get paid for,' said the cleaner.

'I'll just see if the boys have found anything in the rubbish,' said Sgt Lang, 'and make sure they don't leave a mess in the yard.'

'Are they looking for anything in particular?' said the cleaner.

'Green gardening rope or anything that would suggest he owned a bicycle,' said Harry.

'I don't know about a bicycle but there were bits of green rope in the garden beds out the back that I put in the bin.'

Sgt Lang and his team returned to the front yard with a large black plastic bag that held the contents of the recycling bin and a small evidence bag with several small pieces of faded green nylon rope in it.

Sgt Lang approached the cleaner. 'Did you throw anything into the recycling bin?'

'A couple of things,' said the cleaner.

'I'll need a set of your fingerprints.'

The cleaner looked at him and cocked an eyebrow.

'It's okay. We'll destroy them once we've used them to iden-tify which prints on his rubbish belong to Mr Mitchell,' said Sgt Lang. 'We aren't allowed to keep them or use them for anything else.'

The cleaner smiled and held out her hands. 'Okay.'

CHAPTER SIXTEEN

Carl opened the email from Dean Lang and read its contents.

Forensics' tests indicated the rope fibres found in Mitchell's rubbish matched the fibres retrieved from the victims' neck wounds. That's something, thought Carl, but he knew it wasn't conclusive, given the amount of green nylon garden rope in circulation. He scrolled down and read the list of items found in Mitchell's recycling bin, and agreed with Dean's assessment that none of it was incriminating or helpful to his investigation, except for the fact they now had several fingerprints tentatively identified as being Mitchell's.

Carl wondered what had spooked Mitchell. On the surface, they had very little evidence connecting him to Christine Viking's murder and none at all linking him to Kelly Palmer's. He thought about the interview they'd had with Trent Mitchell. Nothing stood out except for Mitchell appearing very relaxed and having a collection of expired betting slips in his wallet.

So, why had he run? It was almost an admission of guilt.

Perhaps asking him where he was the morning Kelly Palmer had been murdered was a mistake, thought Carl.

He looked out across the office to where DC Templar was talking to someone on the telephone. If he is the killer, thought Carl, he may believe we have more on him than we do. And, if he is our man, what's the connection? What links him to the victims?

His reverie was interrupted by DC Templar knocking on the doorframe of his office.

'I've tried all the airlines, Inspector. Mitchell hasn't purchased a ticket to fly anywhere, and they've agreed to let us know if he does,' said DC Templar.

'I saw an ad last night for a cruise leaving from the port. Perhaps he's going by ship,' said Carl.

'What was the name of the cruise line?' said DC Templar. 'I thought they'd stopped sailing from here.'

'Golden Seas Cruises or something like that,' said Carl. 'Nina wants to go on one.'

'I think they're called Silver Seas,' said DC Templar. 'I'll give them a call. Perhaps I can get them to send me a brochure for you.'

'A link to their website will do,' said Carl. 'At least that way I can do some research without Nina knowing.'

'You men are all the same. Why don't you just plan it with her?'

'I will, but I like to be armed with all the facts before I commit to spending that much money on a holiday,' said Carl, 'and, we both know how persuasive she can be.'

DC Templar laughed and headed back to her desk to call Silver Seas Cruises.

Carl wondered what it would be like going on a cruise with a toddler and whether they'd be able to relax enough to enjoy themselves. He assumed they'd have child-minding facilities on board, but doubted he'd be able to persuade Nina to use them.

Lisa was back in his office doorway before Carl had refocussed on his work. 'Mitchell's not booked on any of their cruises.'

Carl looked up from his computer. 'That means he's still here, somewhere.'

'Then it's only a matter time,' said DC Templar. 'There can't be that many places he can hide. We'll find him.'

'I hope you're right, Lisa.'

———

Carl stood in front of the whiteboard holding the details of the Palmer and Viking cases with Harry and Lisa.

'We need to dig deeper into Mitchell's background,' said Carl. 'Start interviewing family and associates. If he's our killer, there has to be something connecting him to the victims.'

'Appears to be a bit of a loner,' said Harry. 'His neighbours didn't seem to know much about him.'

'Try his workmates,' said Carl, 'and, Lisa, see if you can track down his family.'

'Be nice to have something better than the photo from his driver's licence,' said Lisa.

'Perhaps the firm he worked for has a better photo,' said Harry.

'What about online?' said Lisa.

'His Facebook profile has a picture of a pigeon, and his profile on LinkedIn doesn't have an image at all', said Harry.

'Follow up with his friends and connections,' said Carl.

'He doesn't have any friends on Facebook,' said Harry, 'and, all his connections on LinkedIn work for Metropolitan Securities.'

'Maybe he's a troll,' said Lisa.

'Or someone using social media for surveillance or choosing his victims,' said Harry.

'Get Dean's people to take a look at his accounts,' said Carl.

'Don't we need a warrant for that?' said Harry.

'I'll get you one, Harry. The Chief's keen to see some progress on these cases. He wasn't too happy after my last update, and I gather he's getting a bit of stick from upstairs.' Carl smiled. 'If it's Mitchell, we need to stop him before he kills someone else.'

'You know,' said Lisa, 'whatever the link is, it must go back more than five years.'

'Why do you say that?' said Carl.

'The victims don't appear to have had any contact since Viking left City and moved to University five years ago,' said Lisa.

'But, that assumes the link has something to do with them being nurses at City,' said Harry, 'and Mitchell's never been a patient at City, let alone been admitted to the intensive care ward.'

'We're not going to work it out by speculating,' said Carl. 'Start talking to people who know him. There has to be something, and we need to find out what it is.'

———

Harry sat in the chair Fred Sinclair offered him in the offices of Metropolitan Securities.

'So, what's this about, Sergeant?' said Fred.

'Trent Mitchell,' said Harry. 'I was told you were his manager.'

'Reported to me since he joined us.' Fred stroked his chin. 'Be more than ten years. Probably closer to fifteen.'

'Were you surprised he left?' said Harry.

Fred shook his head. 'He'd been talking about it for a while. Reckoned he wanted to see some of the world before he got too old.'

'Any place in particular?'

'Nepal or some place in South America. Said he wanted to go trekking, so I guess that's why he wants to do it now,' said Fred. 'Anyway, why all the interest in Trent?'

'We think he can help us with our enquiries but he's not answering his phone, and he's moved from his last known address,' said Harry.

'And you think I might know where he is?' said Fred.

'Be helpful if you did,' said Harry, 'but I was wondering what you could tell me about him.'

'Like what?' said Fred.

'Like who he associated with at Metropolitan?'

'Trent's a bit of a loner, Sergeant, like a lot of the guys that work here. The sort of work we do kind of attracts people like that, so there's not much social interaction apart from the group events we organize for them.'

'So, no-one who might know how to contact him?'

'Try Jake Smithson. He seemed to get on pretty well with Trent. They often covered shifts for each other. But, apart from Jake, I can't think of anybody else,' said Fred.

'Do you have any contact details for Jake?' said Harry.

———

Harry knocked on the door of the house at the address Fred Sinclair had given him for Jake Smithson.

A teenage girl in a school uniform opened the door and peered at him over the security chain.

'I'm looking for Jake Smithson,' said Harry, holding out his ID. 'Is he home?'

The girl looked at Harry's ID. 'Are you a policeman?'

'Yes,' said Harry. 'Is Mr Smithson here?'

The girl turned away from the door. 'Dad! There's a policeman here to see you.'

A man dressed in a Metropolitan Securities uniform lifted the chain and opened the door to Harry.

'Are you the copper that Fred said would be coming around?'

'Detective Sergeant Fuller,' said Harry, offering his hand.

'Jake Smithson,' said Jake, accepting Harry's handshake. 'What can I do for you?'

'I'm trying to locate Trent Mitchell,' said Harry.

'Haven't heard from him in a while.'

'Are you aware he's resigned?' said Harry.

'Fred did mention that,' said Jake.

'Are you surprised?'

'Hadn't said anything to me about it, if that's what you mean?' said Jake.

'Any idea where he might be?' said Harry. 'He's left where he was living in Harvey Street.'

'Didn't give them a forwarding address?'

'A post office box,' said Harry.

'That's not like Trent. He's usually a stickler for details,' said Jake. 'Have you tried his mobile?'

'He's not answering,' said Harry. 'How well do you know him?'

'He's a hard one to get to know, mate. Doesn't talk much. We mostly helped each other out when things got in the way of our shifts,' said Jake.

'Do you know if he has a girlfriend?' said Harry.

'He used to talk about someone called Helen but he hasn't mentioned her in ages. I assumed she'd left him.'

'Did this Helen have a last name?'

'He only ever called her Helen.' Jake shrugged his shoulders. 'I never met her.'

'Any idea how long it's been since he's talked about her?'

'Be years, mate. At least five or six.'

She could be the connection, thought Harry. She's in the right timeframe. 'You don't know if she was a nurse, by any chance, do you?'

'Sorry. Like I said. Trent kept his cards pretty close to his chest.'

'If you hear from him, ask him to give me a call,' said Harry, handing Jake his card. 'It's important.'

CHAPTER SEVENTEEN

Trent climbed over the gate into the wrecker's yard. There was no-one around. Northfield Auto Wreckers was on the edge of an industrial estate housing a range of businesses servicing the motor trade. He pressed the button that lit up the numbers on his watch and checked the time.

Metropolitan's security patrol wouldn't be checking the yard for another hour but, although he intended to be long gone by then, he couldn't stop feeling nervous about being discovered by one of his workmates.

He walked into the darkness away from the gate, counting the rows of twisted and mangled car bodies awaiting their transformation into blocks of metal by the giant crusher at the far end of the yard, until he arrived at the fifth row.

He made his way along the row of partially dismantled vehicles until he reached the white Ford Transit he'd spotted during his visit earlier in the day. He reached into his overalls, pulled out his screwdriver, and removed the number plates from the van. When he'd unscrewed them, he took a piece of black cloth from his back pocket and wrapped up the plates. Then, he made his way back to the gate, climbed over it and dropped into the street, where he retrieved his bicycle from the shadows and rode into the night.

Twenty minutes later, he wheeled his bicycle into the abandoned warehouse where he'd parked his van and switched the plates. Then, with the bike safely stowed away in the rear of the van, he drove slowly out into the street, only turning on the headlights as he approached the main road that would take him home.

Not wanting to attract attention, he drove along at the speed limit, and smiled to himself when he was overtaken by a police car, which continued on its way without its occupants taking any notice of him.

That was pretty easy, he thought, turning into the side street that would take him to a row of abandoned houses waiting to be knocked over and replaced as part of the urban renewal activity sweeping through the suburbs.

———

In the morning, Trent fished through his possessions until he found Helen's cup with the last three names in it. He held the cup above his head.

'Who's it going to be, sweetheart?'

He closed his eyes and dragged a square of folded paper out of the cup with his finger. He placed the folded square on the box he was using as a table and opened it. The name was: Sarah Cody.

Trent closed his eyes and thought of the attractive young nurse attached to that name. He remembered thinking she was too young to be an intensive care nurse when he'd first met her. He'd always imagined they'd be really experienced, given the serious injuries and illnesses of the patients they had to look after.

He wouldn't be letting her use her youth as an excuse, though. As far as he was concerned, as her righteous judge and executioner, she was responsible for her part in allowing Helen to die.

He slipped the piece of paper into his wallet and finished getting dressed.

With his laptop in his hand, he strolled down the street and around the corner to the coffee shop for breakfast, where he logged on to their free wi-fi network.

While eating soft-poached eggs on toast, Trent ran a Facebook search on Sarah Cody but failed to find a profile that matched what he knew about her. He logged out of Facebook and into LinkedIn. There was no profile for a Sarah Cody that worked as a nurse.

Trent sipped his latte and thought about how he could find her. He opened White Pages and keyed cody into the surname field and s into the initial field of the search engine. The display filled with a list of fifteen addresses but none were located within the state.

Perhaps she's married and changed her name, he thought. But, since Helen had picked her, he knew she must still be around. He decided he'd have to find her the hard way.

He walked back to the house and let himself in. It was too late to watch the nurses coming and going for the morning shift change but he had plenty of time to make his way to City Hospital to observe the nurses coming and going for the next shift change.

CHAPTER EIGHTEEN

Carl read the notes Wayne had attached to the report from Ian Holden's telephone service provider. Holden had apparently travelled to Pemberton in the Riverland the day after he'd been released on bail and Wayne and Nigel had gone there to investigate.

Carl looked up as Harry walked into his office.

'Just got an update on Holden's phone,' said Harry. 'He's either switched it off or its battery's gone flat. They've had no signal from it for days.'

'Obviously doesn't want to be found,' said Carl.

'It's working,' said Harry. 'There's still no sign of him.'

'What's at this Pemberton place?' said Carl, tapping the report.

'A roadhouse and a couple of houses,' said Harry. 'The boys should just about be there by now.'

Carl's mobile phone rang. He looked at the display.

'Anything exciting, Wayne?'

'There's not much here besides a roadhouse in the middle of nowhere, Inspector' said DC Paterson, 'except, for a big truck park next to the roadhouse. The manager reckons around a hundred trucks pass through here most days, and the yard is used as some sort of load transfer station.'

Carl wondered what Holden would have been doing at a roadhouse that catered for truck drivers. 'Anyone recall seeing Holden?' said Carl.

'No, but Nigel's looking at the recording from the security cameras that cover the pumps,' said Wayne.

'I wonder if Holden was meeting Nolan,' said Carl. 'You'd better ask if they recall seeing a green Mack loaded up with cars or seeing Nolan.'

'There are a couple of green Macks parked in the yard here,' said Wayne, 'but none of them carrying cars.'

There must be hundreds of Mack trucks on the roads, thought Carl, and a fair number of them painted green, so Wayne would have to be lucky to encounter anyone who had seen the one Nolan had been driving when he disappeared.

'What's the food like, Wayne? Must be good if it attracts all those truckers.'

'They do a fantastic steak sandwich,' said DC Paterson. 'Even Nigel's had one.'

'Don't eat too many,' said Carl. 'Let me know if you get anything useful.'

———

Carl was on his way downstairs for lunch when his mobile phone rang again.

'What's up, Wayne?'

'Just spoke to a truck driver who reckons he saw someone getting into a green Mack prime mover on the day Holden was here,' said DC Paterson. 'Said he only noticed because the driver showed up in a white SUV with another bloke.'

'Did he know who the driver was?' said Carl.

'Said he thought he looked like Holden when I showed him Holden's photo.'

'Did he speak to him?'

'No.'

It looked to Carl like Holden may have been retrieving the truck Jim Nolan had used.

'Have you traced the truck Nolan was driving yet?' said Carl.

'Not yet,' said Wayne, 'but I'm thinking Holden might have been up here collecting it, Inspector, which sort of suggests he's more involved than he's let on.'

'Sounds like it,' said Carl. 'Did your witness see which way the truck went?'

'Reckons it headed down the road back to the city, but we got something else, Inspector. They filled up the SUV.'

Carl's mind joined two dots. 'Did you say they filled up?'

'Got it on tape, Inspector. The SUV is registered to Bayside Auto.'

Carl pictured the grin on Wayne's face and wondered who else at Bayside Auto was part of the car stealing gang.

'Good work, Wayne! That gives us somewhere to start.'

'Nigel did the legwork on that, Inspector. Says it was easy once he knew what we were looking for. Downside for us, though, is we only got shots of Holden. The other bloke stayed in the car behind tinted windows.'

———

DC Paterson parked next to the white SUV outside Kurt Viking's office. Carl read out the registration number.

'That's the car,' said Wayne.

They went into the office. There was no-one there. They

walked into the workshop, where a young man was working on the engine of one of the three vehicles parked in the service bay. Carl recognized him as the employee who had vouched for Kurt's whereabouts on the day of his ex-wife's murder.

'Hi, Joe! Remember me?'

'You're that policeman that was here a couple of weeks ago, aren't you?'

'That's right. DI West. We're looking for Kurt. Is he about?'

'He's out with a customer on a test drive. Shouldn't be long. Do you want me to call him?'

'No. We'll wait,' said Carl. 'By the way, who drives that SUV parked out the front?'

'That's Kurt's.'

'Nice car,' said Carl. 'Seen Ian lately?'

'Joe shook his head. 'He's still on holidays, as far as I know.' Joe stood up and put down the screwdriver he'd been using to adjust the engine. 'Wish I could get as many holidays out of Kurt as he does.'

A green Toyota drove up to the entrance of the workshop. Kurt and his customer got out and went into the office.

They waited for the customer to leave and then went into the office.

'Morning, Mr Viking,' said Carl.

'What brings you back here?' said Kurt.

'Ian Holden,' said Carl. 'He's failed to report in as required under his bail conditions.'

Kurt nodded. 'There were a couple of your boys here looking for him the other day.'

Carl mentally checked off the report the officers from Uniform had filed on their visit to Bayside Auto. 'When was the last time you saw him?'

'The day after he got out on bail,' said Kurt. 'He wanted time off to sort out a few things.'

'When are you expecting him back?' said Carl.

'First week in July.'

'Is that white SUV out front your car?' said Carl.

'Belongs to the firm,' said Kurt.

'But you drive it?' said Carl.

'Mostly,' said Kurt, 'but sometimes the boys drive it when they need to pick up parts.'

'Who was driving it on the last Tuesday in May?' said Carl.

'The last Tuesday in May?' said Kurt, stroking his chin with his right hand. 'Ian.'

Carl noted that Kurt didn't need to check the car's logbook to know who had been driving it on a day two weeks ago. 'Doesn't he have his own vehicle?' said Carl.

'His Mazda was being serviced that day, so I lent him my car,' said Kurt. 'As I said, he had things to do.'

'Any idea where he went?' said Carl.

Kurt shrugged. 'Didn't say, but he was back before we closed to pick up his car.'

'Where were you that day?' said Carl.

'Here. Do you want to ask Joe?' said Kurt.

Carl turned to DC Paterson. 'Go out and ask the lad.'

'Why so much interest in my car?' said Kurt.

'The last place we've been able to trace Ian to is the truck park at Pemberton in the Riverland. Do you know it?' said Carl.

'Can't say I do. The Riverland's not a place I go.'

DC Paterson walked back into the office. 'Says they were both here all day and that Holden borrowed the SUV while they serviced his car.'

Carl caught the edges of the smile that briefly flashed across Kurt's face.

'What makes you think Ian's been to Pemberton?' said Kurt.

'He was picked up on CCTV when he filled up your car,' said Carl.

'Well, I've no idea why he'd go there unless he was looking for his brother-in-law,' said Kurt.

'What about moving a Mack truck? Did he say anything about that?' said Carl.

'Not that I recall,' said Kurt.

'Funny thing is, Mr Viking, it appears Ian arrived at the truck park in your car with someone else.'

'Well, it wasn't me,' said Kurt. 'Like I said. I lent him my car and he returned it.'

'Anybody with him when he returned it?' said Carl.

Kurt shook his head. 'He was on his own.'

'Have you heard from him since then?' said Carl.

'Told me he was looking for his brother-in-law,' said Kurt. 'Reckons if it wasn't for him, he wouldn't be in trouble with you lot. Maybe you should talk to his sister. She may have heard from him. I certainly haven't.'

———

Carl looked at the houses in the street where the Nolans lived and decided truck driving obviously didn't pay all that well.

DC Paterson rang the doorbell and they waited. Cynthia Nolan had told them she would be home. After a couple of minutes, DC Paterson rang the doorbell again.

'Just a minute!'

They heard the sound of a door shutting and then footsteps approaching the front door of the house.

'Sorry,' said Cynthia, 'was on the phone to my mother. Come in.'

She led them into the front room of the house, where they

sat on worn lounge chairs around a pinewood coffee table covered in newspapers.

'What do you want to know?'

'When was the last time you had contact with your brother?' said Carl.

'He called me the day he was released on bail,' said Cynthia. 'I haven't heard from him since. He's not back inside, is he?'

'We're here because he's skipped bail.'

'I haven't heard from Jim either,' said Cynthia, sinking back into her chair.

'That's more than two weeks now, isn't it?' said Carl.

'I'm really worried. He usually calls me every day when he's away.' Cynthia wrapped her arms together across her chest. 'Do you think something's happened to him?'

'Anything's possible,' said Carl. 'What I do know is Ian retrieved the truck your husband left in the day after he was released on bail.'

'Why would he do that?' said Cynthia.

'I suspect he was covering your husband's tracks,' said Carl. 'I'm not so sure what your brother told me about what he was doing in your husband's truck the day he had his accident is the truth, Mrs Nolan.'

'All I want to know is that they're alright,' said Cynthia. 'Why don't they call me?'

'Ian's mobile appears to be switched off.'

Cynthia looked at Carl. 'Ian? I can't imagine him turning his phone off.'

'I can assure you, Mrs Nolan, it's off. We've been in touch with his service provider,' said Carl.

'Something's not right,' said Cynthia. 'Jim said he'd be back, and it's not like Ian to go away and not tell me when he'd be back either.'

Carl thought she sounded desperate, and wondered about the state of the Nolans' marriage. He knew it was highly likely Nolan and Holden had abandoned the woman sitting in front of him to save their own hides.

'Were you and your husband on good terms?' said Carl.

Cynthia looked at him. 'We've been together for twenty years, Inspector. Jim's never lied to me, and he certainly wouldn't leave me without saying something. Besides, I control all the bank accounts.'

'Does your husband carry much cash with him or use a card?' said Carl.

'He uses his card, mostly. It costs a small fortune to fill up the tank on one of those Mack trucks.'

'Has he withdrawn any money since he disappeared?' said Carl.

'Not a cent,' said Cynthia. 'I check the account every day. He hasn't touched it.'

Nolan was either lying low or he'd been taken out of circulation, thought Carl.

'I'm not sure that's a good sign,' said Carl, 'unless someone else is looking after him.'

Cynthia bit her lower lip.

'Do you have any idea where your husband was going the day he left, Mrs Nolan?'

Cynthia looked at her hands. 'I'm not supposed to know.' She looked at Carl. 'He told me I'd be better off if I didn't know what he was doing to make the cash money. Now, I'm not so sure.'

Carl waited. DC Paterson took out his notebook and pen.

'He was talking to Ian on the phone the morning before they left. I heard him say they had to meet the others somewhere up the river.'

'Do you remember where?' said Carl.

'He didn't say,' said Cynthia. 'The time before, when Greg went with him, they went somewhere down south. I only know that because he bought me back a bottle of wine from the Southern Vales.'

Carl wondered if Nolan had actually been to the Southern Vales or whether he'd simply purchased a bottle of wine for his wife in a bottle shop on the way home.

'How did your husband get involved?' said Carl.

Cynthia wrung her hands together and looked away at the windows.

Carl wondered if she was desperate enough to tell him the truth or whether she'd continue to deny she knew anything. He waited.

'Ian. He told us we'd make enough money to pay off the loan on the truck, and it was easy money. Jim only had to deliver five cars a month, and they paid for the truck.'

'What about the warehouse?' said DC Paterson.

Cynthia blushed. 'Sorry. I didn't exactly tell you the truth about that, did I? We signed the lease but they paid for it.'

'Who's they?' said Carl.

'I don't know,' said Cynthia. 'It was all organized through Ian. He let us know when the cars were ready to be moved. You'll have to ask him.'

I will if I ever get the chance, thought Carl.

'Did you know the cars were stolen?' said Carl.

Cynthia looked at her hands. 'You don't get paid that sort of money for moving ordinary cars, Inspector.' She looked at Carl. 'Am I in trouble?'

Carl felt a twinge of sympathy for her. If his gut feeling about this case was right, she would be paying a higher price for her part than a prison sentence. 'Yes, but nowhere near as much trouble as your husband and your brother seem to have gotten themselves into.'

'What do you mean?'

'I suspect they might not be coming back any time soon, Mrs Nolan, and, if they do, they will be going to prison.'

———

'What did you make of that?' said Carl, as they climbed into the car after leaving Mrs Nolan.

'She's only confirmed what we already know, Inspector. I reckon we should focus on Viking. I don't buy his story, and I'm not sure I believe his offsider either.'

'Why's that, Wayne?'

'Did you get Joe's surname last time you were there?'

'DS Fuller will have those details,' said Carl.

'It's Cotton,' said Wayne, moving the car into traffic as they turned out of the street onto the main road. 'Ring any bells for you, Inspector?'

'Can't say it does,' said Carl.

'I put his old man away for pinching cars around fifteen years ago,' said Wayne. 'The kid looks just like him.'

'That's worth following up.'

'You're not wrong there, Inspector.'

'Look into Viking while you're at it. He was a bit too quick to tell us who'd been driving his car,' said Carl. 'Not sure I'd know off the top of my head who'd been driving my car two weeks ago, especially a work car shared by several employees.'

'Well, let's see what Nigel comes up with, Inspector. He's got a list of the credit cards used to pay for fuel at the roadhouse that Tuesday,' said Wayne.

That could be interesting, thought Carl. 'You reckon they'd be that stupid?'

'They're criminals, Inspector, not rocket scientists. I wouldn't be surprised if they used the company card to fill up that SUV for the trip back to town.' Wayne laughed. 'None of these clowns want to pay for things out of their own pocket.'

Carl's mobile phone rang. He looked at the display: Operations.

'DI West.'

'Got another car for you, Inspector. A beamer taken from a driveway in East Park last night, and he's got a recording of the theft.'

'What's the address?'

CHAPTER NINETEEN

DC Paterson parked in front of 11 Devine Terrace, East Park, and they walked along a paved path that cut across an expanse of lawn up to the front door. DC Paterson pushed the doorbell.

The door was opened by a middle-aged man dressed in grey trousers and a navy blue polo sweater.

'Mr Chester?' said Carl.

'Yes?'

'Detective Inspector West, City Police,' said Carl, holding out his ID. 'This is my colleague, Detective Constable Paterson.'

Mr Chester stepped out onto the veranda. 'An inspector for a stolen car. I'm impressed.'

Carl smiled. 'We're adding you to an existing investigation, Mr Chester. Someone seems to have taken a fancy to cars like yours.'

'I thought the bloody thing was just about theft proof,' said Mr Chester. 'You have to have the remote on you to start it.'

The how question had mystified Carl as well, until Wayne had stumbled across a recording on the internet of a car being stolen from a driveway in London. He decided he'd let Wayne explain when they'd seen the recording from the victim's security camera.

'Where was it parked?' said Carl.

'I left it there.' Mr Chester pointed to a spot on the driveway immediately in front of the garage door. 'I feel a bit silly.' He smiled. 'I forgot to put it in the garage.'

We've all done that, thought Carl, noting the floodlight equipped with a sensor above the garage door. 'Is it insured?'

'Fortunately,' said Mr Chester, 'but it's still a bloody inconvenience.'

'I understand you have a security camera out here somewhere,' said Carl.

'Yes,' said Mr Chester, pointing to the camera above their heads.

Carl looked at the camera and then at the spot on the driveway where the car had been parked. 'Does it cover the driveway in front of the garage?'

'Sure does.'

'Can we have a look at last night's recording,' said Carl.

'Come in, Inspector. I've got it up on my computer.'

Mr Chester led them into his study in the room located immediately inside the front door and adjoining the garage.

'This where you leave your remote, Mr Chester?' said DC Paterson.

'No. I usually leave it on the table just inside the door. Is that important?'

'Could be,' said DC Paterson.

Mr Chester sat at his desk and clicked on an icon on the screen of his computer. 'Here we go.'

'Okay, fast forward until we see something,' said Carl.

'There!' said DC Paterson. 'Go back a bit and let's watch that again.'

Mr Chester adjusted the video and they watched as his car was illuminated by the floodlight over the garage door at 02:13. A few seconds later, a man wearing a hooded sweatshirt came into view. He was holding what looked like a square frame in his right hand and walked away from the car towards the house. As he stepped onto the front veranda, the car's indicator lights flashed. A second person stepped out of the shadows, opened the driver's side door and slipped inside the car. Within seconds, the headlights came on and the car reversed out of the driveway.

They watched the back of the man with the frame in his hands walk down the driveway and disappear.

'How the hell did they do that?' said Mr Chester.

Carl looked at DC Paterson. 'Like to tell Mr Chester what you've found out?'

'That frame thing the first man was carrying,' said DC Paterson, 'that's a signal amplifier. It picks up the signal from your remote and transmits it to your car. The onboard computer thinks you're standing next to the car with your remote and releases the door locks.'

'But you need the remote to start the engine,' said Mr Chester.

'Let's them do that, too,' said DC Paterson. 'They're okay until they switch off the motor. Once they do that, though, they're stuffed. They can't restart it.'

Mr Chester looked at DC Paterson. 'Why would anyone steal a car they can't drive unless they keep the engine running all the time?'

'They're not interested in the car, Mr Chester, they're after the parts,' said DC Paterson. 'They probably had a truck parked around the corner and drove the car into it using a ramp, or they used a flatbed tow truck and dragged it up with a cable.'

'Bastards!' said Mr Chester.

Clever bastards, though, thought Carl. 'Think we could have a copy of that recording, Mr Chester?'

————

Carl sat with Wayne and Nigel as they viewed the recording of the theft of Mr Chester's BMW.

'I reckon the guy in the hoodie is Holden,' said Wayne, pointing at the screen.

'You can't see his face,' said Nigel.

'Look at the way he walks when he goes down the driveway,' said Wayne. 'That's Holden.'

'Looks about the right size,' said Carl, 'but we'll need a better shot than that to convince a magistrate.'

'Well, if it is Holden,' said Wayne, 'at least we know he's out there somewhere.'

'That's something, I suppose,' said Carl, 'but we still need to find him.'

'What about the driver?' said Nigel. 'Any idea who he is?'

'Zoom in on the face through the windscreen,' said Carl.

Nigel adjusted the zoom control. 'Looks pretty young. In fact, it could be a woman.'

'Nah,' said Wayne, 'I reckon that's the Cotton kid.'

Carl looked at the blown-up image on the screen and agreed with Wayne. 'Do we have an address for him?'

'Registrations will have one,' said Wayne.

'Pay him a visit after hours, away from Viking,' said Carl, 'and see if Traffic have any recordings from roads leading into and out of East Park. They may have picked up the truck.'

'That would be handy,' said Wayne.

'I'll get Uniform out interviewing people living in the streets around Devine Terrace. We might get lucky.'

'Okay, Inspector' said Wayne.

'Any joy with those credit cards, Nigel?' said Carl.

'Still waiting on the banks, Inspector. Might not be until early next week.'

Carl stood up. 'I think we're making progress, boys. We know how they're taking the cars, and it looks like we know who's doing it. All we need now is some evidence that will stand up in court.'

'Yeah, and we need to find Holden and his mate, Nolan,' said Wayne.

'Wonder if they saw Nolan as a weak link and eliminated him,' said Nigel.

'Possibility,' said Carl, 'but let's hope they aren't that desperate.'

'They obviously think they're safe if they're still taking cars even after Holden was arrested,' said Nigel.

'Guess he's spun them a good story about what he told us,' said Carl.

'Either that or he's making the most of being out on bail,' said Wayne.

'Doesn't quite make sense to me, though,' said Carl. 'Why would he skip bail and trigger a search that would see him back inside when we pick him up?'

'Probably planning on doing a runner,' said Wayne. 'Maybe that's his farewell performance.'

CHAPTER TWENTY

Ian felt conspicuous and couldn't stop himself from continuously checking the rear-view mirrors for flashing blue lights. Although the BMW tied to the floor inside the back of the truck was hidden from view, Ian knew it was there. What he didn't want was anyone else knowing it was there. And, he sure as hell didn't want to be involved in another traffic accident while it was there.

He'd been on the road ever since they'd taken the car from the house in East Park. He wanted to sleep, but he knew he couldn't do that before he'd delivered the car. That's when he'd get to see Jim, when he'd replaced the car he'd lost in the accident on Port Road. At least, that's what Kurt had told him after they'd returned the Mack to City Truck Rentals.

Ian slowed the truck, pulled off the road onto the shoulder, and stopped. He climbed down from the cabin, stretched his legs, and relieved himself within the trees along the side of the road. As he walked back towards the truck, he wondered what was going to happen when he arrived with the car.

Kurt had told him the boss expected him to do his time, and

keep his mouth shut if he couldn't convince the police Jim had lied to him about the car. Ian wasn't keen on going to jail but Kurt had let him know what would happen if he squealed to the police.

Ian suspected Jim wouldn't come back with him, unless he wanted to join him in jail. He couldn't see that happening, and wondered how Cynthia was going to react when he got back without him, if he went back. He recalled Kurt's suggestion to consider disappearing with Jim if he didn't want to risk going to prison. That option was starting to sound attractive to Ian, now that he was standing on a road in the middle of nowhere.

He climbed back into the truck, put it into gear, and moved back onto the deserted highway, thinking he might simply take the money he'd been promised and disappear, and let Jim worry about Cynthia.

The sun crept over the horizon and forms in the landscape slowly became visible. Ian spotted the sign he'd been told to look out for. He slowed the truck, turned off the highway, and cautiously made his way along the dirt road until he came to a driveway blocked by an ancient Land Rover with two men sitting in it.

Ian stopped the truck and waited. One of the men got out of the Land Rover and walked over to the truck. Ian opened the door of the truck.

'Took your bloody time, mate,' said the man.

'I'm here now,' said Ian.

'Give us a look at the goods,' said the man.

Ian climbed down out of the truck, walked around to the rear, and opened the doors. 'There you go.'

The man glanced inside the back of the truck at the BMW illuminated in the pale dawn light. 'Lock her up.'

Ian closed the doors and slid the lockrods into place. 'Now what?'

'I'll take it from here,' said the man. 'Get your stuff out of the truck.'

'I didn't bring any stuff,' said Ian.

The man shrugged. 'Get in the rover. Jack will take you to where Nolan is.'

'Then what?' said Ian.

'Depends on the boss,' said the man, walking towards the cabin of the truck. 'If he's happy, I should be back with your truck around lunchtime. Then you and Nolan will be free to go.'

Ian walked over to the Land Rover and climbed in beside Jack, who started the engine without a word of greeting.

'Where're we going?' said Ian.

'Up the track a bit.' Jack turned and pointed to the dashboard in front of Ian. 'You might want to hold on if you want to keep your seat.'

Ian felt a stream of icy water trickle down his spine as he grabbed onto the edge of the dashboard. He wasn't sure he'd made the right decision bringing the BMW out here into the vast emptiness of the interior on a promise, and he didn't feel comfortable being alone with the man sitting beside him.

Jack let out the clutch and the rover bumped its way along the driveway towards what looked like a farmhouse to Ian. He hoped someone had breakfast on and that there'd be somewhere for him to lie down and get a few hours' sleep.

———

The Land Rover came to a halt.

Ian looked at the derelict farm buildings. 'This where you're staying?'

Jack killed the engine. 'It's not as bad as it looks. Come on.'

Jack got out of the Land Rover and walked towards the house. Ian followed, expecting to see Jim when they got inside.

Ian stopped when he stepped through the back door. The floor of what once had been the back porch of the farmhouse was strewn with rubbish. He tried the light switch.

'There's no power,' said Jack.

'It's dark in here,' said Ian, feeling nervous about going into a dark house with a bloke that gave him the creeps.

'Your eyes will adjust. Besides, the sun's up, so there'll be plenty of light in the front rooms.'

Ian heard the smirk in Jack's voice even though he couldn't clearly see his face and pushed down the urge to hit him. 'Where's Nolan?'

'In the front bedroom,' said Jack.

'Where's that?' said Ian.

Jack pointed to the door opposite that opened into the dark interior of the house. 'Straight up that passage.'

Ian wondered why Jim hadn't come out to greet them and guessed he must still be asleep.

'Come on, I'll take you to his room,' said Jack. 'No point in hanging around here.'

Ian followed Jack along the dark passage to the front of the house, where Jack opened a door into a room filled with early morning sunlight.

'In here.'

Ian stepped into the room. He blinked and waited for his eyes to adjust to the change in light. The room was empty. There were no floorboards. He took in the hole and the spade stuck in a pile of freshly dug earth next to it in the middle of the floor. He spun around to confront Jack, and saw the pistol in his hand.

'Where's Nolan?'

'In there,' said Jack. He waved the pistol towards the hole in the floor, before bringing it back to point at Ian.

'Why?' said Ian. It didn't make any sense to him. They'd all sworn to secrecy in the event of things going pear-shaped.

'Boss doesn't like loose ends,' said Jack, raising the pistol. 'Get in.'

'Fuck you!' said Ian, lashing out at Jack's pistol hand with his right foot.

Caught off guard, Jack dropped the gun. Ian stepped forward, kicked him in the groin, and then kneed him in the head as he bent over in pain.

Jack fell backwards, his head hitting the wall behind him. He collapsed onto the dirt floor.

Ian picked up the pistol and fired three rounds into Jack's prone body.

Ian felt his heart thumping inside his chest.

He waited and listened.

It was quiet outside. Inside, Jack didn't move or make a sound.

Ian squatted beside Jack's body and checked for a pulse. Nothing. He checked his pockets. Nothing. He must have left the keys in the rover, thought Ian.

He walked over to the hole in the floor and peered in. It was a little over a metre deep. The earth at the bottom looked disturbed. He pulled the spade out of the pile of earth next to the hole and scrapped away at the dirt at the bottom of the hole. He gagged on the smell that wafted out of the hole as he disturbed the soil, and stopped digging when he exposed an arm wearing a wristwatch he recognized.

'Bastards!'

Ian threw the spade onto the ground.

'What the hell am I going to tell Cynthia?'

He glanced at Jack's body on the floor. Jack wasn't the first man Ian had knocked to the ground in a fight but he was the first one he'd killed. Ian closed his eyes and took several deep breaths. He decided he'd process what killing another man meant later.

Ian opened his eyes. He couldn't stay where he was. Jack's mate was sure to come looking for him when he didn't turn up. He took one last look at the wristwatch on the arm at the bottom of the hole. He'd given that watch to Jim for his thirtieth birthday.

'Sorry, mate. I had no idea it would end like this.'

He made his way back through the house to the Land Rover. He picked up Jack's hat from where he'd left it on the driver's seat and climbed in. He dumped the hat on the back seat and looked around him. The keys were dangling from the ignition. There was a box of ammunition and a wallet in the glove compartment. He reloaded Jack's pistol and put it in the compartment beside the box. He pulled out the wallet and opened it. It held a fifty dollar note and a driver's licence in the name of Jack Sloane. The name didn't mean anything to Ian. He slipped the wallet into his pocket, then pushed in the clutch and turned the key. The ancient rover shuddered into life. Ian drove slowly up the driveway in the direction of the road that would take him to the highway.

As he bumped along the driveway, Ian glanced at the fuel gauge. The needle was jumping about below the quarter tank mark. When he reached the highway, he turned towards Pemberton, where he knew there was a roadhouse that sold petrol.

CHAPTER TWENTY-ONE

Carl's mobile phone rang as he was waiting for the elevator to go down for lunch.

'DI West.'

'Bill Norris, Carl.'

Carl wondered why Inspector Bill Norris from the Riverland was calling him.

'Hi, Bill. What can I do for you?'

'Got something in relation to that Jim Nolan you're looking for,' said Bill.

'Oh?' said Carl.

'We had an anonymous caller this morning. Gave us directions to an abandoned farmhouse out by Pemberton. Told us we'd find two bodies there, one being Jim Nolan.'

'And the other?' said Carl, wondering if it would be Ian Holden.

'He didn't say, Carl, but I've just had a call from the patrol I sent out to verify his story. He wasn't kidding. They've found two bodies where he said they'd be. One's on the ground inside the house, beside a grave holding the partially buried remains of the other. He told us the one in the hole was Nolan.'

'Any idea who the caller is?' said Carl, wondering why only one of the bodies had been buried.

'No,' said Bill. 'We haven't had any luck tracing the call.'

'He could be the killer,' said Carl.

'Either that or someone who stumbled across the bodies,' said Bill.

'Got to be someone with something to hide,' said Carl, 'otherwise he'd want his fifteen minutes.'

'Maybe,' said Bill, 'but we've got people doing all sorts of things up here, Carl, people that don't want us poking around and disturbing their activities.'

'Whoever he is,' said Carl, 'he obviously knew who Jim Nolan was and wanted us or somebody to know he's dead.'

'Any ideas?' said Bill.

'Probably someone connected with the cars he was transporting,' said Carl. 'Someone who wanted him out of the way. Makes me think the other body could be Ian Holden. He's been missing since he jumped bail.'

'Better send me a picture,' said Bill.

'Have you spoken to Forensics?' said Carl.

'Not yet,' said Bill.

'I'll let you do that, Bill. Think I'll come up and take a look. Wasn't quite expecting this.'

'Yeah, well life's full of surprises, Carl.'

Carl slipped his phone back into his pocket and returned to where Wayne and Nigel were sitting.

'Sounds like Nolan's dead,' said Carl. 'Buried inside a derelict farmhouse near Pemberton, apparently, and Holden might be dead as well. There's another body next to the grave.'

Wayne and Nigel turned from the screen of Nigel's computer.

'Thought we were dealing with a bunch of car thieves,' said Wayne. 'Not this.'

'Someone obviously doesn't want Nolan and Holden talking to us,' said Carl.

'Too bad Holden didn't spill the beans when he had the chance,' said Wayne.

'Not much we can do about that,' said Carl. 'Meet me downstairs in ten, Wayne. And, you'd better call home. I doubt we'll be back tonight.'

Carl went into his office to collect his travel bag and call Nina. Then, he let Harry know where they were going and headed downstairs to the car park.

———

Four hours later, Carl and Wayne arrived at the abandoned farmhouse hidden in the scrub outside the small settlement of Pemberton. Sgt Dean Lang and his crime scene investigators were setting up their equipment in the fading light of the late afternoon.

'Dr Jonas is inside, Inspector' said Sgt Lang. 'If you go around the front you can access the crime scene through the window from the veranda.'

'Thanks, Dean,' said Carl.

A spotlight on a tripod, powered by a portable generator sitting on the veranda outside the remains of the front door, illuminated the front room. The smell of something dead hit them as they approached the window. Inside, Mike Jonas was bent over a body on the earthen floor.

'Evening,' said Carl, stepping through the window. 'Any idea who he is?'

Mike shook his head. 'No identification on him.'

'How long's he been here?' said Carl.

'Not long,' said Mike. 'I'd say he was shot sometime in the last twenty-four hours or so.'

Carl looked at the body. It wasn't Holden. He noticed the three dark stains in the clothing covering its chest. He compared the face to the image he had of Nolan on his phone. There was no match.

'What about the body in the grave?' said Carl.

'You'll have to wait until we dig him out,' said Mike. 'All I can see at the moment is an arm with a fancy watch on it.'

'That's supposed to be Jim Nolan,' said Carl, 'according to Bill Norris' caller.'

'Let me get this one into a body bag and out of the way,' said Mike. 'Then we can take a look at the other one.'

They watched from the veranda as the crime scene investigators moved the body into a body bag and carried it out of the room, before widening the hole in the floor to allow them to retrieve the body buried in it. The photographer snapped a picture of the face of the body in the hole when it was exposed and showed it to Carl and Wayne.

'That's Nolan,' said Wayne.

'When did he go missing?' said Mike.

'About three weeks ago,' said Carl.

'I'd say he's been dead most of that time,' said Mike.

'We need to find out who his mate is,' said Carl, 'seeing it's not Holden.'

'I wonder if Holden's our mystery caller,' said Wayne. 'Who else would want us to know Nolan was dead?'

'How would he know?' said Carl.

'He must have been here,' said Wayne.

'Someone had uncovered that arm with the watch on it before we got here,' said Mike. 'Probably used that spade over there.'

'I'll check it for prints,' said Dean.

'Anything out in the yard?' said Carl.

'A set of tyre tracks where a vehicle parked,' said Dean, 'and footprints suggesting two people got out of it and walked into the house, but there's only one set going back out to the vehicle.'

'Recent?' said Carl.

'Tracks look fresh to me,' said Dean.

'Are you sure the tracks weren't left by the patrol Inspector Norris sent out?' said Carl.

'They parked at the top of the yard and walked in,' said Dean. 'I spoke to them when we got here.'

———

'Who owns the place where the bodies were found?' said Carl.

'It's an abandoned pastoral lease.' Bill picked up his beer. 'Nobody's lived out there for years, not since the last big drought. That's when a lot of people walked off their properties and never came back.'

'Certainly looks like dry country,' said Carl.

'You're not wrong there, but you should come up after a decent rain. There's so much feed you wouldn't recognize the place. It's green everywhere you look. Trouble is, it doesn't last. Sometimes it doesn't rain for years,' said Bill.

'What about irrigation?' said Carl.

'Too far from the river out there, Carl. Besides, with all the environmental flows they allocate to keeping the river alive these days, there's not enough water to go around even if they could afford to pump it way out there.'

'So, we're not likely to find anyone who may have seen anything out that way,' said Carl.

Bill drained his glass and signalled for the barmaid to refill their glasses.

'There are still a few people living out there. They have to drive past that place to get to the highway. We'll ask them, but we'd have to be lucky,' said Bill. 'It's not like they're up and down that road every day, but they might remember seeing a vehicle go past or at least the dust cloud behind it.'

Carl drained his glass. He didn't like their chances of finding a witness and hoped Dean came up with something they could use to identify the person who had left the scene.

DC Paterson joined them.

'Any news?' said Carl.

'Nigel thinks he's picked up the truck they used to get the car out of East Park. He's trying to follow it through the traffic camera network. Could take a while,' said Wayne.

The barmaid delivered their drinks and dropped a menu onto the table.

'I'll have one of those,' said Wayne.

The barmaid smiled and went to get Wayne a beer.

'Do you think Nolan was bringing the cars up here?' said Bill, picking up his fresh pint.

'We know Holden came up to the Pemberton truck park to retrieve the truck Nolan was driving,' said Carl. 'So, either Nolan met someone and transferred his load or he delivered the cars up here somewhere.'

'That means your cars could be anywhere by now,' said Bill.

'Or out there somewhere,' said Wayne, pointing out the window into the darkness.

'That's a big open space,' said Bill.

'They obviously can't stay there forever,' said Wayne. 'They have to ship them to market, somehow.'

The barmaid delivered Wayne's beer and another menu.

'Why do you think they killed him?' said Bill.

'Probably didn't trust him to keep his mouth shut,' said Wayne.

'If what his wife told us is true, he'd only recently joined the operation,' said Carl. 'I guess they figured we'd come after him after the accident involving his truck.'

'What does that mean for Holden?' said Bill.

'Guess that depends on how he fits into the gang,' said Carl.

'Where do you think he is?' said Bill.

Carl shrugged his shoulders. 'Could be anywhere. Guess we'll have an idea if Nigel works out where that truck went, and if Holden was driving it.'

'Be interesting to find out who the other fellow is,' said Bill. 'His clothing suggests he's a local.'

'You'd better ask around,' said Carl, picking up the menu. 'Time for something to eat.'

CHAPTER TWENTY-TWO

Kurt was locking up Bayside Auto when his mobile phone rang. The ringtone told him it was his wife calling and he wondered what she'd want him to pick up on the way home.

'Hi, honey.'

'Listen up!' said a male voice Kurt didn't recognize.

'Who are you?' said Kurt. 'What are you doing with Georgia's phone?'

'Shut up and listen, Viking!'

Kurt waited. He knew a threatening tone when he heard one.

'Please do what he says, Kurt. He's got a gun,' said Georgia.

Kurt felt his legs turning to jelly and leant back on the door of the workshop.

'Have I got your attention now, Viking?' said the male voice.

'What do you want?' said Kurt, sliding down the door to sit on the ground.

'Shit's hit the fan,' said the voice. 'Holden's disappeared. Probably gone to the police.'

Kurt realized the voice belonged to Shane Lewis, who bought their cars. 'I thought you were taking care of him.'

'Didn't go to plan,' said the voice. 'Someone must have tipped him off.'

'Wasn't me,' said Kurt. 'Where's Jack?'

'Where Holden's meant to be.'

Kurt didn't like where the conversation was going. If Ian was still alive, they were all at risk of going to jail. If he'd bested Jack, thought Kurt, he must know they wanted him dead.

'What do you want me to do?' said Kurt.

'Make sure he keeps me out of it,' said the voice, 'if you want to see your wife and kids again.'

The line went dead. Kurt dropped his head into his hands and took three deep breaths. He lifted his phone and called his father-in-law.

'There's been a fuck up, Tom. Jack's dead and Lewis has taken Georgia and the boys hostage,' said Kurt. 'He thinks Ian's gone to the police.'

'Ian's smarter than that,' said Tom. 'What's Lewis want?'

'He wants me to stop Ian before he drops all of us in it, especially him,' said Kurt, 'otherwise he'll...'

'Don't go there,' said Tom.

Kurt took a couple of deep breaths. 'How am I going to protect Lewis if Ian has already gone to the police?'

'Listen to me, Kurt. We don't know that Ian's gone to the police. Lewis is panicking,' said Tom. 'Where was Georgia?'

'Home,' said Kurt.

'You sure he's got them?'

'He called on her phone,' said Kurt, 'and she spoke to me.'

He waited for Tom to respond.

'What does Ian know about Lewis and his mates?' said Tom.

'Nothing, as far as I know, unless he got something out of Jack.'

'That's not likely,' said Tom, 'but I'm surprised he got the better of Jack.'

Kurt thought he probably should have warned them about Ian's Tae Kwon Do, but it was too late now and he didn't want Tom blaming him for the mess they were in. 'What do you want me to do?'

'Wait for the police to make a move, and deny whatever they claim Ian's told them, if he's told them anything. It's your word against his, unless they can pin something on you,' said Tom. 'Make sure you've covered your arse, and go about your business as if nothing has happened.'

'What about Joe?' said Kurt.

'He'll keep his mouth shut,' said Tom.

'He'll need an alibi for last night if Ian's gone to the police,' said Kurt.

'We can arrange that,' said Tom, 'just in case.'

'I'm worried about Georgia and the boys. Do you think Lewis will hurt them?'

'He's a reasonable man, Kurt. I'd say Jack's death has rattled him. I'll talk to him and get him to bring Georgia and the boys home,' said Tom.

'Okay.'

'Go home and wait,' said Tom. 'I'll call you after I've spoken to Lewis.'

Kurt pushed himself up from the ground and pounded the workshop door with his fists. He wanted to find Lewis and smash the stupid bastard's face in for threatening Georgia and the boys. He toyed with the idea of hunting down Lewis and putting a bullet between his eyes, but he knew Lewis had the upper hand and wouldn't hesitate to carry out his threat, despite what Tom thought about him.

Kurt loved his kids and couldn't bear to think about what Lewis might do to them. He hoped Tom could persuade Lewis to change his mind.

He looked at the traffic streaming past the workshop and wondered how many years he'd get if he couldn't convince the police he had nothing to do with their car stealing racket.

He watched as a battered Land Rover, driven by a man wearing a wide-brimmed hat, turned out of the traffic and came into the yard in front of the workshop. It stopped next to Kurt's SUV.

'We're closed,' said Kurt, as the driver opened his door and got out.

'Get in,' said Ian, pointing Jack's pistol at him.

———

Tom Cotton stared out at the lights illuminating the garden beyond his kitchen window. Things were getting out of hand. First Ian's accident, now this. He wondered why Lewis had abducted Georgia and the boys, his grandkids. He'd known Shane Lewis for years. He was usually level-headed and rarely panicked, so Tom knew Jack's death must have spooked him.

He wondered what Ian would tell the police, if he'd gone to them as Lewis suspected, as he didn't know anything about Lewis' end of the operation. Pity Jack hadn't completed the job, he thought. But dead men didn't tell tales, especially not to the police, so there had to be something else that Lewis knew that he didn't. Tom picked up his phone and called Lewis.

'What do you want?' said Lewis.

'I want to know why you've taken my daughter and my grandsons hostage,' said Tom.

'Insurance, old man.'

'You don't need insurance, Lewis. You only need to wait for things to settle down,' said Tom.

'I don't trust Viking,' said Lewis, 'and, I don't want him taking me down with him.'

Tom counted to three.

'Let me speak to Georgia,' said Tom.

'She's driving,' said Lewis. 'Say something. Your father's worried about you.'

'We're fine, Dad.'

'Satisfied?' said Lewis.

Tom let his breath out slowly. At least Lewis hadn't hurt them.

'I don't think Kurt's your problem,' said Tom. 'He answers to me. We need to silence Ian.'

'Bit bloody late for that,' said Lewis.

'What happened?' said Tom. 'What makes you think he's gone to the police?'

'There's a shitload of cops at the old farm.'

'That doesn't mean Jack's dead' said Tom.

'I went back to the farm when Jack didn't show to confirm he'd done the job. There was a bloody cop car in the yard, and no sign of Jack's rover. I waited for the cops to leave. They didn't. Word is they found two bodies in the house,' said Lewis.

'So, you're assuming one of them is Jack?' said Tom. 'It could be Ian.'

'How would the cops know about the place if Holden didn't tell them?' said Lewis. 'Jack certainly wouldn't have told them.'

Tom knew he couldn't argue with that. 'I guess we'll know soon enough if it's Jack. It won't take them long to identify him, not with his record.'

'Yeah,' said Lewis.

'They can't trace him back to us,' said Tom.

'I made sure of that,' said Lewis.

'How about you bring Georgia and the boys to my place and we work together to find Ian?' said Tom. 'There's no point in us falling out, Lewis. That's not good for business. What do you say?'

Tom waited for Lewis to answer.

'I suppose you're right,' said Lewis.

'Let me see if I can find out where they're holding him,' said Tom. 'I've got a few bent coppers in my pocket.'

'What good will that do us?'

'We'll find out if he's with them or not,' said Tom.

'And, if he is?'

'Accidents happen all the time, Lewis, even inside.'

'Take us about an hour to get to your place,' said Lewis.

'I'll wait up.'

Tom ended the call and scrolled through his list of contacts. When he found the one he wanted, he pushed the call icon.

'Hello, John. Can you talk?'

'Yeah. What can I do you for?'

'Find out where someone called Ian Holden is being held. I understand he's turned himself into your lot in the Riverland.'

'Let me make a few calls. I'll get back to you.'

Tom walked into the family room where Joe was watching TV.

'We have a little problem,' said Tom.

'What's that?' said Joe.

'Ian may have gone to the police.'

Joe sat up. 'I thought Lewis was taking care of him.'

'Something went wrong,' said Tom. 'Lewis has taken Georgia and the kids hostage.'

'Why?' said Joe.

'He doesn't trust Kurt,' said Tom.

'For fuck's sake,' said Joe. 'What are we going to do?'

'I've talked him into bringing Georgia and the boys here,' said Tom. 'Get Rosie to cover for you for last night. If Ian's spilling his guts to the police, they'll be coming for you.'

Tom called Kurt's number. He didn't answer. He left a message for Kurt to call him back.

Tom's phone rang.

'Think your information must be wrong, Tom. We're still looking for him.'

'Thanks, John.'

Tom called his eldest son.

'We need to find Ian before the police do.'

Kurt stared at the pistol in Ian's hand.

'What's going on?'

'That's what I want to know,' said Ian. 'Get in!'

Kurt moved around to the side of the Land Rover and opened the door without taking his eyes off the pistol.

'Don't do anything stupid,' said Ian. 'I know how to use this thing.'

Kurt climbed into the Land Rover and shut the door. 'I thought you were going to disappear with Jim.'

'That was the plan,' said Ian, 'but a few things went wrong.'

'Did you find Jim?'

Ian pushed the pistol into Kurt's cheek. 'Don't give me that did you find him bullshit. You knew damn well where he was all along, didn't you? That's why you sent me up with the last car. To join him.'

'What are you talking about? I swear, Lewis said he'd let Jim go if you two agreed to disappear, just like I told you,' said Kurt.

'Lewis? Is that his first or last name?'

'His name's Shane Lewis,' said Kurt.

'Where can I find him?' said Ian.

Kurt laughed.

'What's so funny?' said Ian.

'He's got a place in the Riverland. It's between the river and that roadhouse at Pemberton,' said Kurt.

'Do you know precisely where?' said Ian.

'No. I've never been there,' said Kurt.

'Then you're not much use to me,' said Ian.

'He's taken my wife and kids hostage,' said Kurt.

Ian leant back against the door and looked at Kurt. 'Why would he do that?'

'He thinks I warned you about Jack,' said Kurt.

'Be nice if you had,' said Ian, 'but you didn't, did you? Thanks for nothing.'

Ian pushed the pistol into Kurt's ear.

'Don't shoot me. I'll do anything you want,' said Kurt. 'Anything!'

'Too late for that.'

————

Inside the Land Rover, the pistol made a loud, sharp noise that reverberated in Ian's ears.

The side of Kurt's head hit the window before his body slumped into the seat.

Ian looked around.

Cars kept streaming past on the road. No-one came to investigate.

Ian searched Kurt's pockets. Found his keys and his wallet.

He placed Jack's hat on Kurt's bloodied head. Then, he slipped the pistol into the pocket of his jacket and climbed out of the Land Rover, locking the doors behind him.

Ian opened the workshop and went into the restroom next to Kurt's office, where he washed his face and hands, and did his best to wash off the spots of Kurt's blood that had splattered onto his jacket. When he was satisfied with his efforts, he locked up the workshop, climbed into Kurt's SUV, and left for the Riverland to find Shane Lewis.

He had every intention of killing Lewis when he found him, whether he had Kurt's wife and kids with him or not.

CHAPTER TWENTY-THREE

Carl was reading the morning paper as Wayne drove them back to the city when his mobile phone rang.

'Morning, Harry.'

'Kurt Viking's been found dead in a vehicle outside his workshop,' said Harry. 'Bullet to the head.'

'Suicide?' said Carl.

'Doesn't look like it,' said Harry. 'His body was found inside a Land Rover registered to someone called Jack Sloane, and his SUV is missing.'

'Did they take anything else?' said Carl.

'Wallet and keys,' said Harry. 'Left his mobile phone.'

'Do we know anything about this Sloane person?' said Carl. 'Or is it a stolen vehicle?'

'He's got a record as long as my arm,' said Harry. 'Mostly for assault.'

Carl pulled the onboard computer towards him. 'Any sign of Holden?'

'What makes you think Holden is involved?' said Harry.

Carl smiled to himself. He liked the way Harry's brain

worked. 'We could be looking at a falling out between thieves, Harry. We found Nolan's body up here yesterday.'

'I heard,' said Harry.

'Who's got the Viking case?' said Carl.

'DI Ryan,' said Harry. 'The chief reckons we have enough on our plate.'

Carl couldn't argue with the chief's logic but he suspected he'd be working closely with DI Ryan to find Viking's killer. 'Anything new on Mitchell?'

'Still looking,' said Harry.

'How's Nigel going with his truck?'

'Reckons he's tracked it from East Park to the Main North Road, so it could have been heading up the river,' said Harry.

'That would explain how Holden got up here,' said Carl.

'Does he have the registration details?'

'Belongs to City Truck Rentals,' said Harry. 'They're expecting it back today.'

'Do we have the details of who rented it?'

'Some company called Arthur Transport. They're sending us a copy of the rental contract.'

Carl ended the call and keyed Jack Sloane into the onboard computer. He waited for the response from the database. When it opened, he clicked on the image of Sloane to enlarge it and read his record.

'Think we know who the other body is, Wayne. This Jack Sloane character.' Carl swivelled the screen towards Wayne. 'Nasty piece of work by the look of it.'

Wayne glanced at the screen. 'Looks like him.'

'Kurt Viking was found dead in Sloane's vehicle this morning,' said Carl.

'Obviously, Sloane didn't drive it down there,' said Wayne. 'Who do you think it was?'

'My money's on Holden,' said Carl. 'I reckon he's Inspector

Norris' caller. Who else would want us to know where Nolan was?'

'Make's sense,' said Wayne.

Carl called Bill Norris and let him know about Kurt Viking's death and Jack Sloane.

'We've come to a dead end with the phone call, Carl. Whoever he is, he's using one of those cheap, pre-paid phones with no caller ID,' said Bill.

'It's got to be Holden,' said Carl. 'How else can you explain Sloane's vehicle ending up at Bayside Auto?'

'Wonder who Sloane was working for?' said Bill. 'He's not known for pinching cars.'

'See what you can find out,' said Carl. 'Somebody must have seen something up your way.'

———

Carl smiled to himself as he read Dean Lang's report. Jack Sloane may not have had any identifying documents on him, but that hadn't stopped Dean from finding out who he was without any help from Carl.

As a frequent inmate in the state's prisons over the course of his adult life, mostly for assault causing bodily harm, Jack Sloane had left a record littered with fingerprints and mugshots for Dean to find.

Carl reread Sloane's file and noted his most recent release date was several years old. He's kept himself out of trouble and managed to stay off our radar for the last few years, thought Carl.

He turned his attention back to Dean's report, wondering if Sloane's only connection to the car stealing gang was being paid to kill Nolan and Holden. He put the report down. How had Holden turned the tables on Sloane? Carl shook his head.

There were things about Holden he didn't know and still needed to find out. If he'd killed both Sloane and Viking, he obviously knew how to use a gun.

He turned back to Dean's notes. The pistol used to kill Sloane had also fired the shot that ended Jim Nolan's life. Carl leant back in his chair. There was no way of knowing who had pulled the trigger to dispatch Nolan. Dean had matched the prints on the handle of the spade found next to the grave with Holden's, which only confirmed his suspicion that Holden had killed Sloane and made off with his vehicle. Carl wondered what had happened to the truck Holden had driven up to the Riverland. There'd been no sign of it at the farmhouse where the bodies had been discovered, and Bill Norris hadn't been able to find it either.

'Got a minute, Inspector?' said DC Beard.

Carl looked up from the report. 'What's on your mind?'

'Got the details on those credit cards from Pemberton. Not good news, I'm afraid,' said DC Beard. 'Looks like they paid cash for their petrol.'

'That's not much help, is it?'

'No, but there might be a way of finding out who was in the car when it returned to Bayside Auto,' said DC Beard.

'How?' said Carl.

'There's a used car place opposite the workshop,' said DC Beard. 'I reckon there's a fair chance they'd have security cameras.'

'You might be pushing your luck, Nigel, but I guess it's worth finding out what they have,' said Carl. 'See if DI Ryan's people have had a look at the recording for the night Viking was killed. They might have pictures of Holden arriving and leaving.'

When DC Beard left his office, Carl closed Dean's report and opened Mike Jonas' report on the autopsy of Jim Nolan.

He noted that the pathologist had estimated Nolan's time of death as the last weekend in May, which meant he'd been killed while Holden was sitting downstairs in the holding cells. At least that rules him out as being Nolan's killer, thought Carl.

With his prints being on the spade, Holden was definitely in the picture for shooting Sloane as far as Carl was concerned, and who knew how much incriminating evidence he'd left behind when he'd killed Kurt Viking. Carl made himself a note to follow up with DI Ryan.

He closed the report and walked out to DC Paterson's desk.

'How do you think they knew where to find the cars?' said Carl.

'I've been wondering about that myself,' said DC Paterson. 'You'd hardly think they wandered around looking for targets, would you?'

'Follow up with the owners and find out who services or cleans their car,' said Carl, 'and see if there's a common link. I doubt anyone owning that sort of car would get it serviced at a place like Bayside Auto.'

———

Carl was packing up for the day when DC Beard came back into his office.

'Checked with DI Ryan's people, Inspector. No security cameras.'

CHAPTER TWENTY-FOUR

DC Templar read the response to the query she'd sent to the Office of the Registrar of Births, Deaths and Marriages.

The first paragraph of the email told her Trent Mitchell was the only child of Robert Ian Mitchell (deceased) and Helen Mary Mitchell (nee Broadbent) (deceased). The second paragraph, contained the names and dates of birth of John Harvey Mitchell, Robert's brother, and Margaret Elizabeth Murphy (nee Broadbent), Helen's sister.

DC Templar entered the names and dates of birth into the Registrations database and waited.

The query response window displayed an address for John Harvey Mitchell at 37 Jacobs Crescent, Portside and one for Margaret Elizabeth Murphy at 78 Cockle Street, Morton Sands.

She printed the addresses, opened White Pages, and searched for their telephone numbers.

When she had the numbers, she telephoned each in turn, and made an appointment to speak with them.

She looked across the room at Inspector West's office. He wasn't in. She called DS Fuller to let him know where she'd be.

'Meet you downstairs,' said DS Fuller.

———

'The only information I've picked up,' said Harry, 'is Mitchell had a girlfriend called Helen a few years ago.'

'Same name as his mother,' said Lisa, as she parked the car in front of 37 Jacobs Crescent.

They walked along a paved brick path through a neat front garden up to a wooden front door, which opened as they approached.

'Are you the police?' said the young woman standing in the doorway.

'Yes,' said Harry, showing her his ID. 'I'm Detective Sergeant Fuller and this is Detective Constable Templar.'

'You look familiar,' said the young woman to Lisa. 'I know you from somewhere.'

'Joni?' said Lisa.

'Oh My God! Mrs Templar! I didn't know you were in the police force.'

'Needed a change,' said Lisa, turning to face Harry. 'Joni was one of my first ever maths students.'

'Pleased to meet you, Joni,' said Harry, offering his hand.

'What are you doing now?' said Lisa.

'I'm nursing at City Hospital, in the maternity wing,' said Joni. 'Why do you want to speak to Dad?'

'We're trying to locate your cousin, Trent,' said Harry.

'You'd better come in.'

Joni led them through the house to the family room where her father was watching golf on TV.

'Look who's here, Dad.'

Mr Mitchell switched off the TV and stood to face his visitors. When he saw who was standing next to his daughter, a broad smile spread across his face. 'The world's best maths teacher! What are you doing here? I was expecting the police.'

'Hello, John, I'm afraid I am the police these days. This is my boss, Detective Sergeant Fuller.'

Harry shook hands with John Mitchell.

'Was that you who called on the phone?' said John, looking at Lisa.

'Yes. I'm sorry, but the name didn't twig until I saw Joni at the door. It's been a long time.'

'How's that husband of yours? Is he still teaching?'

'He's fine. He's one of the Assistant Principals at City High School.'

'Well, what can we do for you? You mentioned something about my nephew, Trent.'

'We're trying to locate him,' said Harry.

'I didn't realize he was missing,' said John, looking at his daughter. 'Did you?'

'To be honest, I haven't seen him for a while,' said Joni. 'He's been kind of off the planet since Helen died.'

'How long ago was that?' said Harry.

They watched as Joni counted off on her fingers. 'Be almost seven years. It was just before I started at City.'

'What happened?' said Lisa.

'They were really into mountain biking. Trent's been into bikes ever since we were kids. Anyway, she came off her bike somewhere up in the hills. Broke her neck and ruptured her spleen. Trent had to ride out to get help. He'd left his phone in the car. She died a couple of days later in hospital.' Joni looked at Lisa. 'He's never forgiven himself for leaving his phone in the car.'

'Which hospital?' said Harry.

'She was in Intensive Care at City,' said Joni.

'What was Helen's last name?' said Harry.

'Drew. Her name was Helen Drew,' said Joni.

'We're investigating the deaths of two nurses that worked in Intensive Care at City,' said Harry.

Joni put a hand to her mouth.

'And, you think Trent might have something to do with it?' said John.

'We don't know,' said Harry, 'but a vehicle similar to Trent's was seen near the scene of one of the murders, at Carrick, and he was staying in the caravan park down there at the time. We've actually spoken to him once and would like to speak to him again, but he's disappeared. Moved out of the house he was renting. Resigned from his job. And, he's not answering his phone or returning our calls.'

'That doesn't sound good,' said John.

'Carrick's his favourite holiday spot,' said Joni. 'He goes down there every year. Sometimes, more than once.'

'Perhaps that's where he's gone,' said John.

'I don't think so,' said Harry. 'The local sergeant hasn't been able to locate him down there either. Any other place he might go that you know of?'

'Not really,' said John. 'He tends to stick to his routine. He's only lived in two places since he left home. He's never been good with change. He likes things to stay the same.'

'He's not alone there,' said Harry.

John smiled. 'I guess a lot of us are a bit like that, Sergeant, but Trent's a little less flexible than most, which is why I'm surprised he's left his job and moved house.'

'Told his manager he wanted to see the world before he got too old,' said Harry.

'God, he's only forty,' said Joni.

'Maybe he's having a mid-life crisis,' said John. 'I know I went off the rails for a bit when I hit forty.'

'Let's no go there, Dad,' said Joni.

'Are there any other cousins?' said Lisa.

'Not on our side of the family,' said Joni.

'What about his mother's side?'

'There are a couple, but they're much older than Trent,' said Joni. 'They're his Aunty Margaret's sons. She's his mother's older sister. I'm not sure Trent has much to do with them.'

'What happened to Trent's parents?' said Lisa.

'Car accident,' said John. 'My brother was way over the limit. Lost control on the way back from Carrick and hit a tree.'

'When was that?' said Harry.

'Before Trent met Helen,' said Joni. 'Must be at least ten years ago.'

'How did Trent take it?' said Lisa.

'Hard to say,' said John. 'He's a lot like his Dad. Robert never let on how he felt about anything. Probably why he drank so much.'

———

The small front yard of the house at 78 Cockle Street was covered in square, sandstone pavers, except for a small garden bed in the centre of the yard with a dead tree in it.

'Minimalist approach to gardening,' said Harry.

'Maybe she's into Zen,' said Lisa.

'I thought they used gravel,' said Harry, pressing the buzzer on the door frame.

They waited. Harry was about to push the buzzer again when he heard the sound of footsteps approaching the door.

The door opened a crack.

'Police,' said Harry, holding his ID out for whoever stood in the darkness of the house to examine. 'We're here to speak with Mrs Murphy.'

'I was expecting a woman,' said a woman's voice from behind the door.

'Hello, Mrs Murphy, I'm the officer that called you,' said Lisa.

The door closed and they listened to the sound of several security chains being released.

'You can never be too careful,' said Mrs Murphy, as she opened the door and let them into her house.

'You're right there,' said Lisa, as they waited for Mrs Murphy to lock her front door before showing them into her sitting room.

'You said something about Trent when you called. What's he been up to that has the police asking about him?'

'We're not sure he's been up to anything,' said Lisa. 'We're trying to find him.'

'Oh. Has he gone missing?' said Mrs Murphy.

'Afraid so,' said Lisa.

'Well, I haven't seen him. He doesn't come to see me very often, you know.'

'Does he keep in contact with your sons?' said Lisa.

'They never mention it if he does. He's not a very likeable fellow, young Trent. Too much like his father, if you ask me.' Mrs Murphy gazed into space. 'I never understood what my sister saw in Robert. The man had no personality unless he was drunk, and look where that got her.'

'Do you think we could have your sons' telephone numbers?' said Lisa, 'just in case he's been in contact with them.'

———

Harry called each of Margaret Murphy's sons, while Lisa drove them back into the city from Morton Sands, only to discover that neither of them had spoken to Trent since they'd last seen him at his parents' funeral.

'Our Mr Mitchell seems to be somewhat antisocial when it comes to members of his extended family,' said Harry.

'Seems to be a bit antisocial all round,' said Lisa, 'otherwise, we'd have a few more people to talk to.'

'We need to find out about this Helen Drew,' said Harry, 'and who nursed her at City Hospital.'

'You think that might be the connection?' said Lisa.

'Could be if Mitchell's our man,' said Harry.

Harry's mobile phone rang.

'Harry, where are you?' said Carl.

'I'm with Lisa, Boss. We're inbound from Morton Sands. Should be in the office in fifteen.'

'Meet me at 18 Lancet Street, Riverside. We've got another one.'

CHAPTER TWENTY-FIVE

Lancet Street, Riverside, was a tidy street of modern, three storey town houses overlooking a section of the linear park that enclosed the Wattle River as it snaked its way through the eastern suburbs on its way from the hills to the coast. Carl parked his silver Ford behind the grey van the Coroner's Office used for collecting bodies.

He slipped into his plastic crime scene suit and walked up to the constable controlling admittance to the crime scene.

'Front room on the left at the top of the stairs, Inspector.'

Carl signed his name on the admittance list and followed the blue plastic sheeting that marked the pathway he was expected to follow into the house, and turned left into the main bedroom off the landing at the top of the stairs.

'Hello, Inspector,' said Dr Worthington. 'We're just about done here.'

Carl smiled. He liked working with Emma Worthington. She was always thorough and very professional, and didn't know most of his personal secrets like Mike Jonas did. He looked down at the naked body of a young woman lying face down on the bed and wondered if he was dealing with the same killer.

'She's been strangled,' said Emma. 'Quite forcibly. That's what made me think of those cases Mike's working on with you.'

'Any sign of sexual assault?' said Carl.

'Looks like it. I'll confirm that after my examination in the lab,' said Emma. 'If you're lucky, we might get something we can use to generate a DNA profile for you.'

Sexual assault was a change for the killer, thought Carl, and he wondered if they were dealing with the same man or a copycat. Either way, a DNA profile would be helpful.

'Best guess on how long she's been dead?' said Carl.

'Not long, Inspector. Probably only a few hours,' said Emma.

'Do we know who she is?' said Carl.

'Her name's Sarah Cody,' said Sgt Lang. 'She's a nurse. Worked at City Hospital.'

Has to be the same killer, thought Carl. Three nurses from the same place was too much of a coincidence for it to be otherwise. He hoped they'd get a break on this one, as he wasn't looking forward to telling the Commissioner they had a third victim, but at least the media would push the story to an extent that should draw the public into helping him find the perpetrator.

'Did she let him in?' said Carl.

'No. The laundry door's been forced,' said Sgt Lang. 'The alarm system was off.'

'Must have thought she was safe in her own house,' said Emma. 'I never turn my alarm on when I'm home.'

'Guess most of us think of alarm systems as a way of deterring burglars when we're not home,' said Carl, looking around the room. 'Who found the body?'

'Her husband. Found her when he came home from work. He's with one of the responding officers out the front,' said Sgt Lang.

'Any foreign prints, Dean?'

'One of the boys is dusting the laundry, Inspector. I'll let you know if we find anything useful.'

———

Carl pulled off his crime scene suit and stowed it in the boot of his car. Then, he approached the constable standing next to the patrol car parked in front of the house.

'I'm looking for Mr Cody,' said Carl.

'He's in the car,' said the constable.

'How's he doing?' said Carl.

'Gone to pieces, Inspector. Can't say I blame him.'

That would make him vulnerable if he had something to hide, thought Carl. 'What's his story?'

'Says he came home around four and found her on the bed,' said the constable.

'Where does he work?'

'Teacher at the local primary school. It's only a couple of streets from here.'

'Have you checked that out?' said Carl.

'Called the head teacher. She confirmed he works there and that he left around three forty-five,' said the constable.

Not likely that he's the killer, then, thought Carl, going on Dr Worthington's estimated time of death. 'What have you got from the neighbours?'

'My partner's still knocking on doors, Inspector, but it

doesn't look like anybody was home in any of the adjoining houses before four o'clock.'

Carl opened the rear door of the patrol car and slipped in next to the victim's husband.

'Mr Cody, I'm inspector West. I need to ask you a few questions.'

Mr Cody turned his tear stained face towards Carl and leant back into the far corner of the seat.

Carl wondered if he was still with him. 'I'm sorry about what's happened to your wife, Mr Cody, but I'm going to need your help if we're to find her killer.'

'I hope you don't think I had anything to do with it. I loved Sarah. She was the world to me.'

Carl raised his hands, palms out. 'I need to keep an open mind, Mr Cody. I'm not pointing the finger at you or anybody else at this stage. It's way too early for that.'

'I assure you, it wasn't me,' said Mr Cody.

'Why was your wife home today?' said Carl.

'She's a nurse. She does shift work.'

'What shift was she on this week?' said Carl.

'Midnight to eight. Has been for the last two weeks.'

That would explain why she was in the bedroom, thought Carl. 'What time does she get up when she works that shift?'

'She's usually up when I get home from school.'

'And, when did you last see her?'

'Last night, when she left for work,' said Mr Cody.

'And, when did you leave for school this morning?'

'Just after eight. It's only a ten-minute walk.'

'Do you always come home at four?'

'I was early today. We were going out to dinner before she went to work. It's my birthday.'

A birthday ruined forever, thought Carl.

'Have you seen anyone hanging about or did your wife mention she'd seen anyone acting strangely in recent weeks?' said Carl.

'She did mention she thought someone had followed her home from work a couple of nights ago, but she only ever mentioned it the once. And, when I asked her last night if she'd been followed, she said she hadn't seen anyone. We thought she'd probably imagined it.'

Might very well be the way her killer had found out where she lived, thought Carl.

'How did your wife travel to and from work?'

'She drove. She had a park in the hospital car park. She didn't even have to leave the building to get to her car, and the place is covered with cameras,' said Mr Cody.

'Which part of the hospital did your wife work in?' said Carl.

'Intensive Care.'

Has to be the same killer, thought Carl, wishing he knew what the connection between the nurses and their killer was. 'Did she happen to mention what type of vehicle had followed her home?'

'Some sort of van, but she said it kept going up the street when she turned into the driveway.'

'White, by any chance?' said Carl, thinking of Christine Viking.

'Yes. A white van. Is that important?'

'Could be,' said Carl. 'If you think of anything else, Mr Cody, please give me a call. It doesn't matter how trivial it seems to you, call me.' Carl handed him his card.

Mr Cody looked at Carl. 'Tell me you'll find the bastard that did this to Sarah.'

Carl squeezed his hand. 'We will.'

———

When Carl climbed out of the patrol car, Harry and Lisa were talking to the constable outside the car waiting for him.

'Let's talk in my car,' said Carl.

They crossed the street and got into Carl's car. They watched as the gurney holding the victim's body was wheeled out of the house.

'What's the story here?' said Harry, once the body had disappeared into the coroner's van.

'Another nurse from the Intensive Care Unit at City. Strangled like the others,' said Carl.

'Any witnesses?' said Lisa.

'Another quiet suburban street of empty house during working hours,' said Carl. 'Seems the victim was the only one home. She was working the midnight shift.'

'Something her killer must have known,' said Lisa.

'Anything linking this to Mitchell?' said Harry.

'Depends what Dean's people find. The killer broke in through the door to the laundry around the back of the house, so we might get some prints, and who knows what bits and pieces he may have left in the bedroom,' said Carl. 'Dr Worthington thinks the victim was sexually assaulted.'

'That's a change,' said Lisa.

'Means he may have left more than a fingerprint or two,' said Carl, 'and the husband says she was followed home one day this week by someone driving a white van.'

'Well, we have something that might link Mitchell to the victims,' said Harry.

Carl turned and faced him as the street lights started coming on along Lancet Street. 'What's that?'

'His cousin, who turned out to be one of Lisa's old students, told us Mitchell had a girlfriend that died in Intensive Care at City Hospital about seven years ago.'

'Does this girlfriend have a name?'

'Helen Drew.'

'You'd better make some enquiries, Harry. We have to stop him before he kills anybody else.'

CHAPTER TWENTY-SIX

Gordon Sharp looked up from his desk in the Forensic Medicine Department at City University, where he was collating the results his investigators had submitted on their work.

'Got a minute, Dr Sharp?' said the young woman standing in his doorway and blocking the light from the window in the corridor behind her.

'What's on your mind, Jasmine?'

'I've found something in the files from City that might be important,' said Jasmine.

'What? A death that should have been reported to the Coroner?' said Gordon.

'No. This death was reported to the Coroner. It's the names of the nurses that caught my eye.'

'Want to explain?' said Gordon.

'They were talking about that nurse who was murdered at Riverside on the radio when I was driving in this morning,' said Jasmine. 'Her name's Sarah Cody.'

'Yes. I heard that report,' said Gordon.

'Well, you can imagine my surprise when that name

showed up in the case notes of the first death I looked at this morning,' said Jasmine.

'If she worked in intensive care, her name will be in the notes associated with a few deaths, don't you think?' said Gordon, wondering why she thought that was important.

'Probably, but two of the other nurses named in the notes have been in the news recently, too, and they were both murdered.'

'Is one of them Christine Viking?' said Gordon. 'I saw something about her murder on TV.'

'Yes,' said Jasmine. 'Christine Viking and Kelly Palmer.'

'Run a query on all the City deaths and see if there are any others linked to those three names,' said Gordon.

'I did that,' said Jasmine.

'And?'

'There's only the one death with those three names in the case notes.'

Gordon joined the dots. 'Are there any other names linked to that death?'

Jasmine opened the page in her right hand. 'There's a Pauline Francis and a Dr Rita Bryant.'

'Who was the patient?' said Gordon.

'A woman named Helen Drew.'

'I think we'd better call the police.'

CHAPTER TWENTY-SEVEN

Carl was about to leave his office for the morning's team meeting when the telephone on his desk rang.

'Inspector, I've got a Dr Gordon Sharp on the line from the Department of Forensic Medicine at City University. Says he has some vital information for you in connection to the nurses that have been murdered.'

Carl wondered what someone working on forensic medicine at City University would know about the deaths of the three women he was investigating. 'Put him through.' He waited until he heard the line click in. 'Dr Sharp. This is Inspector West. How can I help you?'

'I think I might be able to help you find your killer, Inspector, or at least stop him killing anybody else,' said Gordon.

'That sounds promising, Doctor. Want to explain how you can do that?'

'Don't get me wrong, Inspector. I don't want to tell you how to do your job but I've come across some information that could help you,' said Gordon.

'What sort of information?'

'My team is reviewing the notification of deaths to the Coroner by City Hospital, Inspector. You may have heard something about the review on the news. The minister's been making a lot of noise about the issue of incorrect reporting.'

'I recall the minister making some sort of announcement,' said Carl. 'How far back are you looking?'

'Ten years,' said Gordon, 'anyway, one of my assistants noticed the names of those three nurses that have been murdered in the case notes of a particular death at City Hospital, and it's the only death all three are linked to in the records we've been asked to review.'

'What was the name of the patient?' said Carl.

'Helen Drew,' said Gordon. 'She died in Intensive Care in 2010.'

Bloody hell, thought Carl. It had to be Mitchell.

'Are there any other names in those case notes, Doctor?'

'A nurse by the name of Pauline Francis and a Dr Rita Bryant, who signed the death certificate.'

That meant Mitchell had two more targets, thought Carl.

'Thanks, Doctor. I'm glad you called.'

Carl activated the telephone cradle with his right hand and then keyed in the number for David Nelson at City Hospital.

'David Nelson.'

'David, Carl West from City Police. We have a connection between the three nurses that have been murdered but, if we're right, there could be some others in danger. I need some contact details.'

'Who for?'

'A nurse by the name of Pauline Francis and a doctor by the name of Rita Bryant that helped look after a patient by the name of Helen Drew. She died in Intensive Care in 2010.'

'Give me a couple of minutes.'

Carl signalled for Harry to join him in his office while he

waited. 'All three of our victims looked after Helen Drew. It's got to be Mitchell.' Carl held up his hand as David Nelson came back on the line.

'I'm sending you an email with the details, Inspector. Pauline is currently on annual leave and Dr Bryant is now out at University. Do you want me to call them?'

Carl heard the ping of the email arriving and clicked it open. He looked at the contents and saw telephone numbers and home addresses for both Pauline Francis and Rita Bryant.

'Thanks, David. We'll take it from here.'

Carl placed the receiver back in its cradle.

'Harry, I'm sending you this email from David Nelson. Call Pauline Francis and find out where she is. If she's home, get a patrol out to her house, and tell her not to answer the door to anyone until they get there. I'll call University and find out where Dr Bryant is.'

————

Carl called University Hospital. Dr Bryant had not turned up for work as expected and hadn't called in to let them know where she was or whether she was coming in.

Carl tried Dr Bryant's mobile number. His call went through to voice mail.

I hope he hasn't already got to her, thought Carl.

He punched in the number for Operations.

'Get a patrol to this address.' He read the street address from David Nelson's email. 'If Dr Bryant is there, I need to talk to her. If she's not, ask them to question the neighbours and check for signs of forced entry. Keep me informed.'

Harry came into Carl's office. 'I just spoken to Pauline Francis' daughter. She's in Europe with her husband. They won't be back for three weeks.'

'I'm waiting for a call back from Operations. Dr Bryant hasn't shown up for work this morning and isn't answering her phone. They've sent a patrol to her home address.'

'Shit!' said Harry. 'Didn't think he'd strike again that quickly.'

'Let's hope there's some other explanation,' said Carl. 'In the meantime, get Mitchell's details out to the media. He has to be out there somewhere. He can't stay hidden forever.'

'Okay, Boss.'

'I need to bring the chief up to speed,' said Carl.

CHAPTER TWENTY-EIGHT

Trent tried not to think about her. But he couldn't stop thinking about Sarah Cody.

He hadn't expected to find her naked when he'd burst into her bedroom, but he'd surprised her as she was getting ready to take a shower.

The sight of her naked body had aroused him and clouded his mind with lust. She'd looked at the rope in his hand and fallen backwards onto the bed as she'd tried to get away from him. He'd hesitated next to the bed with the rope in his hand looking at her, and wanting her.

He'd expected her to roll off the bed and make for the door, but she'd smiled coyly up at him, let her legs fall apart, and asked if he wanted to fuck her.

He'd watched as she'd run her hands over her breasts and down to the tussock of dark hair below her navel, felt the tightness in his member, and dropped the rope. Then, he'd pulled down his tracksuit pants and his jocks, discarded them on the floor, and mounted her. She'd wrapped her arms around his neck and moved her body against him, making noises of enjoyment as he'd penetrated and exploded inside her.

When he'd pushed himself up from her, she'd rolled off the bed and tried to escape, but he'd been too fast for her. He hadn't forgotten why he was there. He'd grabbed her and thrown her back onto the bed and picked up the rope. She'd kicked out at him, hitting him in the belly with her foot, but he'd grasped her leg and pulled her onto the floor.

She'd managed to stand, but he'd slipped the rope around her neck and twisted it behind her head, pulling her warm naked body towards him until she'd stopped breathing. Then, he'd let her fall face down onto the bed.

Every time he thought of her, the scene played through his mind. He couldn't let it go. He knew it should not have happened but he wanted it to happen again.

Trent looked at Helen's coffee cup on the upturned box he was using as a table in front of him. He couldn't feel her presence. That meant she was upset with him for his lapse in self-control. She'd always been jealous. In life, she'd hated it whenever he'd looked at another woman, and had always subjected him to the silent treatment. Sometimes for days. He wondered how long he'd have to wait. This was the first time he'd betrayed her and had sex with another woman.

He knew he couldn't hide anything from her now and that he'd have to ask for her forgiveness and perform acts of penance to atone for his sin, before she'd speak to him again and tell him which one he'd have to deal with next.

Trent knew he'd have to stop thinking about Sarah Cody and what it felt like fucking her, before any of that could happen but, for the moment, Helen would have to wait. He couldn't resist reliving the experience.

———

When he heard on the van's radio that the police were asking members of the public to report any sightings of him or his Ford, Trent shaved his head and let his beard grow. He stopped going to the gym as a casual member, where he'd been making use of the showers, so he could keep a low profile and avoid the public gaze.

After a week of living without access to hot running water, he joined the lines of homeless men dressed in crumpled and dirty clothes queuing at the men's shelter for food and a hot shower.

Once a week, he made his way to the laundromat four blocks from the abandoned house he called home to wash his underwear and the clothes he wore when he wasn't blending in with the homeless.

After two weeks, he resolved to let the memory of Sarah Cody go and get on with his mission before the police found him. Each day, he sat before Helen's coffee cup and reached out to her, asking for her forgiveness, but failed to make contact.

There were days when he wondered if he'd made a mistake listening to her in the first place but the nightmares had stopped, so he knew that wasn't it. She was obviously still jealous of what he'd done with Sarah Cody and the way she had crept into his thoughts and dreams.

Then, a morning came when he thought that maybe he'd done enough and she didn't want him to kill the others, as they had not been responsible for her death. But, he wondered how he was going to know for sure if she wouldn't guide him one way or the other. He knew he couldn't stay where he was forever.

He picked up her coffee cup and held the fingers of his right hand over the opening.

'If you want me to continue, direct my fingers to pull out a name.' He waited. Nothing happened. He felt no urge to lower his fingers into the cup and draw out one of the last two names.

'That's it! I'm moving on.'

He picked up the cup and threw it against the wall. It shattered, and the last two squares of paper fell into the dust on the floor.

Trent looked at the shattered pieces of the cup strewn across the floor and felt alone. He dropped his head into his hands. He had no idea what he was going to do now that it had come to an end. He hadn't thought that far when he'd agreed to Helen's demands to avenge her death.

CHAPTER TWENTY-NINE

Carl called the team together.

'Harry, get on to Metropolitan Security and get the details of the bank account they paid Mitchell's salary into. He has to eat, so we might be able to track him through his credit card.'

'Okay, Boss.'

'Do we have a mobile number for him?' said Carl.

'We got one from his cousin,' said Lisa.

'Get it tracked,' said Carl.

'For the time being, Dr Bryant is a patient in her own hospital, thanks to the accident she had on the way to work this morning, and Pauline Francis is safely out of the country for another three weeks. Hopefully, we'll find Mitchell before she gets home.'

'Too bad we couldn't get a more recent photo of him,' said Lisa.

'We will just have to go with the one from Registrations and the one Metropolitan supplied,' said Carl. 'At least they're clear.'

'They both look like mugshots,' said Wayne.

'Do we have any evidence putting this Mitchell at the scene of the crime?' said DCI Rankin, from the back of the room. 'I hope we're not jumping to conclusions based on these people all being named in the case notes of a death at City Hospital in 2010.'

'It's all circumstantial at the moment, Chief,' said Carl, 'but, we have a possible motive. He had the opportunity at Carrick, and his behaviour suggests he doesn't want to be found.'

'What about the rope found in his rubbish?' said Harry.

'Think we're going to have to do better than that,' said DCI Rankin. 'I've got some of that rope in my garden shed at home.'

'We should have Forensics' report from the Cody crime scene later today,' said Carl, 'and, it looks like he spent more time there than at either of the other locations. Hopefully, they'll pick up something we can use to identify him.'

'And, who knows what the post mortem will tell us', said Harry.

'I hope something tells us Mitchell was there,' said DCI Rankin, 'otherwise, finding him will be a waste of time.'

'That was the problem when we had him in after the Viking murder,' said Carl. 'Nothing to connect him to the victim apart from being in the area at the time.'

'Well, we need to pin something on him this time, Inspector, otherwise you'll need to start looking for someone else,' said DCI Rankin.

———

Carl made his way down to the basement morgue for the post mortem examination of Sarah Cody's body.

Emma Worthington was suited up, waiting for him, when he arrived in the morgue where Sarah's body lay stretched out on a stainless steel bench under the glare of the room's bright lights.

Carl watched Emma examine the skin of the body through a magnifying glass.

Emma stopped at the neck and leant in close. She picked up her tweezers and lifted a fibre from the ugly purple wound in Sarah's neck. 'Green rope fibre,' said Emma, as she placed the fibre in an evidence bag.

I'm going to need more than that, thought Carl.

'There's a lot of tiny black fibres on her breasts,' said Emma, 'probably from clothing.' She picked up a damp cotton swab and used it to lift several fibres from the victim's skin. 'Could be from the killer's clothing, seeing she was naked when she was assaulted.'

Matching them with the killer's clothing would be a long shot, thought Carl. It would probably be something made in China and worn by half the population.

Emma moved her attention to the lower abdomen. 'This might be a little more exciting for you, Carl. This one doesn't look like it belongs to her.' She picked up a pubic hair and placed it in an evidence bag. 'Wrong color.'

Then she looked closely at the genital area. 'Either she's been raped or engaged in some pretty rough sex,' said Emma, 'and someone's left enough semen here for me to get you a DNA profile.'

'That's the best news I've had all day,' said Carl.

'Might take a while to get your results,' said Emma. 'They have a bit of a backlog.'

A call from the Commissioner might help, thought Carl.

Carl waited while Emma completed her examination of the body before heading back to his office.

———

When Carl arrived back in his office, there was an email with an attachment from Dean Lang in his inbox.

Carl read the attached report. The crime scene investigators had lifted green nylon rope fibres and several fresh semen stains from the carpet in Sarah Cody's bedroom, and a clear foreign fingerprint from the sliding glass door the killer had forced in the laundry.

Dean had run the fingerprint through their database. It matched one of the prints lifted from the rubbish Mitchell had left behind at Harvey Street.

Carl dialled DCI Rankin's number.

'Chief, Dean's people have lifted a print from the Cody crime scene that matches one of Mitchell's, and we have a semen sample from the victim's body to test.'

'Are we sure it's not the husband's?' said DCI Rankin.

'Dean's taken a swab from the husband,' said Carl. 'You might want to get the Commissioner to lean on them, Chief.'

'I'll suggest it to him when I brief him,' said DCI Rankin. 'I know he's keen for a result.'

After updating DCI Rankin, Carl called the team together in front of the whiteboard.

'We've got a print that puts Mitchell at the Cody crime scene, and he's left more than enough semen behind for Dr Worthington to get a clear DNA profile. All we have to do is find him.'

CHAPTER THIRTY

DC Templar knocked on the door of Carl's office.

'Looks like Mitchell switched his phone off the day he moved out of Harvey Street, Inspector.'

'Keep them on it,' said Carl, 'in case he comes back on line. Any luck with the bank?'

'He pulled five thousand in cash out through their ATM in Portside in the week before he moved, but he hasn't used the account since.'

Carl leant back in his chair. It looked like Mitchell had planned his disappearance almost from the day they'd questioned him about his whereabouts in Carrick on the day of Christine Viking's murder.

'How long do you think five grand will last him?' said Carl.

'That would depend on where he's living,' said Lisa. 'If he's not paying rent, I guess he could survive for a couple of months or more on five thousand dollars.'

'Where can you live and not pay rent?' said Carl.

'On a friend's couch,' said Lisa, 'but he doesn't appear to

have any friends. Maybe he's camping out but that would be rough this time of year.'

'Perhaps he's found a squat,' said Carl. 'He's been driving around the city for fifteen years, so I guess he'd know where to look.' Carl stared out at the city skyline through the window and wondered where he'd go if he was looking for somewhere to hide. 'Get on to Metropolitan and ask them for a copy of the patrol routes he's been servicing. They might give us somewhere to start until someone spots him and calls it in.'

———

As Lisa left his office, Carl turned his attention back to the email he'd received from DI Ryan.

Holden's fingerprints had been found all over the Land Rover Kurt Viking had been killed in. Forensics had determined Viking, Sloane, and Nolan had all been killed with the same pistol. Holden was the main suspect for the murders of Sloane and Viking, while Sloane was being regarded as the possible killer of Nolan. DI Ryan had appealed to the public for help in locating Holden and Viking's missing SUV.

Carl wanted evidence connecting Holden and Viking to the thefts, and he'd tasked Wayne and Nigel with finding it.

Wayne had followed up his suspicion that Joe Cotton had helped Holden steal the BMW from East Park, but Cotton's girlfriend had sworn he'd been in bed with her at the time the BMW had been taken from the driveway in Devine Terrace, East Park.

Carl was almost ready to call it quits for the day when Wayne knocked on his door. 'Got a minute, Inspector?'

Carl waved him into his office. 'What have you got?'

'Tom Cotton,' said Wayne. 'Young Joe's father.'

Carl leant back in his chair and waited.

'He runs a car detailing business,' said Wayne. 'It's called Bayside Clean Cars.'

'Any of our victims use it?' said Carl.

'All of them,' said Wayne. 'They offer a mobile service that comes to you.'

'Any connection to Bayside Auto?' said Carl.

'Funny you should ask, Inspector. Appears Cotton has come a long way since the last time I saw him,' said Wayne. 'He's the owner of three businesses. Not bad going for an ex-con.'

'What's the third one?' said Carl.

'Bayside Used Cars.'

'Is that the place over the road from Bayside Auto?' said Carl.

Wayne nodded. 'It's managed by Tom's brother, Eddie'.

'Find out anything on Viking?'

'Tom Cotton's his father-in-law,' said Wayne, 'and he was living beyond his means from what I can tell. His missus drives a BMW and their home's a mansion in the foothills. Can't see how a guy who was running a three-bay workshop could make that sort of money, especially when it wasn't even his own business.'

'Does his wife work?' said Carl.

Wayne shook his head. 'She's got two little kids. The oldest is only four.'

'You think Tom Cotton's behind this?'

'Too big a coincidence for me, Inspector. Cotton's got form and three sons, and I wouldn't be surprised if they were all in on it.'

'Do you know where the other sons work?'

'One sells used cars with his uncle, and the other one manages the mobile arm of Bayside Clean Cars.'

'We need to break young Cotton's alibi,' said Carl. 'Run a

background check on his girlfriend and see if her story stacks up.'

'I've got Nigel looking into Arthur Transport,' said Wayne. 'Be nice to know who rented that truck Holden took up the river.'

CHAPTER THIRTY-ONE

Shane Lewis made his living dismantling wrecked and stolen cars and selling parts on the used spare parts market. He operated his business from a farm in the Riverland and moved his merchandise around the country inside the trucks Arthur Transport used to carry citrus fruit to markets in each state capital.

The downside of the luxury end of his business, as far as Shane was concerned, was his reliance on a supply of stolen cars from people he didn't control. In recent years, he'd come to rely on Tom Cotton's network and, until Holden had stuffed up, things had run smoothly and profitably. He'd been able to order cars on demand to get the parts his customers wanted, and Tom's people hadn't experienced any problems with the police in the more than five years they'd been working together.

Whenever he'd discovered a weak link in his supply or distribution network, Shane had contracted Jack Sloane to remove that link, and Jack had always delivered until Holden. Despite days of playing scenarios through his mind, Shane still couldn't work out how Holden had got the better of Jack. He had no doubts about how he'd killed Viking. The details were in the paper.

He knew Holden couldn't finger him. What worried him, though, was the people Holden could finger, and some of them could implicate him, and he was relying on those same people to hunt down Holden and eliminate him before the police found him. Despite Tom Cotton's promises, he didn't like their odds. The police had everyone in the state on the lookout for Holden. He'd seen that in the paper as well.

He decided he'd have to put the business into hibernation if they survived. That was the only way to keep the police from finding him. It wasn't like he could sell it, well not the luxury end of it, where the real money was. He might even have to disappear to keep out of prison, if they didn't find Holden first.

Shane stood on the front veranda of the farmhouse and looked across the darkness towards the shearing shed that housed his dismantling business. The shed hadn't been used for shearing sheep since the last drought, when he'd decided to move on from sheep to dismantling upmarket cars, a move that had introduced him to Tom Cotton and transformed his fortunes.

He was about to go inside and call his son when he noticed a small, red light flicker briefly in the window of the shearers' quarters attached to the shed. He stopped and stared at the window. Someone had to be inside the shearers' quarters. He hadn't heard anyone approach. It was a long walk into the homestead from the road if they'd come in on foot. He stepped into the house, picked up his rifle, and crossed the yard to investigate.

When he reached the shearers' quarters, he opened the door and flicked on the light. The place was empty. He shrugged and thought he must have imagined it. He turned off the light and shut the door. As he stepped into the darkness, a hand grabbed him from behind. He felt something hard press into the side of his head.

'Drop it, Lewis! Or I'll blow your stupid head off!'

Shane rested his rifle up against the side of the building.

'Inside!'

Shane felt himself being pushed through the door into the shearer's quarters. He stumbled and fell onto the floor. The light came on. He looked up. Ian Holden stood over him holding a pistol in his hand.

'I can cut you a good deal,' said Shane.

Ian stepped closer and pointed the pistol at Shane's head.

'Say hello to Jack, arsehole!'

CHAPTER THIRTY-TWO

Trent looked at the two small squares of paper on the floor amid the dust covered, shattered fragments of Helen's coffee cup. He knew what he had to do.

He reached out and picked up the square he felt drawn to and opened it: Rita Bryant.

Trent closed his eyes. He could picture her, all prim and proper in a white coat with a stethoscope dangling from her neck. She'd been pretty the last time he'd seen her, the day she'd signed Helen's death certificate and done her professional best to console him.

He spent several moments imagining what she'd look like without her clothes and then rebuked himself, when he felt his erection pushing against his jeans. He didn't want Helen thinking that was his objective. He'd promised her it wouldn't happen again.

He picked up his laptop and walked down to the coffee shop, where he could charge its battery and use their free wi-fi while he had a coffee and a lemon tart.

Dr Rita Bryant was easy to find on LinkedIn. He read her

profile. She was working at University Hospital. He couldn't locate a profile for her on Facebook and she wasn't listed in the White Pages. Trent sipped his coffee. He wasn't in a hurry and, besides, it was much warmer in the coffee shop than in his unheated squat. He nibbled on the lemon tart. It reminded him of all the times Helen had bought him one after they'd been on a ride.

'Are you okay, sir?' said the girl cleaning the table beside him.

Trent looked up. 'Sorry?'

'Are you alright? You look upset,' said the girl.

Trent smiled. 'Just thinking about someone I haven't seen for a while.'

The girl smiled and went back to her table cleaning. Trent watched her out of the corner of his eye and tried his best to ignore the voice inside his head telling him she was cute.

Trent closed his laptop. He decided he'd have to use the same method he'd used to find Sarah Cody. He would stake out the car park at University Hospital and then follow her home from work. It would be easy after that, just like it had been with the others.

He slipped the last piece of the tart into his mouth and made his way outside onto the footpath. He was about to head home when a police car turned into the street and parked opposite the coffee shop.

As the two officers walked across the street to the coffee shop, Trent turned and made his way along the footpath in the direction opposite to his intended path. He knew he had time to take the long way home, and no-one was waiting there for him to arrive at some pre-agreed time.

When he turned the corner at the end of the street, he laughed to himself, knowing the police had looked right at him and not seen him.

The one thing that Trent thought made watching nurses easy was the set pattern of their shift changes. The nurses changed shifts at eight in the morning, four in the afternoon, and at midnight. He only had to spend around three hours each day watching them.

It had only taken him three days to locate Sarah Cody, so Trent was optimistic about finding Dr Bryant. When he hadn't spotted her after a week of standing around in the cold watching the entrance to the hospital during the daily shift changes, he wondered if she was on leave or if Helen was still punishing him for what he'd done with Sarah Cody.

He spent his nights asking Helen for her forgiveness, dreaming of Sarah Cody, and thinking he was going mad, but he persisted.

On the Monday morning of his third week of surveillance, Trent spotted Dr Bryant arriving for the start of the morning shift as a passenger in a blue BMW driven by a man. He'd expected her to drive herself and assumed the man driving the car had to be her husband. When Dr Bryant left the hospital that afternoon, shortly after four, Trent followed the taxi she caught to a house in East Park and wrote down the address.

He returned to the street in East Park at seven the next morning and parked his van three houses down from Dr Bryant's driveway and waited. At seven thirty, a blue BMW driven by a man pulled out of the driveway and slowly made its way along the street. As it went past his position, Trent saw Dr Bryant sitting in the passenger seat talking on her mobile phone.

He waited until nine o'clock. When the blue BMW had not returned, he drove his van down the street and parked it around the corner at the first intersection he came to, and then walked back to Dr Bryant's house. He walked up the driveway and rang the front doorbell. There was no response. He went around the back through the side gate. There was no dog in the backyard.

He read the sticker on the back window that told him the house was protected by a security system and smiled, assuming, like Sarah Cody, she'd turn off the alarm when she was home, even if she was home alone.

Trent looked at his watch and decided he'd wait until she was on the midnight to morning shift, when she'd be sleeping during the day and her husband and her neighbours would be at work. He felt a rush of arousal as he envisaged extracting a Sarah Cody moment from Dr Bryant before paying her for her part in allowing Helen to die.

Feeling guilty, he dismissed the thought before it could develop into a full-blown sexual fantasy and distract him from his mission. He checked the yard for hiding places, then made his way around to the front of the house, and walked along the footpath to where he'd left his van.

CHAPTER THIRTY-THREE

DC Paterson had been a detective for more than thirty years. People had lied to him, confessed to him, and tried their best to confuse him. He knew Rosie Munro wasn't telling him the truth about the night her boyfriend had helped Ian Holden steal a BMW from East Park. All he had to do was get her to admit it.

He'd done his research. He'd asked a couple of her girl-friends what they'd been up to that night, and they'd told him about a night spent with Rosie at the Merlin, and how they'd been asked to leave at three in the morning because Rosie had started a fight. He'd checked their story with the security guards at the Merlin and obtained a copy of the CCTV recording of the girls' eviction.

'I don't believe your story, Rosie,' said DC Paterson. 'I don't think you spent the night of Tuesday the thirteenth of June with Joe Cotton at all.'

'You can believe whatever you want,' said Rosie, 'but that's where I was.'

DC Paterson turned to DC Beard. 'Bring up the recording

from the Merlin.' He turned back to Rosie. 'I'm giving you one last chance to correct your story, Rosie. If you don't tell me the truth, I'm going to take you back to the station and charge you as an accessory to the theft of a motor vehicle.'

Rosie crossed her arms across her breasts and stared at him.

'Show her the video.'

DC Beard held his iPad where Rosie could see it and pressed play.

'This video was recorded by the Merlin nightclub at five minutes past three on the morning of Wednesday, the fourteenth of June,' said DC Paterson. 'Bring back any memories?'

He smiled as he watched the color drain from Rosie's face. 'Unless you have an identical twin sister, Rosie, I'd like you to explain how you could have been in bed with Joe Cotton at two am that same morning.'

DC Paterson waited.

Rosie Munro sat in silence. Her eyes darted from one policeman to the other, and then to the door open behind them.

'Don't even think about it,' said DC Paterson. 'Joe asked you to lie for him, didn't he?'

Rosie nodded. 'What will happen to me? Will I go to jail?'

'You'll be charged with providing a false alibi,' said DC Paterson. 'My best guess is you'll get off with a good behaviour bond, provided you haven't stolen any cars.'

'Honest to God, I've never stolen a thing in my life,' said Rosie.

DC Paterson wished he had a dollar for every time someone had spun him that line.

'What do you know about Joe?' said DC Paterson.

'He's going to beat the living shit out of me when he finds out,' said Rosie.

'Then he's not worth protecting,' said DC Paterson. 'What do you know about him?'

'I didn't know he stole cars,' said Rosie. 'He told me he was a mechanic. He works for his old man.'

'How long have you known him?' said DC Paterson.

Rosie counted on her fingers. 'Six months. I met him at the Merlin.'

'Okay, let's get a statement from you about Joe asking you to lie for him and then you'd better call a lawyer.'

———

Carl's mobile phone rang as he walked across the lobby of Police Headquarters towards the coffee shop next door.

'How did it go, Wayne?'

'She's given us a statement confessing Joe asked her to lie for him,' said DC Paterson.

'Bring her in and charge her,' said Carl, 'then go and pick up Cotton.'

Carl slipped the phone back into his pocket and walked into the coffee shop. DCI Rankin was already seated at the table near the window that looked out onto the plaza in front of the building. Carl ordered a latte and joined the chief inspector.

'Cotton's girlfriend has confessed to lying for him,' said Carl.

'Bit hard for her to do otherwise with that recording from the Merlin,' said DCI Rankin.

The waiter delivered Carl's latte to the table.

'Hopefully young Cotton will roll over,' said Carl.

'I wouldn't count on it,' said DCI Rankin. 'Any luck with the banking records?'

'Nothing out of the ordinary,' said Carl. 'If Viking was getting anything from the sale of the cars it must have been in cash.'

'If Viking wasn't involved, why did Holden kill him?' said DCI Rankin. 'There has to be a connection, Carl. Keep looking.' The chief inspector drained his cup. 'What about Mitchell? Any news?'

'Nothing,' said Carl. 'It's almost a month since his last attack and there's been no sign of him.'

'I'm going to have to scale back on the protection for the others,' said DCI Rankin. 'I don't have the money to keep up that level of surveillance.'

Carl nodded. He'd been expecting the chief inspector's decision. 'We've schooled them up on not travelling alone and upgrading their household security.' Carl sipped his latte. 'They're aware of being potential targets, so it should be harder for him to surprise them, and they've got Operations' number in their phones.'

'You'd think he would have acted by now if he was going to,' said DCI Rankin. 'It's not as though these people are hard to find, and he didn't waste any time taking out the first three.'

'Perhaps he thinks they're no longer around, seeing they were out of circulation in the weeks following his last attack,' said Carl.

'We need to find him, Carl. No-one likes the idea of a serial killer being loose in the city, especially upstairs.' The chief inspector raised his eyebrows.

'I can't understand why nobody's seen him, given the media coverage he's had,' said Carl.

'Either he knows how to keep a low profile or he's left town.' DCI Rankin looked at his watch. 'I gotta run. Keep me posted on Mitchell.'

Carl watched the chief inspector make his way out of the coffee shop and wondered where Mitchell was hiding. They'd searched all the likely places along the routes Mitchell had patrolled when he was with Metropolitan Security without sighting him or his van. Carl doubted he'd left town because Mitchell had recently withdrawn a thousand dollars from his account through an ATM in Morton Sands, only a couple of blocks from where Carl lived.

Carl finished his coffee and headed back to his office on the third floor. As he waited for the elevator in the lobby, he thought Mitchell must have a knack for hiding in plain sight and wondered if they'd ever see through his disguise.

———

Carl looked through the two-way mirror into the interview room where Joe Cotton sat with his lawyer, William Maynard.

'What did he say when you picked him up?' said Carl.

'Very little,' said DC Paterson, 'but he didn't appear all that surprised.'

'Maybe he'd heard about us arresting his girlfriend,' said DC Beard.

'You watch from here, Nigel. Come on, Wayne, time to get this show on the road.'

Joe Cotton sat upright when they entered the interview room and glared at DC Paterson.

'Mr Maynard,' said Carl. 'We meet again.'

'Inspector,' said William Maynard, crossing his arms and leaning back in his chair.

DC Paterson switched on the video recorder and stepped them through the opening interview protocol.

'Mr Cotton, where were you in the early hours of the morning of Wednesday, the fourteenth of June?' said Carl.

'Like I told your mate,' said Joe, looking across the table at DC Paterson, 'in bed with my girlfriend.'

'That would be with Rosie Munro?' said Carl.

'Yeah,' said Joe, 'with Rosie. Didn't she already tell you?'

'Oh, she told us alright,' said Carl, 'it's just that I don't think she told us the truth.'

'My client has an alibi backed by a statutory declaration,' said William Maynard, 'so, why are we going through this charade?'

'Your client should have asked his girlfriend a few questions before getting her to lie for him,' said Carl.

'She's not lying,' said Joe. 'I spent the night at her place.'

'Not according to Ms Munro,' said Carl, taking a copy of Rosie Munro's statement from his folder and passing it across the table to William Maynard. 'Unfortunately for your client, Ms Munro was not at home between midnight and three-o-five on the morning of Wednesday, the fourteenth of June, Mr Maynard. She was out with her girlfriends at the Merlin night-club,' said Carl.

'Bullshit!' said Joe.

'We have a recording of them being evicted at three-o-five that morning, Mr Cotton. Would you like to see it?'

Joe Cotton sat and glared at his lawyer. 'They're making this stuff up!'

'Can we see the recording?' said William Maynard.

'Show them,' said Carl.

DC Paterson opened his iPad, placed it on the table in front of Joe and his lawyer, and pressed play. They sat and watched the recording of Rosie Munro being evicted.

'Note the time stamp,' said Carl, pointing to the figures in the lower right-hand corner of the image.

'Stupid bitch!' said Joe.

Think you might be the stupid one, thought Carl. 'So, where were you if you weren't with Rosie?'

Joe glared at Carl.

'Perhaps I can help you remember,' said Carl. 'I have another recording taken that morning in the driveway of 11

Devine Terrace, East Park. It shows two men stealing a BMW, and one of them looks a lot like you, Mr Cotton.'

'Wasn't me,' said Joe. 'I don't steal cars.'

'Can we see the recording?' said William Maynard.

At least his lawyer knows I'm not bluffing, thought Carl. 'Show them the recording.'

DC Paterson opened the file on his iPad and pressed play.

'That could be anybody,' said William Maynard.

'It's not me,' said Joe.

'Show them the enhanced image of the face of the driver,' said Carl.

DC Paterson opened the image file and turned the iPad back so they could see it. Joe Cotton took one look and slumped back in his chair.

'I'm sure if we used face recognition software to compare that with a photograph of your client, Mr Maynard, we'd get a match,' said Carl.

'That may not stand up in court,' said William Maynard.

'I think it will,' said Carl, 'the courts are considering a lot more electronic evidence these days, Mr Maynard.'

'Still think you're pushing the envelope, Inspector.'

'You need to bring yourself up to speed on what we can do with technology, Mr Maynard. Using facial recognition, for example, we've identified the other person as Ian Holden.' Carl turned to Joe Cotton. 'You and Holden both worked for Kurt Viking. Was he involved?'

'That's two questions,' said William Maynard, 'and you're asking my client to incriminate himself.'

'I'm asking him to tell me the truth,' said Carl. 'He's already incriminated himself by asking his girlfriend to lie for him.'

'I've got nothing more to say,' said Joe.

'Any idea where Ian Holden might be?' said Carl.

Joe remained silent.

'Any idea why he killed Kurt?' said Carl.

'What makes you think Ian killed Kurt?' said Joe.

'Let's say he left enough evidence behind for us to work it out,' said Carl, 'and, if he killed Kurt, I guess you could be next.'

'Yeah, right,' said Joe. 'Why would he want to kill me? I don't know what he's been up to.'

'You might be safer with us, Mr Cotton, if Ian's out there eliminating the people he worked with.'

'I never worked with him,' said Joe. 'You're just trying to scare me.'

'I could be saving your life,' said Carl.

'Anything else?' said William Maynard.

'Things could go a little easier for you if you tell us who else is involved,' said Carl.

Joe crossed his arms on his chest and glared at Carl.

'Joesph Cotton, I'm charging you with the theft of a motor vehicle and attempting to pervert the course of justice,' said Carl.

———

Carl's mobile phone rang as he was processing the paperwork associated with Joe Cotton's arrest.

'DI West.'

'Bill Norris, Carl. Got some news for you.'

'I'm listening, Bill.'

'There was a fire at the Lewis place, last night. It's a farm about an hour north of here. Been in the same family for the last hundred years or so. Anyway, the shearing shed burnt down last night. Pretty sure it was arson.'

'What makes you think that?'

'We found a body in what had been the shearers' quarters,' said Bill.

'Any idea who it is?' said Carl.

'The body's pretty badly burnt but it could be the owner, Shane Lewis. There's no sign of him at the property.'

'Name doesn't ring a bell, Bill. What makes you think I'd want to know?'

'Remember that truck Holden drove up here?'

'The one with the BMW on the back?'

'We found what's left of that truck and a BMW in the ashes of the shearing shed, along with a pile of car parts,' said Bill. 'I think we know where your stolen cars were going.'

Something big has obviously gone wrong within the group stealing the cars, thought Carl.

'Any buildings survive the fire?' said Carl.

'The homestead,' said Bill, 'and a few other sheds.'

'Think you should search them, Bill?' said Carl.

'I've got a CSI team coming up from the city.'

'Keep me in the loop,' said Carl. 'I wonder if Holden's taking out the principal players.'

'Playing a mean game if he is,' said Bill. 'His tally is up there with your serial killer, if he's behind this.'

Carl put his phone back into his pocket and walked out to the squad room.

'Wayne, see what you can find out about someone by the name of Shane Lewis.'

'Where does he live?' said DC Paterson.

'In the Riverland,' said Carl. 'Someone burnt down his shearing shed last night, and Inspector Norris' people have found the burnout remains of the truck Holden used to transport the BMW from East Park to the Riverland in what's left of the shed. Seems that's where our cars were going.'

'Do you want me to find this Shane Lewis?' said DC Paterson.

Carl shook his head. 'They found a badly burnt body in the

ashes. Inspector Norris thinks it's Lewis. See if we can link him to anyone we know.'

'Sounds like a serious fallout between thieves,' said DC Paterson.

'I wonder if Holden's planning to wipe out their entire operation,' said Carl.

'Could be his body,' said Wayne, 'if this Lewis was expecting him after what happened to Viking.'

'I guess so,' said Carl, 'but we'll have to wait for Forensics and whatever they uncover from the scene. Hopefully, they'll find something in the homestead that will help us work out who else is involved, if Lewis was the mastermind.'

'I've still got my money on Tom Cotton,' said Wayne.

CHAPTER THIRTY-FOUR

Carl sat on the edge of DC Paterson's desk. 'Dr Jonas has identified the body from Lewis' dental records,' said Carl.

'I guess that confirms he was receiving the vehicles from
Holden and his mates,' said DC Paterson.

'Be nice to know who Lewis was selling the parts to,' said
Carl. 'Are you having any luck with the hard drive Dean
bought back from the Lewis' place?'

'Nigel's playing with it,' said DC Paterson. 'He thinks
Lewis must have stored his inventory records in the cloud.
There's nothing on his hard drive that looks like an inventory
database or list of customers, but he appears to have several
cloud accounts, which we can't get into.'

'I guess his business records could have been stored in the
shed that went up in flames,' said Carl.

'I suppose,' said DC Paterson, 'but he was a little careless
with his bank account login details. They're all here in his pass-
word manager.'

'Find anything interesting?'

'Well, for a farmer with no sheep, he has a lot of transactions on his wool account, and it appears he's paid a small fortune to Arthur Transport,' said DC Paterson, 'and what's interesting about that, Inspector, is Arthur Transport paid the rental on the Mack truck Jim Nolan used.'

'How do you know that?' said Carl.

'I followed up the invoice City Truck Rentals sent us for the truck Holden used. They told me that lease wasn't the only one Arthur Transport had paid for.' Wayne searched through the pile of papers on his desk. 'Here you go. This is a copy of the lease for the Mack made out to Nolan Transport, and this is a copy of the rental company's bank statement showing the payments linked to the invoices they gave to Nolan.' Wayne looked up. 'The bank's confirmed the payments came from an account controlled by Arthur Transport.'

'Any idea who owns Arthur Transport?' said Carl.

DC Paterson smiled. 'Edward Anthony and Margaret Lynette Cotton.'

'Eddie Cotton?' said Carl. 'That's interesting.'

DC Paterson nodded. 'If Eddie's involved, Inspector, I'd say Tom's in on it, too.'

Carl thought Wayne was probably right. 'Who runs the business day to day?'

'Brad Arthur, according to their website,' said DC Paterson. 'They're based in the Riverland.'

That would be convenient for someone like Lewis who wanted to move stolen car parts out of the Riverland, thought Carl. 'We'd better find out who he is. I'll give Inspector Norris a call and see what I can find out.'

'Okay,' said DC Paterson. 'Perhaps we should find out where his trucks go. That might help us locate Lewis' customers.'

'See if you can find any money coming into Lewis' accounts, that might be easier to trace,' said Carl.

'I'll let you know,' said DC Paterson. 'He's got seven different accounts that I know of.'

Carl stood up. 'If they own a trucking company, why on earth did they drag Nolan into it?'

'I guess they needed someone with a heavy vehicle licence when they wanted to shift several cars at once,' said DC Paterson. 'From what I can tell from their website, Arthur Transport only operates light trucks.'

'That decision looks like it might be their undoing,' said Carl, 'provided we can get some firm evidence to back us up.'

'Still think Holden killed Lewis, Inspector?' said DC Paterson.

'If it wasn't Holden, the answer's going to be somewhere in those accounts.'

———

Carl glanced at the trucks parked in the yard as DC Paterson parked their car outside Arthur Transport, and noted they were all small trucks with an enclosed back.

They entered the office, where a middle-aged man sat behind a desk reading the morning paper.

'Brad Arthur?' said Carl.

'Who wants to know?'

'Inspector West, City Police,' said Carl, showing him his ID.

'You're a long way from home, Inspector.' The man put down his paper, stood, and offered his hand to Carl across his desk. 'I'm Brad. What can I do for you?'

'I'd like to know what you were transporting for Shane Lewis,' said Carl.

'Used car parts,' said Brad. 'He was running a wrecking

business to keep his farm afloat. Guess you know his place was torched last week.'

'Yes,' said Carl, 'but I'm not investigating that. Did you ever see any of the cars he was wrecking to get those parts?'

Brad shook his head. 'He brought his stuff into the depot. We didn't go out to his place to collect. We charge extra for that, and he wasn't prepared to pay.'

'Where did he send his used parts?' said Carl.

'All over,' said Bart.

'Can you be a little more specific?' said Carl.

'I'll have to look that up,' said Brad. He sat down and moved the mouse on his desk to wake his computer. 'Might take me a while.'

'We'll wait,' said Carl.

Ten minutes later, Brad handed Carl a printed list of addresses. 'As I said, all over.'

Carl read through the list. There was an address in every state capital except for City.

'Tell me, Mr Arthur, why did you pay the rental on a Mack prime mover from City Truck Rentals in May?' said Carl.

'What?' said Brad.

'Show him the invoice,' said Carl.

DC Paterson handed a copy of the invoice he'd obtained from City Truck Rentals to Brad, who read the invoice and then looked up at Carl.

'This is made out to Nolan Transport, Inspector? What's it got to do with me? And, besides, what would I want with a Mack prime mover?'

Carl thought Brad was either a good actor or totally confused by the invoice.

'Who pays your accounts?' said Carl.

'The owner,' said Brad. 'I send him the invoices we have to

pay and our customers pay us electronically. We don't do anything for cash these days.'

'How do you get paid?' said Carl.

'My salary goes into my account, same as the drivers,' said Brad.

'Who's the owner of the business?' said Carl.

'Eddie Cotton. He's married to my sister.'

'Can you give me his contact details?' said Carl.

'Sure.'

While they walked out to the car after leaving Brad Arthur, Carl took out his mobile phone and called Harry.

'Where are you, Harry?'

'Where you asked me to be, Boss.'

'Is Eddie at work today?'

'I can see him,' said Harry. 'He's on the phone.'

Carl smiled. He had a good idea who Eddie was listening to. 'Take him into custody and hold him until I get there.'

———

'Mr Cotton, I understand you own a trucking business in the Riverland. Is that correct?'

Eddie Cotton looked at William Maynard, who nodded.

'Yes. I own Arthur Transport with my wife. It was her father's business.'

'And your brother-in-law, Brad Arthur, is the Operations Manager?'

'Yes. That's right,' said Eddie.

'Do you know someone called Shane Lewis?' said Carl.

Eddie scratched his head. 'He's one of our customers, I think.'

'Do you know him or have you just seen his name on an invoice?' said Carl.

'I've never met him,' said Eddie. 'Brad handles the customers.'

'What is the point of this?' said William Maynard. 'It's not a crime to own a trucking business.'

Carl held up his hand in front of him. 'And, do you pay the accounts, Mr Cotton?'

'Yes,' said Eddie. 'I'm sure Brad explained all that to you.'

'What's that got to do with anything?' said William Maynard. 'Your sergeant, here, told me my client was being charged with dealing in stolen cars.'

'We're getting there, Mr Maynard,' said Carl, taking a piece of paper out of the folder on the table in front of him. 'Did you pay this invoice, Mr Cotton?' He handed Eddie a copy of the invoice made out to Nolan Transport that DC Paterson had obtained from City Truck Rentals.

'Why would I pay that? It's made out to some other company.' Eddie handed the invoice to his lawyer.

Before William Maynard could protest, Carl slipped a second piece of paper out of his folder. 'This is a copy of a transaction on City Truck Rentals' bank account, Mr Cotton. The number I have highlighted in yellow is the account the payment came from. I've had it traced.' Carl looked up from the paper at Eddie. 'It belongs to Arthur Transport, and City Truck Rentals have confirmed that's the rental payment for one of their Mack prime movers, the one described in that invoice, Mr Cotton, the one Jim Nolan used to transport stolen cars up to Shane Lewis before he was killed.'

Eddie Cotton shook his head slowly from side to side.

'How do you explain that?' said Carl.

Eddie shrugged. 'Obviously a mistake by the bank, Inspector. They make them all the time.'

'That's a fairly large payment for you not to have reported it to your bank, Mr Cotton,' said Carl, 'and your bank has confirmed the transaction was authorized by someone using your internet banking login.'

Eddie looked at his lawyer.

'My client will not be answering any more of your questions, Inspector,' said William Maynard.

'That's his prerogative, Mr Maynard, but anything he does say that assists us with our investigation could help him later.'

'I have nothing more to say,' said Eddie.

'Read him his rights, Sergeant, and then charge him with dealing in stolen cars and for being an accessory to murder,' said Carl.

'Murder?' said Eddie. 'I haven't killed anyone.'

'Someone killed Jim Nolan, Mr Cotton, and you helped set him up. That makes you an accessory.'

'I had nothing to do with it,' said Eddie.

'So why did you pay Nolan's invoice?' said Carl.

Eddie crossed his arms on his chest.

'Who do you take your orders from Eddie? I don't think you have the brains to run an operation this size,' said Carl.

'What the fuck would you know about running a business?' said Eddie.

'Your brother seems to know a lot more about running a business than you do, Eddie. After all, you work for him, don't you?' said Carl.

'So, what?' said Eddie.

'Perhaps I should drag your wife in and charge her instead of you,' said Carl, 'seeing Arthur Transport really belongs to her. What do you think?'

'You leave my wife out of this,' said Eddie. 'She has nothing to do with any of this.'

'I only have your word for that, Eddie. For all I know, your wife could have authorized the payment for the Mack,' said Carl. 'Maybe she's the one running the car stealing business with your brother, and they're letting you manage the used car business to keep you out of trouble.'

'You're full of shit,' said Eddie.

'All you have on my client, Inspector, is payment for a truck rental,' said William Maynard, 'and paying someone else's invoice is not a crime, as far as I know.'

'You really need to pay more attention, Mr Maynard. There is more to this story than that payment.' Carl looked from William Maynard to Eddie Cotton. 'Anything more you'd like to tell me, Eddie?'

'No,' said Eddie.

'Sure you don't want to tell us why you paid this invoice?' said Carl, taking another paper out of his folder. 'It's for the truck Ian Holden used to take the BMW your nephew helped him steal up to Shane Lewis.'

Eddie looked at his lawyer and rolled his eyes.

'Charge him, Sergeant.'

CHAPTER THIRTY-FIVE

Trent fingered the rope in his coat pocket for the umpteenth time. He'd been standing behind the shed in Dr Bryant's back-yard for nearly an hour, waiting for her to arrive home from work.

After observing Dr Bryant's movements for three weeks, he'd realized she was working a regular eight to four shift, Monday to Friday, with weekends off.

He'd watched her house. Most days she was alone in the house between four thirty, when a taxi dropped her off, and six, when the man she lived with arrived home from work, except for the days when a teenage schoolgirl let herself into the house at four in the afternoon.

Although he'd struggled with lustful thoughts about what he'd like to do to the schoolgirl, Helen had reminded him she wasn't on the list, and he'd resolved to complete his mission for her without letting his sexual desires get the better of him.

Today was the Monday of a week when the schoolgirl was not due to be letting herself in at four. Trent had arrived at three forty-five just to make certain the girl hadn't changed her routine. She hadn't. He checked his watch: four twenty-five. He heard the dull thud of a car door closing. Dr Bryant had arrived home.

He waited for her to settle into the house. He didn't want to make his move until she had deactivated the security alarm. He wrapped his scarf around his face, pulled his woollen hat down over his ears, stuffed his hands back into the pockets of his coat, and waited.

He looked at his watch again: four forty-two. He poked his head around the back of the shed. There was a light on in what he knew was the kitchen but he couldn't see the doctor through the window. He made his way around the shed to the back door and raised his right foot. He kicked the door with force. The impact of his boot landing next to the handle splintered the doorframe. He pushed the door open with his hand.

Whoop! Whoop! Whoop!

Trent turned and ran down the side of the house onto the driveway and then into the street. He sprinted along the footpath and rounded the corner into Sixth Street, where he'd left his bicycle leaning on a fence. It was gone. He kept running until he reached the end of the street. There, he slowed to a walk, took off his coat and scarf, and caught his breath before turning into Lime Avenue.

He strolled along Lime Avenue as if he didn't have a care in the world, until he reached the bus stop. He stood at the stop with his coat and scarf folded over his arm, and waited for a bus to arrive.

After what seemed like an eternity to Trent, the 284 bus heading towards the city came along Lime Avenue and stopped.

As he climbed into the bus, a police car with flashing blue lights sped past, going in the direction from which he'd come.

Shit, that was close, thought Trent, as he took a seat on the bus.

CHAPTER THIRTY-SIX

Carl's phone rang.

'DI West.'

'Operations, Inspector. There's been an attempted break in at Dr Bryant's house.'

God, thought Carl, Mitchell's found her.

'Is she okay?' said Carl.

'He ran when her alarm went off. We've got patrols searching the area and there's someone with the doctor.'

'I'm on my way,' said Carl.

Carl slipped his phone into his pocket and picked up his coat. 'Harry!'

'What's up, Boss?'

'Get your coat. Someone's set off the alarm at Dr Bryant's. Probably Mitchell.'

'Is she safe?' said Harry.

'Yes,' said Carl. 'Uniform are searching the area.'

'Let's hope they find him.'

'Come on, let's have a word with her and see what happened.'

Thirty minutes later, Harry parked their silver Ford behind the patrol car in front of Dr Bryant's house. They made their way past the Forensics' van in the driveway to the front door. Carl rang the doorbell. The door was opened by PC Chan.

'Hello, Lily,' said Carl. 'How is she?'

'A bit shaken but otherwise okay, Inspector,' said PC Chan.

'Did she see him?' said Carl.

'A tall guy dressed in black wearing a scarf. She only saw the back of him as he ran down the driveway, I'm afraid,' said PC Chan.

'Response time?' said Carl.

'First patrol, seven minutes,' said PC Chan. 'That was us. Backup within fifteen.'

That was quick, thought Carl, but not quick enough to stop him, especially if he had wheels.

'What's the chatter?'

'He was seen running down the street by the lady opposite. Turned into Sixth Street. We're still door knocking in Sixth, Inspector.'

'Any sign of a white Ford Transit van?' said Carl.

'Not that I know of,' said PC Chan.

'Thanks, Lily. Where is the doctor?' said Carl.

'In the kitchen,' said PC Chan. 'It's at the back of the house. Adam's with her.' PC Chan smiled. 'Small world, Inspector. The doctor knows Adam's mother.'

———

Carl and Harry made their way to the back of the house where a CSI officer was inspecting the damaged door in the laundry.

'Anything useful?' said Carl.

'A few finger prints, Inspector' said the officer, 'and a muddy footprint. Looks like he'd been waiting for her behind that shed.' He pointed to the garden shed in the backyard. 'A few footprints up there but nothing else I'm afraid.'

'See what you can do with the fingerprints,' said Carl, hoping Mitchell hadn't changed his habits since he'd broken into Sarah Cody's and left his prints on the door he'd forced.

They walked into the kitchen where Dr Bryant was chatting with PC Monks.

'Dr Bryant,' said Carl.

'We meet again, Inspector,' said Dr Bryant.

'This is Detective Sergeant Fuller, my right-hand man,' said Carl.

Dr Bryant smiled at Harry and turned back to Adam Monks. 'Make sure you say hello to your mother for me, Adam.'

'I will,' said PC Monks.

'Can I get you gentlemen something to drink? A coffee, perhaps?' said Dr Bryant.

'No need to go to any trouble, Doctor,' said Carl. 'We won't be staying. I just wanted to make sure you were okay.'

'I think I'll survive, Inspector.' She smiled. 'I guess he didn't count on us having that perimeter alarm you suggested.'

'Did you see him at all?' said Carl.

'I tried to take a photo of him as he was running down the driveway, but he was too quick. Probably wouldn't have been much use anyway. I only saw the back of him.'

'Hopefully someone in Sixth Street saw him,' said Carl.

'There's a bus stop just around from where Sixth Street meets Lime Avenue, you know. That's where Robert's daughter catches the bus to school when she stays with us. I wonder if that's where he was going.'

'We'll check, but if it's Mitchell, we know he drives a van and rides a bike, which he could have parked around the corner in Sixth or Lime.'

'I'm sure you know what to do, Inspector,' said Dr Bryant. 'Do you think he'll be back?'

'Hard to say,' said Carl, 'but I'd stay alert. There's no way of knowing how determined he is.'

'What about the back door?' said Dr Bryant. 'I don't feel safe without being able to lock it.'

'Forensics will secure the door and turn your alarm back on once they've finished,' said Carl. 'PC Monk and his partner will stay with you until that's done.'

'And Robert will be here soon,' said Dr Bryant. 'I always feel much safer when he's around.'

———

After leaving Dr Bryant, Carl and Harry met with the sergeant coordinating the search for the man who'd fled from her house.

'Anything?' said Carl.

'We've got three sightings of him running along Sixth towards Lime, Inspector, and one of him catching the 284 into town from the stop on Lime just before five.'

'Anyone chasing up the bus?'

'I've got someone interviewing the driver and getting a copy of the recording from the onboard camera,' said the sergeant. 'Oh, and I've got a bicycle a kid found in Sixth Street.' The sergeant smiled. 'I think you'll like this, Inspector. It's an,' he peered at his notebook, 'Allez Sprint DSW. Isn't that the sort of bike you're looking for in relation to the murder of that nurse near City Hospital?'

Be great if he could link Mitchell to Kelly Palmer through the bike, thought Carl.

'Get it to Forensics,' said Carl, 'and get the kids prints.'

Carl allowed himself a moment of satisfaction.

'That would link Mitchell to the murder of Kelly Palmer, if it's his bike,' said Harry.

'Let's hope he's left some prints on it,' said Carl, 'otherwise it'll be nothing but coincidental in the mouth of a lawyer.'

———

Carl read the report from the officers who had tracked down the driver of the 284 bus.

The driver remembered a bearded man in black clothing getting onto the bus in Lime Avenue, not only because of his dishevelled appearance, but his obnoxious body odour. But, he hadn't noticed when or where he'd left the bus.

The officers had reviewed the recording from the bus' security camera and discovered that the man in black identified by the driver had alighted in the city centre at five thirty-five, around the time Carl had arrived at Dr Bryant's.

Carl wondered if they'd be able to track him using the footage from the CCTV cameras covering the city centre. He called the Camera Control Centre and requested access to their footage.

Then, he clicked on the link to the video file and watched the grainy recording of the passengers getting on and off the 284 bus. He watched a man dressed in black, with a black coat and scarf over his arm, get onto the bus and swipe his card on the ticket validator. When the man sat down and faced the camera, Carl froze the image. He pulled up the image of Trent Mitchell from Registrations.

The man on the bus had a beard but his eyes matched those staring at Carl from the photograph of Trent Mitchell supplied by Registrations.

Carl walked to the door of his office. 'Harry. Got a minute?'

'What have you got, Boss?'

Carl showed him the two images.

'Both look like Mitchell to me,' said Harry. 'I bet we'd get a match if we ran facial recognition on them.'

'Do that,' said Carl, 'and then get over to the Camera Control Centre. See if you can track him through the city. If he catches another bus, that should help us narrow the search. Take Lisa with you.'

'Do we know where he got off?'

'The location is in this report. I'll send it to you,' said Carl. 'I'll be releasing this to the media.' Carl pointed to the image from the bus video. 'Someone must have seen him.'

'Better release that image to Operations as well, Boss. Should make it easier for Uniform to spot him.'

CHAPTER THIRTY-SEVEN

DC Paterson worked his way through the transactions in the bank account Lewis had designated as his wool account. It was tedious work, but one of Wayne's favourite stories was how the FBI had used accounting records to bust Al Capone for tax evasion, and he wanted to bust Tom Cotton.

Wayne knew it would take forever to trace the payments into the account. They were all cash deposits which had been made at different branches of the bank across the country. Just thinking about the logistics of organizing the security camera recordings and trying to identify the people involved gave him a headache.

But, analysing the outgoing payments was different. There was a clear trail for him to follow as, apart from the transfers into what Lewis had described as his operating account, all of the outgoing transactions went to Arthur Transport.

It puzzled Wayne that the payments Lewis had made for transporting his merchandise to market had come out of his wool account, even though he knew Lewis hadn't been operating a wool business for years. He thought they should have come from his operating account, which made more sense to him from an accounting perspective.

He traced all the transfers into Lewis' operating account and identified the outgoings as payments of the farm's running expenses, including Lewis' supermarket purchases.

There had to be a reason why Lewis had used the account that way, thought Wayne. It looked like he had purposely kept the transport expenses separate from what he had recorded as expenses in the operating account.

In the end, Wayne asked Brad Arthur for a list of the invoices he'd issued to Lewis over the last twelve months, and that's when he realized there were more payments to Arthur Transport than there were invoices.

'We need to get hold of the accounts for Arthur Transport, Inspector.'

'Why's that, Wayne?'

'To follow the money trail. Lewis was sending money to Eddie in addition to paying for using his trucks,' said Wayne. 'Look at this.' He handed DI West a copy of the list of transactions he'd been working on. 'There are no invoices connected to the payments I've marked.'

DI West ran his finger down the page. 'That's a considerable amount of money, Wayne.'

'Timing is interesting, too, Inspector,' said Wayne. 'There's a payment every month. Makes me think there must be some sort of agreement between Lewis and Eddie Cotton.'

'Why don't you ask Eddie?'

'I reckon I'll get straighter answers from the accounts,' said Wayne.

'Okay. Get the paperwork into the bank,' said DI West.

'Any news on Holden?' said Wayne.

'Still no sign of him,' said DI West.

'Be great if we could get him to spill the beans,' said Wayne.

'We have to catch him first,' said DI West, 'but if you find what you're looking for in those accounts, we may not need him to nail Cotton.'

———

It took the bank a week to supply a copy of the transactions spanning the last twelve months for Arthur Transport. Wayne looked at the transactions, focusing on the withdrawals and transfers to other accounts. He marked off the regular payments to Brad and his team of drivers. Then he went through the others, starting with the larger amounts. There were several to Bayside Auto.

Wayne wondered why a company located in the Riverland would pay a city based mechanical workshop to service its trucks, especially when it was also paying money to Riverland Motors.

He called Brad Arthur.

'Who services your trucks, Mr Arthur?'

'Riverland Motors,' said Brad. 'Why do you want to know that?'

'You haven't had any serviced by Bayside Auto in the last twelve months by any chance?' said Wayne.

'Never heard of them,' said Brad. 'We always use Riverland Motors. They're just across the road.'

'Thanks,' said Wayne.

Wayne walked over to DI West's office and knocked on the doorframe.

DI West was on the telephone and waved him in. Wayne sat and waited.

'Good news,' said DI West, putting down the receiver. 'Holden's been arrested. We should be able to talk to him in the next day or so.'

'Great,' said Wayne.

'What did you want to see me about?'

'Money,' said Wayne. 'Eddie probably thinks he's clever moving money through his accounts, but I think he's stuffed up. Take a look at this.' He passed the inspector his highlighted copy of Arthur Transport's bank statements. 'He's paid thousands of dollars to Bayside Auto.' Wayne smiled. 'I just spoke with Brad Arthur. He reckons their trucks are always serviced by Riverland Motors.'

'Are those payments on here?' said DI West, looking through the pages Wayne had given him.

'The green ones,' said Wayne. 'Brad claimed he'd never heard of Bayside Auto.'

'Might be time to have chat with Tom Cotton,' said DI West.

'How do you want to do it?' said Wayne.

'Bring him in. Let's make it formal.'

———

Tom Cotton sat at his kitchen table and stared into the darkness that hid the back garden. It had taken him years to build his empire but he'd built it, despite the setback of spending five years in prison. Now it looked like it was imploding.

Eddie was sitting in the Remand Centre, charged with dealing in the proceeds of crime and as accessory to murder. Joe was out on bail, but he'd been charged with stealing a car and perverting the course of justice for getting his girlfriend to lie for him. And, to make matters worse, he'd just learnt from his police source that Ian Holden had turned himself in.

Tom had come out of retirement and hired a mechanic to keep Bayside Auto open. He'd put his oldest son in charge of Bayside Used Cars, and started searching for another outlet now that Lewis was out of the picture for good.

He realized it was too late to get anyone to silence Ian. He would have spilt his guts by now, if he was going to. He had nothing to lose and Tom couldn't see why he'd spare him.

Tom turned the cold coffee cup in his hands and cursed the day he'd let Ian talk him into using his brother-in-law to drive the truck ferrying the cars to the Riverland. In Tom's mind, if that hadn't happened Ian wouldn't have been driving Nolan's truck on Port Road, and that accident would never have happened, and Lewis would not have panicked.

What a fuck up, thought Tom. Four people dead, a ruined business, and the man I want dead alive and talking to the cops.

Tom looked at his reflection in the window and wondered if he'd live long enough to see the world outside of prison again. He doubted it. He'd get life if the cops pinned Nolan's murder on him. And the worst part was he'd miss out on seeing his grandsons growing up.

The doorbell sounded. He let Joe answer the door. It was probably his new girlfriend.

He heard footsteps coming down the passageway towards him.

'The police are here, Dad. They want to talk to you,' said Joe.

Tom turned from the window. There were two uniformed officers and a detective in a crumpled suit. He thought he recognized the detective.

'Get your coat, Mr Cotton,' said DC Paterson. 'You need to come with us.'

'Will I need a lawyer?' said Tom.

'You can call one from the watch house,' said DC Paterson.
'Call Maynard,' said Tom, 'and tell him what's happening.'
'Okay, Dad.'

CHAPTER THIRTY-EIGHT

Carl was reading through Wayne's analysis of Bayside Auto's bank account when the telephone on his desk rang.

'DI West.'

'Bill Norris, Carl. Got a minute?'

'Sure.'

'I've just had an interesting chat with Logan Lewis, Shane Lewis' lad,' said Bill.

'Where's he been all this time?' said Carl.

'Holidaying in Bali with a couple of mates,' said Bill, 'but he was working for his father.'

'In what capacity?' said Carl.

'Helping him strip down cars or driving them interstate,' said Bill. 'He's shit-scared, so he's talking.'

'Did he tell you where the cars were coming from?' said Carl.

'Said they were getting them from Tom Cotton,' said Bill.

Sounds like Wayne was right all along, thought Carl. 'Does he know about the payment arrangements?'

'He's got access to his father's accounts,' said Bill, 'and he's shown me how they paid Cotton through Arthur Transport. Eddie Cotton sent them bogus invoices. We've got copies.'

Think we're going to make this stick, thought Carl. 'Making any progress on who killed Lewis?'

'I'm waiting for an update from Des Ryan, but I hear your mate Holden is the prime suspect,' said Bill.

'I'm waiting to talk to Holden myself,' said Carl. 'Be nice to have all the pieces of the puzzle.'

'I'll be sending details interstate about who Lewis was selling to,' said Bill. 'If nothing else, we'll be shutting down a major stolen vehicles operation.'

'Send me a copy of young Lewis' statement, Bill. I'm waiting for Wayne to bring Tom Cotton in for a chat. Could come in handy.'

———

Two hours later, Carl sat across the table from Tom Cotton and William Maynard.

'Do you have access to Bayside Auto's bank account, Mr Cotton?' said Carl.

'I own the business,' said Tom.

'But do you access the bank account?' said Carl.

'Yes.'

'So, you'd be aware that over the last few months Bayside Auto received a considerable amount of money from Arthur Transport, a trucking company located in the Riverland?' said Carl.

'That's Eddie's company,' said Tom. 'I'd say he paid for servicing his cars out of the wrong account. Does it all the time.'

Good try, thought Carl. 'Bayside Auto must service a lot of cars for him.'

'You'll have to ask Eddie,' said Tom.

Carl placed a photograph of Shane Lewis on the table in front of Tom. 'Know this man?'

'No.'

'This is Shane Lewis, Mr Cotton. He paid the same amount of money to your brother's trucking company as Eddie paid to Bayside Auto,' said Carl. 'Are you sure you don't know him?'

'Why would I know him?' said Tom.

'Do you use a mobile phone, Mr Cotton?' said Carl.

'Doesn't everybody?'

'Would the number of yours be 0419 654 897?'

'I guess you already know that if you're asking me.'

'Why would your number appear on the call list of Shane Lewis' phone if you don't know him?' said Carl.

'He must have called a wrong number,' said Tom. 'Happens all the time.'

'You misunderstand me, Mr Cotton. Your number appears on the list of numbers that called Shane Lewis in the days before he was murdered.'

'I must have called the wrong number,' said Tom.

'And spoke to him for more than five minutes?' said Carl. 'You're lying to me.'

Tom didn't respond.

'Did you know Lewis had a son?' said Carl.

'I don't know anything about him,' said Tom, 'so, how would I know that?'

'The boy knows all about you, Mr Cotton. He worked with his father. He's given us a statement and access to his father's accounts,' said Carl.

'He's probably told you a pack of lies to protect his own arse,' said Tom.

'Maybe,' said Carl, 'but your bank records don't lie, and they tell us who withdrew money from your accounts, Mr

Cotton. It appears you've withdrawn a considerable amount of cash from Bayside Auto's account, money which is the proceeds of crime, in fact, your payment for the stolen cars you supplied to Shane Lewis.'

Tom looked at his lawyer, who shook his head slightly.

'I'm not answering any more questions,' said Tom.

'I'm charging you with dealing in the proceeds of crime and as an accessory to murder and attempted murder, Mr Cotton.'

'What, you're not charging me with stealing cars?'

'It's all in the wording, Mr Cotton. Ian and Joe were stealing the cars for you but you were the one selling them to Shane Lewis. That's called dealing in the proceeds of crime,' said Carl. 'I'm sure Mr Maynard can explain it all to you.'

'I had nothing to do with killing anyone,' said Tom.

'Someone sent Jim Nolan to his death, Mr Cotton. I think it was you.'

'Well, you're wrong there. Lewis was the one who panicked and killed Nolan. I'm not taking the wrap for that!'

'So, why did you send Ian Holden up to him?'

'That was Kurt's idea. Had nothing to do with me.'

'Good luck with convincing a jury with that one.'

'It's the truth!'

'Tom,' said William Maynard. 'Leave the arguing to me.'

———

Carl's mobile phone vibrated in his pocket as he and Wayne made their way up to their offices on the third floor of Police Headquarters. He pulled it out and looked at the caller display. It was DCI Rankin.

'Get anything out of Cotton, Carl?'

'He started out denying everything, but the accessory to murder rattled him, Chief. He's blaming Lewis for killing

Nolan and Viking for setting up Holden,' said Carl. 'I don't think he's realized he's incriminated himself by blaming the others.'

'Maynard asleep at the wheel?' said DCI Rankin.

'Don't think he was expecting Tom's outburst,' said Carl.

'So, you're happy with the way it went?'

'We've also got a statement from Lewis' son implicating Tom and Eddie, and a money trail that's going to be hard to dispute, Chief. Think we're on a winner with this one.'

'Good,' said DCI Rankin. 'Before you go, I've just got off the phone from Des Ryan. Holden wants to talk. He's looking for a plea bargain.'

Would have been better for Holden if he'd spoken to me when he had the chance, thought Carl. 'Let's hear what he has to say, Chief. Be nice to have all the pieces, but I think we have enough to convict Cotton without his testimony.'

'Could be icing on your cake, Carl,' said DCI Rankin.

'Better keep Des involved, Chief. I don't want him accusing me of raining on his parade.'

'I think he knows it's a team effort, Carl.'

'When will Holden be here?'

'They're bringing him down tonight.'

'Okay. I'll set up an interview with Des for tomorrow morning. By the way, Chief, does Holden have a lawyer? I doubt he'll want to be represented by Maynard, if he's going to spill the beans on the Cottons.'

'Better alert the duty lawyer,' said DCI Rankin, 'and make sure it isn't Jessika Walsh. We don't want any subsequent lawyer he takes on accusing us of stacking the deck.'

CHAPTER THIRTY-NINE

Harry watched the man in black get off the 284 bus and walk away from the camera.

'He's knows he's on camera,' said Lisa. 'Look at the way he walks with his head down.'

'Didn't stop him looking at the camera on the bus,' said Harry.

'Perhaps he thought it wasn't on,' said Lisa.

'I'll bring up the recording from the next camera,' said the technician.

They watched the man they believed was Trent Mitchell walk towards the camera mounted on top of the traffic lights at the intersection of East and North Terraces. He crossed East Terrace and walked to the bus stop opposite the stop where he'd alighted from the city bound 284 bus.

'He must smell something bad,' said Harry. 'Look at the way people are moving away from him.'

Twelve minutes after he'd gotten off the 284 coming into the city, the man boarded the 284 heading back towards East Park.

'Zoom in. Let's see if we can read the number of the bus on the back window,' said Harry.

They waited while the technician paused the video and bought the rear window of the bus into focus.

'5147,' said the technician.

Harry rang City Buses.

'I need the recording from the camera on bus 5147,' said Harry.

'Which trip, Sergeant?'

'The 284 leaving East Terrace at five forty-seven last night,' said Harry.

'Give me a minute.'

Harry drummed his fingers on the desk.

'You're out of luck, Sergeant. The camera on that bus is stuffed.'

Just my luck, thought Harry. 'Can you tell me who was driving the bus on that run?'

'Operator 286. That's Michael Wilson. He starts his next shift from the Portside depot at two.'

'Can you let the depot know we want to speak to him?' said Harry.

'No problem, Sergeant. Is there anything else you need?'

'Thanks,' said Harry.

Harry slipped his mobile phone into the pocket of his trousers. 'There's no recording. We need to speak to the driver. He starts his next shift from Portside at two.'

Lisa checked her watch. 'We better get a move on, Sarge, or we'll miss him.'

Five minutes later, Lisa drove their car out of the basement car park of the Camera Control Centre and joined the traffic heading towards Portside on Port Road.

'Why do you think he caught the 284 going back towards Dr Bryant's?' said Lisa.

'Not sure,' said Harry, 'but I guess he could have parked his van out there somewhere and had to find a way back to it, especially after that kid pinched his bike.'

'Why not just catch the bus going the other way in the first place?' said Lisa.

'I'd say he caught the first bus that came along,' said Harry. 'I doubt he would've wanted to hang around after setting of the doctor's alarm.'

'Suppose he could be living somewhere off that route,' said Lisa.

Not likely, thought Harry, unless he knew someone who owned a mansion.

———

Michael Wilson was waiting for them when they arrived at the Portside bus depot.

Harry showed him the still image from the video taken on the city bound 284. 'Remember this guy getting onto your bus on East Terrace last night?'

Michael touched his nose. 'Bit hard to forget, mate. Pretty bad BO.'

'Recall where he got off?'

'Stop 25.'

'Where's that?' said Harry.

'Just before the corner of Thirtieth and Lime,' said Michael. 'It's the second to last stop on that route, right in front of the shopping centre.'

Forty-five minutes later, Lisa pulled into the car park of the East Park Shopping Centre.

'Must be around two hundred spaces here,' said Harry.

'Can't see any cameras,' said Lisa.

They walked to the entrance and read the opening hours displayed on the glass sliding doors.

'They're open to nine,' said Lisa.

'God only knows how many cars there would have been here around six thirty last night,' said Harry.

'Look over there,' said Lisa, pointing to three white vans parked in the corner of the car park, close to a door in the side of the building.

'The front one is a Ford,' said Harry.

They walked across the car park to where the vans were parked.

'Doesn't have Mitchell's rego number,' said Lisa, 'and it looks like a newer model to me.'

Harry walked around behind the vans and read the signage across their rear doors. 'They belong to the supermarket.'

They went into the supermarket and asked to speak to whoever drove the vans parked in the car park. The manager called the drivers into his office.

'Anybody notice a white 2012 Ford Transit parked out front between four and six thirty yesterday?' said Harry.

'There was a dirty white Ford parked a couple of spaces down from where we park,' said one of the drivers. 'It was there when I did a delivery run about six but it was gone when I got back at seven.'

'Anyone note the registration number?' said Harry.

The three drivers shook their heads. 'There are always cars in the car park,' said one of them.

'Anybody see this guy?' said Harry, showing them the image of the man in black on the 284 bus.

The three drivers shook their heads.

'Any security cameras covering the car park?' said Harry.

'The cameras only cover the mall, Sergeant,' said the manager.

They interviewed the people working in the shops with a view of the car park.

'I thought it was a bit strange,' said the young woman in the beauty salon. 'There was this old bloke, looked like a hobo. Anyway, he parks his grotty van and then gets this flash bike out of the back. You know, one of those ones like you see on the TV when they show the Tour de France, and he goes for a ride.'

'What time was that?' said Harry.

'Around three,' said the young woman. 'I'd just come back from my coffee break, otherwise I wouldn't have seen him.'

'Which way did he go?' said Harry.

'Dunno. I only saw him ride across the car park. I didn't see where he went.'

'Did you see him come back?' said Harry.

'No, but the van was gone when I went home.'

'What time was that?' said Harry.

'We close at nine.'

———

Carl met with Harry and Lisa for a briefing on their findings.

'Looks like he parked his van at the East Park Shopping Centre and rode his bike around to Dr Bryant's,' said Harry. 'All he had to do was ride down Lime until he got to Sixth.'

'Just as well that kid thought it had been stolen,' said Carl, 'otherwise, he wouldn't have been on the bus.'

'I wonder if he's using stolen plates on his van,' said Lisa. 'I mean, he's driving it around the suburbs and every patrol in the state is looking for it. It's not like it's invisible.'

'Might as well be,' said Carl, 'but I take your point.'

'Just doesn't make sense to me,' said Lisa.

'Update the bulletin, Harry,' said Carl. 'Get them to run a check on the rego number of every white Ford Transit they see.'

'Anything from the public, Boss?' said Harry.

'Crime Stoppers have been inundated with calls from people claiming to have seen him. Uniform are following up but I'm not hopeful,' said Carl. 'Seems Mitchell has been everywhere and nowhere at the same time.'

CHAPTER FORTY

Trent picked up the newspaper and scanned the story on the front page through the plastic wrapping. There was a picture of him sitting on the bus. His appearance was described as unkempt. He scratched his armpit. He'd hadn't thought about there being a security camera on the bus. He'd only wanted to get out of the area as quickly as he could when he'd discovered someone had taken his bike, and catching the bus had made sense at the time. Staring at the picture, he told himself walking back to where he'd left the van would have been a better idea. Too late, now he thought.

He looked up and down the street. There was no-one about. He dropped the newspaper back onto the driveway he'd picked it up from and continued walking along the footpath.

When he got back to the house, he had the cold shower he'd been putting off for weeks, trimmed his beard, and shaved his head. He searched through his clothes and dressed in blue jeans, a pale-yellow shirt, and the faded light-blue sweater Helen had given him for his thirtieth birthday.

He sat in what had been the kitchen thinking about what

had happened and decided he must have made a mistake and mixed up the names, otherwise Dr Bryant would be dead. Helen had told him he wouldn't fail her if he followed her instructions.

He looked at the fragments of Helen's coffee mug on the floor. Perhaps he shouldn't have lost his temper when she'd made him wait after what he'd done with Sarah Cody. He squatted and picked up the last piece of paper with Pauline Francis written on it and slipped it into his pocket. Dr Bryant would have to wait her turn.

Trent spent the afternoon in the warmth of the laundromat located in the local shopping centre, a twenty-five-minute walk from the abandoned house he called home, washing his clothes in an effort to erase any similarities between his appearance and the image the police were circulating of him as being unkempt and homeless.

The next morning, he took his laptop to the coffee shop and logged onto their free wi-fi network. Between sips of coffee and mouthfuls of blueberry muffin, he searched for Pauline Francis.

She didn't appear to have a social media presence. Trent wondered if the police had worked out the connection between Helen's death and the names on his list, and told her to delete her social media accounts. He knew the police were looking for him. He knew they weren't stupid, and assumed they must have worked out by now what he was doing and why he was doing it. He shrugged; they hadn't stopped him yet.

He tried White Pages. There were fifty-six entries for people with the surname Francis. He had no idea which suburb she lived in, so following her home from work looked like his only option. It had worked for Sarah Cody and Dr Bryant, so there was no reason why it wouldn't work again.

Trent knew he hadn't seen Pauline Francis while he was watching Dr Bryant come and go from University Hospital.

That meant she had to be working at City Hospital, if she was still nursing.

He drove into the city and parked as close as he could to the hospital, and sat at the bus stop opposite the entrance. He watched the nurses parade in and out at the end of the day shift.

He knew he'd made the right decision when Pauline Francis walked out of the hospital and got into a taxi. He wrote down the number of the taxi and watched it slowly make its way along North Terrace towards the spot where he'd parked. He crossed over the street and got into his van as the taxi went past in the slow stream of traffic heading towards the city centre.

Half an hour later, Trent watched Pauline Francis get out of the taxi and walk up the driveway of a house in Northfield, a house within walking distance of where he was living. He couldn't believe his luck. He wrote down the address and drove home. That night he dreamed of Helen.

The following morning, he walked to Pauline's house to have a look around. There was a dog in the backyard that barked as soon as he walked across the driveway. It sounded like a little lapdog with an oversized ego. He kept walking and glanced at the house. There was a very obvious blue light attached to a security alarm on the front gable. He wasn't keen on breaking in after what had happened at Dr Bryant's. As he walked home, he knew there had to be a way of getting to her without setting off the alarm or the dog.

As he walked, an idea popped into his mind and he knew what he had to do. He chuckled; Helen was always full of bright ideas.

CHAPTER FORTY-ONE

Ian Holden accepted the offer of a duty lawyer sitting in on his interview to protect his rights, and Saul Wakefield, who had been on the list for as long as Carl had been in the force, spent fifteen minutes with him before the interview started advising him of his rights.

Carl arrived for the interview with DI Ryan and DC Paterson.

'Morning, Mr Wakefield,' said Carl, as he shook hands with the lawyer. 'Ready?'

'When you are Inspector.'

DC Paterson switched on the recording equipment and stepped them through the interview protocols.

'What's on the table, Mr Holden?' said Carl. 'I understand from DI Ryan that you've admitted to killing Kurt Viking.'

'I can give you everyone involved,' said Ian.

'Does that include Jack Sloane?' said Carl.

'That was self defence,' said Ian.

'What are you looking for in return?' said Carl.

'I want consideration of, what was that word?' Ian looked at his lawyer.

'Mitigating circumstances,' said Saul Wakefield.

'Yeah, that,' said Ian. 'I don't want to be seen as a cold-blooded killer.'

'We're prepared to listen to what you have to say,' said Carl, 'but, we can't make any promises. The final decision on any plea deal will be made by the Prosecutor's Office after they've read your statement.'

'Mr Wakefield explained that,' said Ian.

'Are you prepared to continue?' said Carl.

'Yeah. I got nothing to lose,' said Ian.

'Want to start at the beginning?'

'How far back do you want to go?'

'Tell us how you got into stealing cars,' said Carl.

'Started in high school,' said Ian. 'We did it for fun back then. Just a bit of joyriding.'

'Who was the we?' said Carl.

'Jim and me,' said Ian.

'Jim Nolan?' said Carl.

'Yeah. We've been mates since high school.'

'What about the cars you've been pinching lately?' said Carl.

'That started when I met Kurt,' said Ian. 'A couple of weeks after I started working for him, one of the owners forgot to leave his keys. Kurt bet me I couldn't open the car. I thought it was a game. When I opened it, he wanted to know how I knew how to break into cars.'

'How did that lead to stealing cars?'

'You don't make much money working as a mechanic for someone else,' said Ian. 'Kurt asked me if I'd like to make some extra cash, and it went from there.'

'Was it just you and Kurt?' said Carl.

241

'Do you know Tom Cotton?' said Ian.

'We know him,' said Carl.

'We worked for him. He owns the workshop, and he owned Kurt.'

'Want to elaborate on that?'

'Kurt was married to Tom's daughter. Whatever she wanted, she got. She had Kurt on a string, which was the same as Tom having him on a string.'

Carl rubbed his chin. He still couldn't align that description of Kurt Viking with the man he'd met, even though he'd now heard it from more than one source.

'What about Joe?'

'He started working with us a couple of years ago. He's good with cars.'

'How did Nolan fit in?'

'When we started pinching high-end cars, we needed a truck. It's easy enough to get them started but if the engine cuts out, you're stuffed. It's a lot safer to get them onto the back of a truck as soon as you start them. Jim had the right sort of truck and he needed the money. I talked him into it.'

'So, what went wrong?'

'That bloody accident on Port Road,' said Ian. 'None of the others trusted Jim to keep his mouth shut.'

Carl made a note. That was different to what Tom Cotton had told him.

'Who helped you the day you retrieved the Mack from Pemberton?' said Carl.

'How do you know I did that?'

'There's a security camera covering the fuel pumps. You filled up Kurt's SUV,' said Carl, 'and, we have a witness who remembered you taking the truck out of the yard.'

'Oh. I went up with Kurt. He drove the SUV back. Took me home from the rental place.'

'Tell us about the BMW you and Joe took from East Park?' said Carl.

'How do you know about that?' said Ian.

'Remember the security light coming on?' said Carl.

'Yeah.'

'The owner has a camera trained on the driveway. Want to see the recording?'

'Has Joe said anything?' said Ian.

'He's denying he was there,' said Carl.

'The little shit was there alright. The amplifier we used to start the cars is his.'

'What happened when you took the BMW to the Riverland?'

'They were supposed to let Jim go. We were going to piss off into the great blue yonder,' said Ian. 'Didn't happen.'

'Tell us about Jack Sloane?' said Carl.

'Jim was dead when I got there. Buried inside that farm-house. Jack pulled a gun on me. Wanted me to get in the hole before he shot me,' said Ian. 'Lazy bastard.'

'So, how did Jack end up dead if he had the gun?'

'I surprised the cocky bastard,' said Ian. 'All those Tae Kwon Do lessons my mum paid for trying to keep me out of trouble. He didn't see it coming, and when I had the gun, I shot him before he could get up.'

'Were you the one that told us about the farmhouse?'

'Yeah. I wanted Jim to get a decent burial at least. Not be left to rot out there in the middle of nowhere.'

'What happened to the car?' said Carl.

'I handed it over when I got there,' said Ian.

'Who to?' said Carl.

'I'd never seen him before,' said Ian.

'Is this him?' said Carl, slipping a photo of Shane Lewis across the table to Holden.

'Looks like him,' said Ian.

'So, why did you shoot Kurt?' said Carl.

'He sent me up there to get killed,' said Ian. 'I trusted him.'

'Why did you shoot Shane Lewis?' said Carl.

'Who's he?' said Ian.

'This guy,' said Carl, tapping the photograph on the table.

'I didn't shoot him,' said Ian. 'I couldn't find him.'

Carl looked at DI Ryan.

'Know anything about ballistics, Mr Holden,' said DI Ryan.

'Not really,' said Ian.

'It's the science we use to link bullets to the guns that fired them,' said DI Ryan.

'So, you can tell I used the same gun to shoot Jack and Kurt?' said Ian.

'In fact, Mr Holden, that gun was used to kill your friend and Shane Lewis as well. How do you explain that?' said DI Ryan.

'I sure as hell didn't shoot Jim,' said Ian. 'He was my best mate.'

'But you shot Shane Lewis, didn't you,' said DI Ryan.

Ian Holden looked at his hands. Carl wondered if he was going to deny it again.

'Yeah,' said Ian. 'He had it coming for what he did to Jim.'

'And, you torched his shed,' said DI Ryan.

'How else was I going to destroy the business?'

'You could have come to us earlier,' said Carl. 'After shooting Sloane would have been a good time.'

'Guess I wasn't thinking straight,' said Ian.

'I'm not sure the Prosecutor's Office will want to cut you a deal, Mr Holden, but we'll pass on your request,' said Carl.

Carl played the recording of the interview with Ian Holden to DCI Rankin.

'He might get some slack from a jury,' said DI Ryan, 'but I doubt the Prosecutor's going to want to do a deal. What do you think?'

'We don't need his testimony,' said Carl. 'The statement we have from young Lewis and the money trail through their accounts should be enough to put the Cotton's away.'

'Think he's asking a bit much given he's admitted to two murders,' said DCI Rankin, 'but, I'll have a chat with the Prosecutor's Office.'

'Pity he didn't think to talk to us sooner,' said Carl. 'We might not have been able to stop Nolan's death, but the others could have been avoided.'

'Forget about Holden for the time being, Carl. The Commissioner wants some good news on Mitchell.'

'He's not alone there, Chief.'

CHAPTER FORTY-TWO

Carl surveyed the blackened walls and smouldering roof beams that had been Pauline Francis' house.

He knew the family had survived the fire, even though Pauline's daughter had been taken to City Hospital suffering from smoke inhalation.

'Looks like a petrol bomb through that window,' said the Fire Inspector, pointing at the smashed window in front of them. 'Found the remains of the bottle inside. They're lucky they had a smoke alarm.'

'So, no chance this was accidental?' said Carl.

'Somebody wanted this place to burn,' said the Fire Inspector.

Carl turned to SC Charlie Head who had responded to the initial call-out. 'Any witnesses, Charlie?'

'Woman across the street says she heard the sound of glass breaking and someone running around two, but nothing really useful,' said Charlie.

'Find out if anybody in the surrounding streets saw a white van,' said Carl.

'You think it's Mitchell,' said Harry.

'She's one of the nurses that looked after Helen Drew,' said Carl. 'Who else would it be?'

'What if she isn't the target?' said Harry. 'What if this is someone having a go at her husband? Or a random attack?'

'Too much of a coincidence to be anybody else, Harry,' said Carl.

'I'm not so sure, Boss. I'd like to take a look at the husband. We could be making a mistake.'

Carl scratched his head. Harry had a point and, he had to admit, arson wasn't Mitchell's usual MO. 'Okay, let's cover that angle but I still think this has to be Mitchell.'

'If it is, said Harry, 'he's going to be pissed when he finds out she's still alive.'

'I hope so,' said Carl. 'We need him to make a mistake.'

'Bit of a change if it is him,' said Harry. 'Arson's a long way from strangulation.'

'Maybe he's getting desperate after what happened at Dr Bryant's,' said Carl, 'or he's trying to throw us off his trail.'

'Wonder if he'll have another go at Dr Bryant,' said Harry.

'If he does, that could be the mistake we need,' said Carl. 'The chief's put Protective Services back onto providing her security.'

———

Pauline and Neil Francis sat close to each other in the interview room on the ground floor of Police Headquarters.

'Do you think it was him?' said Pauline.

'Hard to say,' said Carl. 'Could be.'

'What does that mean?' said Neil.

'Depends who was the intended target,' said Carl, 'if there was an intended target. It could be a random attack.'

'I don't have those sort of enemies,' said Neil, 'and I didn't think Pauline did either, until you told us about this Mitchell.'

'What about your daughter?' said Harry. 'Has she been in any sort of trouble? Received any threats?'

'Grace is a good kid,' said Neil. 'She's either studying or working.'

'Go out much?' said Harry.

'With her girlfriends mainly,' said Pauline. 'She's been part of the same group for years. They went to school together. She's never said anything about anyone hassling her.'

'Boyfriend?' said Harry.

'Not that we know of,' said Pauline.

'How is she?' said Carl.

'They're keeping her in overnight for observation,' said Pauline. 'I expect she'll be discharged in the morning.'

'That's good,' said Carl. 'Has anyone threaten you at all, Mr Francis?'

'Most people don't even know I exist,' said Neil. 'I work in the archives at the State Library.'

'Any disputes with your neighbours or anything like that?' said Carl.

Neil shook his head. 'We've lived in the same house for the last twenty years, Inspector. We moved in when it was a new sub-division. We know all the neighbours. We've never had anything like this happen before.'

'If you think of anything, Mr Francis, you can reach me on this number,' said Carl, handing him his card. 'I guess your mobile will be the best way of contacting you for the time being.'

'Our insurance company is putting us up in the Welford,' said Neil. 'You can always leave a message there.'

———

DCI Rankin came into Carl's office as he was shutting down his computer.

'The Commissioner's not happy, Carl. The minister's breathing down his neck demanding answers, and he's spitting chips about the press calling us the Keystone Cops.'

Time for the Commissioner to suck it up, thought Carl. Taking flak from the press and the minister was why he was the one being paid the big bucks. Carl wasn't exactly feeling excited about the progress of the case either but he knew complaining about it wasn't going to help him find Mitchell.

'I'm doing my best, Chief,' said Carl.

'I'm not criticising your efforts, Carl,' said DCI Rankin. 'What everybody wants to know is why we haven't found him?'

'It's not from lack of trying,' said Carl. 'We've got every officer in the state looking for Mitchell and his vehicle.'

'You'd think those eyes would give him away,' said DCI Rankin, pointing to Mitchell's photograph on the wall behind Carl.

'You'd think so,' said Carl, 'but the only people who've seen him are the passengers on the 284 bus and a shop assistant out at East Park.'

'We've got his photograph everywhere,' said DCI Rankin.

'Maybe that's part of the problem,' said Carl. 'The public are tuning him out.'

'Or they don't care,' said DCI Rankin.

'Find that hard to believe, Chief. More like they're dealing with too many distractions,' said Carl.

'You don't suppose someone else is behind this arson attack, do you?'

'Bit too much of a coincidence for me, Chief,' said Carl. 'We've spoken to the husband. Hard to see him as a target, and the daughter's a uni student. No boyfriend, apparently. I've asked Harry to talk to their neighbours and run some back-ground checks just in case.'

'Good.' DCI Rankin looked at his watch. 'How's young Sophie?'

'Mobile,' said Carl. 'We've had to childproof the house.' He pulled out his phone, opened the message Nina had sent him, and clicked on the video of Sophie walking around their kitchen. 'Take a look at this.'

DCI Rankin watched the video and laughed. 'Give her a hug from me when you get home.'

CHAPTER FORTY-THREE

Trent listened to the mid-morning news on the radio in his van. Pauline Francis and her family had survived what the police were calling an arson attack on their house. He knew he'd try again if Helen wanted her dead, but he was in no hurry. It was time to let the police run around in circles for a while. He was certain there was no way they could connect him to the fire. He'd made sure of that.

He changed into a fresh set of clothes and caught the bus into the city, where he ambled through the city centre and bought himself lunch in a sandwich bar on the plaza. After lunch, he walked to East Terrace and caught the 284 bus to East Park.

He got off the bus in Lime Avenue and strolled along the footpaths until he reached the street where Dr Bryant lived. He walked past her house on the opposite footpath. There was a security guard sitting in one of the chairs on her front veranda. Trent smiled to himself. He'd obviously done enough to spook her into taking extra precautions at home, but those precautions meant he'd have to find a way of getting to her somewhere else if Helen still wanted her killed.

He walked around the block and back to the bus stop on Lime Avenue. After a fifteen-minute wait, he caught the 284 back into the city and then the 175 out to Northfield.

On his way home, he stopped in at the local supermarket where he purchased batteries, to power the portable camp lantern that lit his makeshift kitchen, and the ingredients for the meal he intended to cook on his camp stove that night.

Later that evening, Trent stood in his dimly lit kitchen cooking. The house shook as a low-flying helicopter passed overhead. He guessed it was the State Rescue helicopter trans-ferring someone to City Hospital. He hoped that night's passenger would get a better outcome than Helen had.

He picked up the saucepan and scraped the braised steak and onions he heated in it onto a piece of fresh bread. As he ate, he wondered how he was going to get Dr Bryant alone in a place where he could administer the justice she deserved. It was highly unlikely he'd be able to get to her in her house, unless he was prepared to wait until everyone assumed he'd given up.

He thought about the possibility of sneaking into the hospi-tal, before dismissing that option as too dangerous. There were too many people and too many cameras in the hospital.

'How would you do it, sweetheart?' he said to the empty room.

He waited for Helen to respond.

When she didn't, he took that to mean he had to wait. She'd tell him when it was time.

When he'd finished eating, he wondered if it might be time to scout out another place to hide or consider taking a holiday interstate, where there'd be less people looking for him.

He decided he'd sleep on it before making a final decision. After all, he'd managed to stay invisible since leaving Harvey Street.

CHAPTER FORTY-FOUR

Harry read the report from the crime scene investigators. The evidence they had uncovered confirmed someone had thrown a petrol bomb through the front window of the Francis' house, but there was nothing in the report identifying who that someone might be.

Harry suspected Mitchell was the culprit but knew they couldn't ignore the possibility that someone else had carried out the attack.

He ran a query on Neil Francis through the database. Nothing. He ran one on Pauline. She was clean. He ran one on Grace and got a hit. He pulled the file. She'd been arrested during a student protest the year she'd started at City University. He couldn't see that being a motive for anyone to firebomb her house.

Harry drove out to Northfield with Lisa and interviewed their neighbours. By all accounts, Neil and Pauline were friendly with everyone in their street.

They interviewed Neil's colleagues. No-one had a bad word to say about him.

They spoke to Grace and her friends. They had no idea who would want to hurt her.

'Could be a random attack,' said Lisa, 'or they firebombed the wrong house.'

'Guess that's possible,' said Harry, 'but I'm inclined to agree with the boss.'

'Big change in MO,' said Lisa.

'Yeah, that's what I thought,' said Harry. 'But who else could it be?'

'We've got nothing linking him to the scene,' said Lisa.

'Opportunity and motive,' said Harry.

'Wish we could find him,' said Lisa.

'He can't hide forever,' said Harry. 'He'll slip up. They always do.'

CHAPTER FORTY-FIVE

On a bright spring day in early October, a little over two months since the arson attack on Pauline Francis' house, PC Lily Chan stayed with the patrol car while her partner, PC Adam Monks, went into McDonalds to get himself a burger for lunch. She scanned the car park, taking in the group of boys standing around a new looking sports car parked next to a dirty white Ford Transit van.

Lily looked at the list of vehicles they were meant to be on the lookout for. She was pretty sure there was a Ford Transit on the list. She noted the registration number: SRBC465. Lily got out and walked towards the van to get a better look at the number. It was SRAD734. She wrote it down and returned to the patrol car.

Adam was still inside the restaurant, probably talking to the girl behind the counter, thought Lily. She keyed in the registration number of the van to check its status. It came up as being cancelled. She checked the notes field and read that the cancellation had been lodged by Northfield Auto Wreckers.

Lily keyed in the registration number for the van on her list. It was registered to Trent Mitchell. That name rang a bell in Lily's head. Nigel had been talking about him for months. She knew he was wanted in connection for a string of murders, and for an attempted break in she and Adam had attended in East Park.

She picked up her radio, pressed the call button twice, and watched the van while she waited for Adam to respond.

The door of the restaurant opened. A tall bearded man with a shaved head followed Adam out into the car park and walked towards the van.

'Something's not right here, Adam,' said Lily, when Adam got into the car. 'The rego on that Ford over there belongs to a vehicle that's been scrapped.'

'Aren't we looking for a van like that?' said Adam.

'Trent Mitchell,' said Lily. 'Let's go, before he leaves.'

Adam started the car, drove across the car park, and blocked the van's exit.

Lily jumped out of the car as soon as it stopped, walked up to the driver's side window, and tapped on the glass.

The man rolled down the window.

'This your vehicle, sir?' said Lily.

'Yeah,' said the man. 'Is there a problem?'

'It's not registered,' said Lily. 'Can I see your driver's licence, please?'

The man reached for the keys in the ignition.

'I wouldn't do that' said Lily, opening the door and putting her hand on her holster.

The man let his hands drop and sank back into his seat.

'Your driver's licence,' said Lily.

The man pulled a wallet out of the rear pocket of his jeans, extracted his driver's licence and handed it to Lily.

Lily glanced at the name on the licence: Trent Mitchell. She looked at the photo. It didn't look much like the man sitting in front of her except for the eyes.

'Get out of the car, Mr Mitchell, and put your hands behind your back.'

Trent Mitchell stared at PC Chan. 'You're arresting me for driving an unregistered vehicle?'

'No, Mr Mitchell, I'm arresting you on suspicion of murder.'

———

The telephone on Carl's desk rang.

'DI West.'

'Operations, Inspector. We've picked up Trent Mitchell for you.'

'Where?' said Carl.

'Outside the McDonalds at Northfield.'

Even killers have to eat, thought Carl. 'Thank God for that.'

'Think you'd better thank PC Chan, Inspector. She spotted the cancelled plates on his vehicle.'

'Is he alive?' said Carl, hoping Mitchell hadn't resisted arrest. If he had, he wouldn't be the first suspect Lily Chan had shot.

'He didn't resist arrest, Inspector.'

Carl heard the laughter in his voice. 'He's a lucky man, then.'

Carl called DCI Rankin's number. 'Uniform have picked up Mitchell, Chief.'

'Thank God,' said DCI Rankin. 'I'll let the Commissioner know.'

Carl walked into the Incident Room. 'We've got Mitchell!'

The room erupted in cheers.

'Just got a text from Lily,' said Nigel, when the noise died down. 'Says we owe her big time for not shooting him.'

'I'll drink to that,' said Carl.

CHAPTER FORTY-SIX

Trent Mitchell sat in the interview room. He was dressed in blue jeans and a light blue sweater. His head was shaved. His beard neatly trimmed. He didn't look much like the man in the image taken from the 284 bus or the person in the photograph on his driver's licence to Carl, except for the piercing blue eyes.

Next to Mitchell sat Anne Hilton, the duty lawyer, who was there to protect his rights.

'You've been a hard man to find, Mr Mitchell,' said Carl. 'Where have you been since you left the house in Harvey Street?'

'Around,' said Trent.

'Can you be a little more precise?' said Carl.

'Not really,' said Trent.

'Why did you leave your job?' said Carl.

'Needed a holiday,' said Trent.

'Any reason why you turned your mobile phone off?' said Carl.

'A man's entitled to some privacy,' said Trent.

'Makes it difficult to call you,' said Carl.

Trent shrugged.

'Why have you got stolen plates on your vehicle, Mr Mitchell?' said Carl.

'So you'd leave me alone,' said Trent.

'Why did you want to be left alone?' said Carl.

'You were trying to frame me for killing that woman in Carrick,' said Trent.

'There was no need to hide if you didn't kill her,' said Carl.

'I've seen how you stitch up people like me on TV,' said Trent.

Carl pulled a photograph of the bicycle retrieved from Sixth Street, East Park, from his folder and slid it across the table. 'Recognize this bike, Mr Mitchell?'

'No.'

'It was found in Sixth Street, East Park, late in the afternoon of Monday, the twenty-fourth of July, by a lad who thought it had been stolen. He didn't think anybody who owned a bike like this would just leave it in the street,' said Carl.

'He's probably right,' said Trent. 'Looks expensive.'

'Did you steal it?' said Carl.

Trent looked at Carl.

'It's got your prints all over it.'

Trent looked at Anne Hilton. 'Told you they'd try and frame me.'

'Ever been to this house?' said Carl, placing a photograph of 18 Lancet Street, Riverside, on the table.

'Seen a lot of houses that look like that,' said Trent. 'Where's this one?'

'Riverside,' said Carl.

'Can't say I know it,' said Trent.

Carl placed a photograph of Sarah Cody on the table.

261

Trent blushed, which wasn't the reaction Carl was expecting.

'This is Sarah Cody. She lived in this house. Ever meet her?'

'I don't think so,' said Trent.

'She was a nurse at City Hospital,' said Carl.

Trent didn't respond.

'She nursed Helen,' said Carl.

Trent crossed his arms.

'We know about Helen, Mr Mitchell. I've spoken to her parents. They blame you, don't they?' said Carl.

Carl waited. Trent didn't say anything.

'I've spoken to the Coroner's Office, Mr Mitchell. You made a complaint against the doctor and the nurses that looked after Helen before she died.'

'If they'd done their job properly she'd still be alive,' said Trent.

'Is that why you killed them?'

'I haven't killed anybody,' said Trent.

'You weren't very careful with this one,' said Carl, tapping the photograph of Sarah Cody. 'You left a fingerprint on the laundry window when you broke into her house, and plenty of semen for us to test, which I'm sure will match the sample we took when you arrived here.'

'Wasn't me,' said Trent. 'You're just stitching me up with planted evidence, just like they do on TV.'

Carl smiled at Anne Hilton, who was writing on her legal pad. 'We'll send you a copy of the analysis if you take on his defence.'

Anne nodded.

Carl slid another photograph across the table. 'Recognize this house?'

'Why would I?' said Trent.

'This is where Dr Bryant lives. She's the doctor that signed Helen's death certificate.'

'Is that so?' said Trent.

'It's around the corner from where your bike was found in Sixth Street on the day you tried to break into Dr Bryant's house,' said Carl.

'They're doing it again,' said Trent. 'Can't you make them stop?'

'They're only telling you what they think they know,' said Anne. 'You don't have to agree with them.'

'Recognize this man?' said Carl, sliding the image taken from the security camera on the 284 bus across the table.

Trent glanced at the grainy image of a man sitting on a bus. 'Doesn't look like anybody I know.'

'Heard of face recognition software, Mr Mitchell? We use it to compare different photographs of the same person. We've compared this to the photograph on your driver's licence. Want to know what we found?'

'What?' said Trent.

'This is you,' said Carl, pointing to the image on the table.

'So, I was on a bus,' said Trent.

'Trouble is, Mr Mitchell, you got onto this bus at the stop on Lime Avenue, East Park, on the day a man meeting your description tried to break into Dr Bryant's house, and that bus stop is just around the corner from Sixth Street, where your bike was found.'

'It's not my bike,' said Trent.

'Where were you around two in the morning of Thursday, the third of August?' said Carl.

'Asleep,' said Trent.

'Can anybody vouch for that?' said Carl.

'What do you mean?' said Trent.

'Was anybody with you?'

'I live alone,' said Trent.

'You weren't in Northfield, by any chance, throwing a petrol bomb through the window of this house?' Carl slid a photograph of the smoking remnants of Pauline Francis' house across the table.

'Wasn't me,' said Trent.

Carl leant over and picked up the evidence bag holding the contents the Duty Sergeant had removed from Mitchell's pockets.

'Recognise this stuff?' said Carl, placing the clear plastic bag on the table.

'It's my stuff,' said Trent.

Carl used his fingers to move a small piece of paper away from Mitchell's wallet and flipped the bag so they could read the writing on the piece of paper.

'Why do you have this piece of paper with Pauline Francis written on it?'

'That's not mine,' said Trent. 'You put that in there.'

'Pauline Francis is the name of one of the nurses that looked after Helen,' said Carl. 'Someone fire bombed her house on the morning of the third of August. I think it was you.'

'You can't prove that,' said Trent.

'I might not have to,' said Carl. 'I think we have a pretty good case linking you to the murders of Kelly Palmer, Christine Viking, and Sarah Cody. You really shouldn't have raped her.'

'I didn't rape her. She begged me to screw her!'

Carl looked across the table at Anne Hilton.

'Do you want to start again, at the beginning, Mr Mitchell?'

————

'Everybody blamed me,' said Trent. 'It was all my fault because I'd introduced her to mountain bike riding. Fuck! She only fell off a bloody bike! Kids do that every day. If the people in the hospital had done the right thing, she'd still be alive.'

'That was seven years ago,' said Carl. 'Why now?'

'She wouldn't leave me alone.'

'Who?' said Carl.

'Helen.'

Carl looked at Anne. 'What do you mean? Helen's been dead for seven years.'

'She might be dead to you,' said Trent, 'but she's not to me. I see her every night.'

'Tell me about that,' said Carl.

'She wanted me to get the Coroner to open a case on her death. I tried. They wouldn't listen to me. Said they'd already reviewed her death and there was nothing to investigate.'

Carl glanced at his notes. 'That was more than six years ago.'

'She's been pestering me ever since to avenge her death. The only way I could get her to give me any peace was to do what she wanted,' said Trent. 'I begged God to help me. He ignored me. Left me with no other choice.'

'Why did you start with Kelly Palmer?'

'I wrote their names on pieces of paper, like that one,' said Trent, pointing to the evidence bag. 'Then it was like a lucky dip. Her name came out first.'

'How did you kill her?' said Carl.

'Strangled her with a rope,' said Trent. 'It was easy.'

'And Christine Viking?'

'Same way.'

'How did you get her to open her door?' said Carl.

'Just knocked,' said Trent.

'What happened with Sarah Cody?' said Carl.

'She was naked when I broke into her house,' said Trent. 'She tried to trick me.' Trent looked at Carl.

'With sex?' said Carl.

Trent blushed and looked at his hands. 'Helen wasn't happy about what happened, even though I killed her, like I'd promised.'

'Tell me about Dr Bryant,' said Carl.

'She'd be dead if it hadn't been for that alarm,' said Trent. 'I didn't expect that. I thought she'd turned it off.'

'How did you find them after all this time?' said Carl.

'I looked them up on the Internet or I followed them home from the hospital,' said Trent. 'It wasn't hard.'

'Why did you firebomb Pauline Francis' house?' said Carl.

'That was Helen's idea,' said Trent. 'She said I didn't deserve to kill her.'

'Oh, why was that?' said Carl.

'Because I failed with the doctor,' said Trent.

'Well, it's over now, Mr Mitchell,' said Carl.

'Might be for you,' said Trent, 'but I still have to deal with Helen, and she's not happy I'm in here.'

———

DCI Rankin read the transcript of Mitchell's confession.

'Prosecutor's going to want a psychiatric assessment after he sees this, Carl.'

'Out of our hands, Chief,' said Carl. 'As long as he's off the streets, I don't care whether he's in prison or some psychiatric hospital.'

'Too bad you didn't arrest him after the Viking murder,' said DCI Rankin.

Carl crossed his arms. 'He had an alibi, Chief, and no-one positively identified him as being at the scene, but I take your point.'

'Don't blame yourself, Carl. There's nothing like hindsight

to remind us we all make mistakes. God knows I've made more than enough myself over the years.'

'Thanks, Chief. Coming to join the celebrations?'

'Make sure PCs Chan and Monks are there,' said DCI Rankin. 'I want to thank them. In person.'

'They're in the Commissioner's office,' said Carl. 'Nigel's gone to make sure they get to the pub.'

CHAPTER FORTY-SEVEN

Carl pushed open the door into the lounge bar. The wave of raised voices nearly knocked him off his feet. The lounge bar of the Criterion was packed with police officers. Carl thought every officer who'd worked on the case had to be there.

He scanned the room looking for Harry and the rest of the team.

'Over here, Boss!' Harry waved his hand in the air.

Carl pushed his way through the crush of bodies in uniform to join his team, a small group dressed in suits, standing around a table in the centre of a sea of officers in blue uniforms.

'Where's Lily?' said Carl.

'They should be here any minute,' said Wayne. 'Just had a text from Nigel.'

Carl picked up the beer Harry pushed across the table to him and raised it in a toast. 'Let's hope the bastard gets life.'

The others raised their glasses.

The level of noise went up several decibels.

Carl turned and saw PCs Chan and Monk standing in the

doorway. The crowd parted, making a gap for them to get to the bar, where several drinks sat waiting for the heroes of the day.

Nigel came in with DCI Rankin. The noise level dropped. The chief inspector stood on a chair. Wayne passed him a glass of beer.

'Let's all raise a glass to Lily and Adam,' said DCI Rankin. 'Job well done!'

'And praise the Lord Lily didn't shoot the bastard!' called a voice from the crowd.

'Next time,' said Lily.

The room erupted with laughter.

Carl ordered another round of drinks and sent a text message to Nina. It was going to be a long night.

A NOTE FROM PETER

If you enjoyed **_Twisted Justice,_** you can help other readers share your enjoyment by telling them about the book and writing a review.

Drop by at **www.petermulraney.com** and join my **Crime Readers Group** to download a free copy of **_Deadly Sands,_** and be one of the first to know when my next book will be released.

ACKNOWLEDGMENTS

A book is a community project. I'd like to acknowledge the emotional support I received from Toni during the writing of this book, and the editorial assistance provided by Francesco during the massaging of the original manuscript into the final book.

This book has also received assistance from the members of my Street Team, who act as beta readers and provide feedback that always improves the quality of the final product.

It's also great to have readers who write reviews and spread the work among their friends.

A big thank you to you all.

ALSO BY PETER MULRANEY

Inspector West series

After

The Holiday

Holy Death

Whistleblower

The East Park Syndicate

Inspector West Collection One

Inspector West Collection Two

Stella Bruno Investigates series

The Identity Thief

A Gun of Many Parts

Bones in the Forest

A Deadly Game of Hangman

Taken

Fallout

Stella Bruno Investigates: Books 1 to 6

The Identity Thief Collection

The Fallout Collection

Ryan Holiday PI Short Stories

Rosie

Framed

Living Alone series

After She's Gone

Cooking 4 One

Sanity Savers

Living Alone (Collection)

Living Alone Journal

Novella

The New Girlfriend

Everyday Business Skills

Everyday Project Management

Everyday Productivity

Everyday Money Management

Writings of the Mystic

Sharing the Journey: Reflections of a Reluctant Mystic.

A Question of Perspective

My Life is My Responsibility: Insights for Conscious Living

My Life is My Responsibility Workbook

I Am Affirmations: The Power of Words

Beyond the Words: Reflections on I Am Affirmations

Mystical Journey: A Handbook for Modern Mystics

Sharing the Journey Coloring Books

Mandalas

Mandalas by 3

Sharing the Journey Coloring Journals

Sharing the Journey Coloring Journal

Sharing the Journey Coloring Journal ~Discovery

Sharing the Journey Coloring Journal ~ Reflection

.

www.ingramcontent.com/pod-product-compliance
Lightning Source LLC
Chambersburg PA
CBHW030633110726
47901CB00002B/423